ARTHUR McCANN AND
ALL HIS WOMEN

Leslie Thomas was born in South Wales in 1931 and when his parents died, he and his younger brother were brought up in an orphanage. His first book, *This Time Next Week*, is the autobiography of a happy orphan. Aged 16, he became a reporter on a weekly newspaper in Essex and then did his National Service in Malaya during the Communist bandit war. *The Virgin Soldiers* tells of these days; it was an immediate bestseller and has been made into a film with Lynn Redgrave and Hywel Bennett.

Returning to civilian life, Leslie Thomas joined the staff of the *Evening News*, becoming a top feature writer and travelling a great deal. His second novel, *Orange Wednesday*, was published in 1967. For nine months during 1967 he travelled around ten islands off the coast of Britain, the result of which was a lyrical travelogue, *Some Lovely Islands*, from which the BBC did a television series. He has continued to travel a great deal and also written several television plays. He is a director of a London publishing house. His hobbies include golf, antiques and Queen's Park Rangers Football Club. His other books include *The Love Beach*, *Come to the War*, *His Lordship*, and, most recently, *Onward Virgin Soldiers*. His next novel, *The Man with the Power*, will be published by Pan in 1975.

By the same author in Pan Books

ORANGE WEDNESDAY
THIS TIME NEXT WEEK
COME TO THE WAR
THE VIRGIN SOLDIERS
ONWARD VIRGIN SOLDIERS
HIS LORDSHIP
THE LOVE BEACH

ARTHUR McCANN AND ALL HIS WOMEN

LESLIE THOMAS

PAN BOOKS LTD
LONDON AND SYDNEY

First published 1972 by Michael Joseph Ltd
This edition published 1974 by Pan Books Ltd,
Cavaye Place, London SW10 9PG

ISBN 0 330 24092 7

The quotation on page v from 'The Sea and the Mirror'
contained in *Collected Longer Poems* by W. H. Auden
is reproduced by kind permission of Messrs Faber and
Faber Ltd

Printed in Great Britain by
Richard Clay (The Chaucer Press), Ltd, Bungay, Suffolk

At Dirty Dick's and Sloppy Joe's
We drank our liquor straight,
Some went upstairs with Margery,
And some, alas, with Kate;
And two by two, like cat and mouse
The homeless played at keeping house.

W. H. AUDEN
'The Sea and the Mirror'

Although I have never kept proper records I know that, during the past twenty years, I have had women in London, New York, New Guinea, Barry Dock, Liverpool, Hartlepool, Sydney, Lydney, Paris, Harris, Bora Bora, Pago Pago, Hong Kong, Kings Lynn, Florence, Adelaide, Fanny Bay, Natal, Pentecoste, Corpus Christi, Bilbao, Balboa, Brest, Leghorn, the Hindu Kush and the Rann of Kutch; five Newports, three Kingstons, two Birminghams, God knows how many places starting in Saint, San or Sante, dozens called Port Something, and a minor Australian settlement known as Birdsville.

Not necessarily in that order.

I recall the towns, the cities and islands, and the ships that took me there better than most of the women, which is, I suppose, to be expected. But some of the women were beautiful. (My father, a prize swine, always said: 'Never open your eyes in the morning and have to close them again'.) Some were clever, some were happy, some were sweet and good. I even thought once or twice, that they were truly mine.

My father is well known for having bedded five of his wife's six sisters. My grandfather died at the door of a cheap dance hall and my great-grandfather is buried in a ship's barrel in Port Desire in South America. His wife thought he had gone to Bristol for the day.

With this pedigree it is, perhaps, little wonder that my life has been both adventurous and empty. I have searched this world, tried everything and found nothing. All I wanted was a true, endearing, enduring, undying, sensual, sensible, sexual, spiritual, all-embracing, all-everything, exclusive and particular love. Again and again and again. Women have been my failing and my failure. I seem to be a man who simply cannot say no. You could say it has been my hobby.

But looking back on it now, I see it has been both a long and foolish journey. Oh, Mrs Nissenbaum of Riverdale, New York (and your tragic dog, Errol Flynn); Oh, Belinda with whom I spent my wedding night (although I was married to Pamela); Oh, Pamela, for all the years the port to which the hapless sailor returned (but who admitted other vessels); Oh, Monique at Port de Loupe and Rose Kirby of England; Oh, the young girls, and those old enough to make me know better, that I have held in my clasp through torrid nights and cold, in all hemispheres, creeks, continents, backwaters and famous cities. Oh, the lies, the thrills and the pain. Oh, Angie. Oh, God. Oh, shit.

To tell you the truth I don't know what the hell I am doing on the freezing deck of this ship, five thousand tons of rust and rubble if I ever saw it. I can't help feeling that somewhere, years ago, there was a mistake, a big mistake as far as I'm concerned. I've turned all the wrong corners and here I am in the icy Thames on a day like toothache, London one side, marshes the other, and January every bloody where. It's worse than Phillips Elbow.

The crew are aboard, miserable bastards, and the skipper is playing the piccolo in his cabin. I don't know whether he's drunk or whether he just likes the piccolo, because I've only just joined myself. Chief Officer Arthur McCann, recently relieved of captain's duties (in painful circumstances) sailing for the south, which is a place you then sail from to go north or east or west. Eventually you disappear up your own jacksie; or reach Port Desire.

I don't mean necessarily the actual place where my great-grandfather sits dead in his private barrel. But some stinking hole like that. As I said, my great-grandmother really thought he had gone to Bristol for the day. But he sidled away to South America and while he was making love to a twelve-year-old Indian girl a potty dog bit him on the arse and he died the terrible death of rabies. I know this for a fact because I've been to the place and I got a native to read the story on his grave. The Indians thought he was a secondary god so they buried him sitting in this barrel and put a headstone over him. That he died in Port Desire only filtered back after years and my great-grandmother was too old and deaf to care then, anyway. She was always sewing ribbons on her hat saying she was going to Bristol to look for him.

I've watched this crew come aboard today. I know some of them of old and they know me. Hobbling up the gangway with their belongings like refugees staggering five hundred miles instead of fifty yards from a taxi. You can actually see the grumbles growing on their faces when they see the ship. By the end of the first week they'll all know me and I'll know them.

They're like wandering children. If they had a survey on which profession *cries* the most the seafarer would come top. Usually for himself. They are afraid because the sea is big, going out on a voyage like infants trembling towards the lavatory in the dark. They boast about the places they've been and seen and yet they often don't know the world is round. All they know is they set out and they come back, and at the end they say they'll never go to sea again. They always say that.

But I'm one of them anyway, a one-man Flying Dutch-man, condemned to sail this way and that until death. And with no reason now. At forty-two where is there any place for me, better than any other? Unless the girl in Auckland or Gosport meant what she said, which she didn't.

I have had my adventures, however, and although I look enviously tonight at the lit buses taking men to their homes, sitting there on the top decks behind their papers, out of the snow; although I envy them, in my discomfort, for their comfort and for their everyday loves, I know that not one has ever been to Bodie's brothel in the Arctic.

The night they auctioned off the new girls at Phillips Elbow, the thick snow of the new winter was humming down from the Pole and there was a fresh skin of ice right across the

9

river. They did the auction at Bodie's place, each man discreetly approaching either Mr or Mrs Bodie and mentioning a price he was willing to pay to be first with one of the new season's crop.

Bodie's is the most northerly house of ill-repute in the world, well above the Arctic Circle (unless something hitherto unsuspected is happening at Novaya Zemlya). Nobody can get in and out of Phillips Elbow, except by occasional ski-plane, for at least four months of the year, so the anxiety to be first with any of the fresh consignment is understandable because they quickly get worn out. Inside as well as out it was a wild night; by tradition, Mr and Mrs Bodie trying to fight off the eager hands of the trappers and lumbermen as the girls walked with professional allure among them in the big bar. The noise was tremendous, smothering the tunes played by the three-piece string band, also newly arrived for the winter. Before the evening was through they were soaked in beer anyway. Music came a bad third at Bodie's.

I had a pain that night, low in my chest, and I was not enjoying the novel festival as much as I should have been. I was just as new there as the girls for I had only flown in on the ski-plane that afternoon, relief captain for the *SS Northern Swan*, lying in the cold Phillips River.

A bottle of whisky in each fist, my predecessor, Captain Happy Harrington, had reportedly gone off into the forests saying he was going to feed the grizzlies and had not been seen since. The river would be iced up in a week and the ship had to be loaded and clear before she was trapped in the Arctic until spring.

'Last steamer of the year,' the pilot had said banking over the jagged river and the settlement spread at the bend that gave it the name of Phillips Elbow. 'She's nearly there. Sure won't be anybody on the field.'

I could see my new command sitting alongside the blunt jetty just before the river took its sharp turn. Two thousand tons and even from the plane she looked as though she leaked. Moving up towards her was a fat river steamer, smoke streaming joyously from its pencil funnel. I could see there were already blobs of ice on the river. 'Which field?' I said.

'Landing field,' he answered laconically. 'They'll all be waiting for the steamer. Look at the cars making for the landing stage down there, and all those guys waiting.'

'Nobody to see us down, then,' I said with concern looking over the side to where the red shirts were dotted like poppies by the river.

'Nope,' he said. 'I guess we'll have to let ourselves in.'

It was then that I first felt the pain. I thought it might have been the discomfort occasioned by the prospect of the unassisted landing. I curled up for a moment but it went and I straightened in the seat.

'You laughing about something?' said the pilot.

'No, I had a pain,' I said.

'If you don't have one now, you sure soon will,' he replied morosely. 'The grub down there is the worst anywhere in the world. Guts-acheville, it certainly is.'

'There's a man on the landing strip,' I pointed out with relief. He was waving the orange discs.

'Devotion to duty,' grunted the pilot. He turned the nose down and we went across the river, then the congregation of men at the landing stage. They were so engrossed with the approaching steamer that scarcely a face turned up to the ski-plane. As we came into the landing strip the man with the discs waved them indiscriminately a few times, then turned and bolted towards the landing stage. The pilot hummed understandingly and set the plane down. We reached the exact point where the orange discs were lying in the thin snow. The hurried footprints set off from there.

'Is the steamer that important?' I said to the pilot. 'I suppose it's the mail's coming in.'

'Females,' he said. I jumped down and he threw my bag out and followed it.

'Oh, women,' I said.

'Sure, female women. It's the last steamer in for the season and they always bring the new girls on it.' As he said this he was apologetically, but quickly striding away from me and then he broke into a run and went off like a horse in the direction taken by the disc man's footprints.

I picked up my bag and walked after him. The pain came on biliously again, stopping me, then receding. I went into the shack at the end of the airstrip but there was no one there, only a tethered husky asleep by the stove. A telephone began to ring. I picked it up. 'Sammy,' said an urgent voice. 'Sammy.'

'Sammy's gone to the steamer,' I said with confidence.

'What they like?' he almost screamed. 'What they like?'

'Who?'

'Ferchristsake!' he shouted. 'The wimmin! The new wimmin.'

'I don't rightly know,' I said.

'Yer don't know! You sweet or som'ing?'

'I've just got here,' I said irritably. I had the pain again. 'Anyway the steamer's not in yet.'

'Listen, mister,' he said like a threat. 'I don't care for the sound of you. I'm stuck up here on Monro Mountain and I can't get down because o' my leg, and you can't even be civil to a man.'

'I'll get Sammy to call you,' I promised evenly. 'But I don't think there's going to be much left over. Everybody's down there waiting. Why don't you hobble down?'

He let out a half cry, half moan. The husky looked at me sleepily. I went out and followed yet another set of tracks towards the town. All roads led to the jetty for soon they were joined by others and then more, curving in to the main path like the branches of a tree.

As I trudged further down into the small wooden town I began to realize fully what a remarkable day that was in Phillips Elbow. Apart from a few women, standing at their doors looking sadly or sarcastically towards the jetty, the settlement was empty. Puzzled dogs wandered about the main street. Some of the women looked malevolently at me as I passed and one called an obscenity in my direction as though I were responsible for the weaknesses and behaviour of the entire male sex.

Then a young woman, clinging like a classical portrait of despair to a doorpost, called to me: 'Tell Neddy Shanks his wife is waiting for him, please mister. Tell Neddy Shanks to come back.' She crouched close to the doorpost and hugging it began to weep.

'I'll tell him if I see him,' I promised, because I was sorry for her.

'The bastard will be in the front line, mister,' she sobbed after me. I nodded but went on without turning.

At the jetty the events were amazing. I suppose that being cut off from the world for so much of time has an effect on people that we who are free to come and go as we wish cannot understand. The men were six deep, jostling and pushing, cursing each other, waiting for the gangplank of the steamer to be lowered. She was standing against the jetty now, two cables ahead of my own ship. There were some people on the deck, watching and waving, but no assembly of women.

'Harry!' bawled an anxious voice from the shore. 'Are they aboard? Have they come, Harry?'

A man grinned from the top deck rail and shouted back. 'They sure are Benjie. They're just powdering their noses down below.'

This information was greeted with a whoop of anticipation that I had only heard in the wildest of westerns. The men were on tiptoe, eyes afire, tongues lapping over lips. But before the expected troupe came ashore there came another diversion. A small motor bus pulled up at the jetty and a dozen women, wretched wenches, deep in furs, and cigarette smoke, disembarked and filed like prisoners towards the steamer's gang plank. I was amazed at the treatment they received. Shameful insults were thrown at them, and enormous male raspberries; some were even pushed and jostled as they flounced through the mob, each carrying a small hand-case and attempting a defiant swing of the buttocks. I realized immediately that this was the return of the last consignment of whores, weary, reviled, but not without spirit. One of the larger women returned a rudery

13

delivered from the front rank of tormentors with a powerful push that sent one of the shorter men careering back into his companions.

But, such was the anticipation for the new arrivals, that there was no serious scene. The final veteran woman reached the top of the gangway, turned her raddled face to the crowd, shouted mysteriously; 'You've all got it!' and raised two stubby fingers as an illustration or a curse.

Yells and foul language flew after her, but then a new anticipatory silence dropped over the men. There must have been a hundred or more, quickly quiet as though some miracle was about to be wrought. I remembered Neddy Shanks. Sometimes I do tactless things out of a sort of inborn and idiotic perversity, bordering on supreme stupidity. This was one of them. 'Neddy Shanks,' I called out. 'Neddy Shanks.'

Various men pointed towards the front row, where Mrs Shanks had correctly forecast her husband would be stationed. 'What d'you want? Who is it?' I saw, to my relief that he was a small man, tough and weasel-featured, but small, and I waved in a comradely manner and called: 'Your wife asked me to tell you to go home.'

All round me huge faces burst with merriment, men began rolling to one side and another with laughter and from the front I detected a swift passage being forced between the bodies and I knew that Neddy was coming after me. He arrived angrily from between the shoulders of the men immediately in front. 'My wife?' he snarled, looking up nastily. 'What you been doin' with my wife, mister?'

'Nothing at all,' I said with caution. The pain had come back. I felt myself go white. I hoped he would not hit me in that region. 'I was just passing and she asked me to give you the message.'

I did not like the look of him at all, but a sudden shudder in the crowd took his attention away. The girls were on the way. He began to make a return burrow through the big men, calling back to me: 'You keep away from that decent married woman, pal, or I'll be attending to you.'

The girls were greeted with a deep, happy, roar from the men of Phillips Elbow. The first one, face and body enveloped in what Chicago or Montreal imagined an Eskimo wore, stood nervously at the top of the gangway, with the others pushing timidly behind her, and in the middle of them a sharp looking couple, Mr and Mrs Bodie, urging them ashore.

I suppose there were about twenty girls. They came ashore and were immediately pushed and touched and embraced by the ecstatic northerners. Kisses and pinches rained on them despite the violent tactic employed by the Bodies to keep the men at bay. Although he was red-faced and in late middle age Mr Bodie, using arms and hands like buffers, pushed the biggest men aside, calling: 'Get off, pigs! Get off or you're on my blacklist!' Mrs Bodie was repeating this threat in a squeaky English voice like a retired Sunday School teacher, 'Blacklist! Blacklist!' It apparently carried a good deal of power because the men began retreating and waving their hands impotently in the air around about the troupe of new arrivals. Safely through the crowd the girls mounted the bus which had recently disgorged their used predecessors and drove off through the surrounding excitement, fists and hands banging on the outside of the windows, and promises shouted in the rudest terms.

When the bus had gone the men of Phillips Elbow stood around discussing, then arguing over, what they had seen of the arrivals, but the party was over and they began to go back towards the town. Some of them, including unmistakably Neddy Shanks, began to run.

Even the most charitable estimate of the majority of the new girls at Bodie's that night would not have given them much chance of avoiding starvation in any location other than immediately behind the lines of a nasty battlefield or somewhere like Phillips Elbow.

The bar was like a barn, full of acrid smoke and smells and noise, the lofty roof rattling like a loose sail in the northern wind. MacAndrews, the inebriate chief engineer of my new command, was with me to try and drink away his depression over the strange departure of Captain Harrington. He was almost incidental to the proceedings that night, hanging morosely on to a bottle and a glass, and moaning: 'But he *loved* bears. He really *loved* them.' Every half an hour my pain would come back, sharper and filling the cave just under my lungs. The next morning we were due to sail. The ice would be thick in a few days.

Men were sitting ten to a table and the new girls were wobbling in and out of the narrow openings. Hands and suggestions went out towards them, but both Mr and Mr Bodie cruised around like escorting gunboats with a convoy, knocking away the most demanding grasps and crying their dire cry: 'Blacklist! Blacklist!' This continued to be a potent deterrent because the men forced themselves back, howling with the agony of the sacrifice, sometimes, and banging their fists with exasperation on the deal tables, as the whores paraded. Most of those girls would have looked better if they had kept their furs wrapped around them. Some were anxious and overweight, rolling dangerously against outstretched limbs and beer and whisky bottles stacked on the tables' edges.

One, with more bulges than it would seem biologically possible on one human body, rolled her ridiculously dark eyes enticingly and sucked heavily on her teeth. Another, who must have been forty-five and twelve stone, wore a gym slip, school blazer, and thick black stockings. There were two or three with thin, consumptive-looking features who, I thought at the time, would be lucky to see the spring. Others were ugly but obviously confident of other attributes, looking about with expressions which indicated that they had seen all this before, and worse, which made me wonder where the hell they had been.

Some were not so bad, I suppose, provided there was nowhere else to go (and in Phillips Elbow there isn't, except the Hudson's Bay Mission Cinema) and you had drunk enough not to care. One was just beautiful.

Because I was not familiar with that region I thought at first that she must be Eskimo. She stood more or less shyly towards the back of the room, smiling quietly at the musicians, who, until then, had not been subjected to any flung beer. Strangely, she was not attracting the attention that the other girls were getting. The customers were avidly making their bids to Mr and Mrs Bodie, pointing at the girls and naming their price, while the owners wrote quickly in little notebooks, Mrs Bodie with a silver pencil. Perhaps the girl was too far in the shadow, perhaps she was too slim and small for men who eat a three pound steak and eight eggs for breakfast. Perhaps they thought she looked too exclusive. I did.

Her cheekbones were high, pushing up against her slant eyes; she had a small pursed mouth and black hair pulled away severely from her face. She was the only one of the girls with a dress to her throat. Around her neck she wore a modest crucifix on a gold chain.

MacAndrews was at the table beside me, head in arms, still moaning: '*Liked* bears. He really did.' I stood up and walked by the girl, smiling as I did. She smiled back encouragingly, diminishing any passing thought I had that she might have come in from the mission to save everybody. I went around the tables to where Mr Bodie was taking bids in his busy book. 'Excuse me,' I said. 'Can I have a word with you?'

'Sure, sure,' he nodded backing away from the trappers at the table. 'You're the guy who's come up to take the *Northern Swan* out, ain't you?'

'That's right.'

'I know everything in this town,' he said. 'Even on a change-over day. You don't look too good, mister.'

'I've got a bit of a pain,' I said holding my chest.

'Don't have a pain here,' he warned. 'You'll die. The doctor's the sickest man in these parts. He can't do nothin' for himself, poor bastard. What's your name again?'

'Captain McCann,' I said. 'Arthur McCann.'

'Meet the lady wife,' he said civilly. 'Mirabelle, come

over here.' Mrs Bodie looked up from the bidders surrounding her and greeted me effusively.

'Captain McCann,' said her husband as I bowed and she treated me to a quaint old curtsey. 'Come to take the place of Harrington what's been ate by they bears.'

'Mirabelle's English,' he said to me cosily.

'From Droitwich Spa,' added Mrs Bodie. 'That was when it was a *nice* place. Before they put up all the wireless masts.' She sighed genteely: 'Poor Captain Harrington. Those bears are so beastly, Mr McCann.'

I frowned conventionally. 'You think that's what happened, do you?' I said.

'Listen,' Mr Bodie sniffed grimly. 'They grizzlies ain't keepin' him to bring up as one o' their own. That only happens in books.'

'Poor Captain Harrington,' repeated Mrs Bodie. She immediately brightened, however, and said: 'Don't let's talk about that. We're all having such a happy time tonight. I always think this is a lovely occasion in Phillips Elbow, Captain.'

'Highlight of the social year,' confirmed her husband. 'What do you think of our new playmates?'

'The girls? Oh, very nice indeed.'

Mrs Bodie beamed. 'I'm so glad, Captain, that you approve. We have to cast our net wide for girls like this, you know.'

'I can imagine,' I said. 'Is that one an Eskimo?'

'Good heavens, no!' exclaimed Mrs Bodie looking in the direction of my nod. 'She's *very* exclusive. From eastern parts, I believe, isn't she, Ewart?'

'From Korea,' said her husband. 'She's a Korea girl.' He beamed. 'Hey, just get that! Korea girl! It's a funny!'

I laughed loudly and felt the pain stretch in my inside. Mrs Bodie gave her husband an old-fashioned girlish push. 'Ewart! Really, you *are* a caution.'

'Exclusive,' murmured Mr Bodie. 'Very exclusive, Captain.'

18

'I can see that,' I agreed.

'In fact,' he confided, 'I think maybe I made a mistake with that one. She's too exclusive and that ain't no good in a place like Phillips Elbow. See I've only got two bids for her, and the sort of money these two jerks want to spend they can't afford to hold one of her hands between them.'

He glanced challengingly at me: 'Hundred bucks,' he said. 'Our Special Introductory Offer. And for that you get the Big Bear Suite, which is our best.'

'Our very best,' echoed Mrs Bodie. 'And she seems such a nice girl. Well worth the money.'

I only had seventy, so I went back to MacAndrews, who was lying insensible across our table, and took thirty from his wallet. It was only a loan, of course, but when everything happened afterwards it was overlooked and I never saw him again. He probably wondered who had robbed him.

'Each of our suites is named after a figure in our history,' said Mr Bodie proudly as he took us upstairs together. The girl was holding my hand comfortingly. The pain had gone away for a while. 'Wolfe, Montcalm, Strathcona and so on. Big Bear and Poundmaker.' He paused and then said: 'They last two was Indian Chiefs.'

The Korean girl was looking at me with faint, assured amusement in her narrowed eyes. She moved without a sound.

'What a good idea,' I said politely to Mr Bodie.

'We like it,' he said. 'And you have our best suite. Have a good night, Captain, and God bless you both.'

He went away as though to pray. I touched the girl's elbow so that she went in front of me. She seemed very young and shy, but she closed the door behind us with professional assurance.

'Good and fine,' she said with chiming voice. 'What you called?'

'Captain McCann,' I smiled. 'Arthur.'

'Captain McCann Arthur,' she repeated carefully. 'I call you Captain, okay?'

'Okay. What shall I call you?'

'Anything,' she shrugged. She was carefully folding down the cover on the double bed, a charming touch of domesticity.

'How 'bout Maggie. You like Maggie, Captain?'

'Yes, I like you, Maggie,' I said seriously. She really was small, beautiful. Her features were broad but accentuated with those fine cheekbones and she had Oriental freckles on her nose.

The room was comfortable, probably luxurious for those parts. There was a full-grown grizzly bear rug on the floor topped with grimacing head, and a rough drawing of an Indian, presumably Big Bear on the wall above the bed. There was also, for no sound reason I could imagine, a tourist poster of the Vatican. A blind at the window moved irritably with a finger of wind that was getting in from the night outside.

'Do you think you're going to like it?' I asked. She was undoing my tie with accustomed charm. There was a strong musky smell coming from her neck.

'I like it if you like it,' she said bluntly.

'I mean the place,' I said, embarrassed. 'Phillips Elbow.'

'I don' think so,' she sighed. 'I was in San Francisco. That much better. But I guess I need vacation. I thought this place was ski resort.'

'You made a bad mistake,' I said.

'Maybe. Maybe not. Maybe I find gold nugget.' She unbuttoned my shirt and rubbed her small hands against my chest. 'Now,' she added with a sign of finality. 'You tell me where you from and then we quit the family stories and where you come from, this, and where you been, that. You din pay hundred bucks to talk, Captain. Okay?'

She indicated that this had closed the subject except for the question of my homeland.

'I'm from England,' I said.

'I hear of England,' she nodded slickly. 'You have nice Royal people. Okay. No more little talk now.'

'Suits me,' I said. It did too. She undressed me almost

pedantically, folding my clothes neatly, which pleased me because I'm of tidy habits. I remember now how Pamela brought that up. She looked closely at each bit of me which became revealed, even giving my knee caps a brief twist as though to see if anything would fall off me. Then, without fuss, she put both tiny hands between my legs and lifted my whole sexual assembly as if making a guess at the weight. She dropped to her knees and ran a surveyor's eye along the upper edge of my extended thing, pressed the front end down and let it jump up under its own spring.

'Is it all there?' I inquired. She had taken nothing off yet.

'Sure. Very nice,' she said. 'It work very good.'

'It has up to now,' I answered.

She ignored the remark and standing up said with nurse-like formality, 'Bath in there.' She pointed to a screen at one corner of the room. Reluctantly, wondering now if the night was going to be all I had hoped, I went behind the screen. On the floor half full of warm water was an enamel bath emblazoned with the words 'Canadian Pacific Railways'. Feeling foolish I stood in it, I felt as uncertain and exposed as I did the first day I paddled as a child in the sea at Barry Island. After a few moments she came around the screen, unfussily still businesslike, but now naked.

At that moment I got a new fearful spasm of pain about my midriff. I bent forward, almost double, and it brought tears to my eyes. I half-straightened when she appeared, but I knew than I had something serious going wrong. If this had not gone so far, if we had not been there, facing each other naked, I would have gone back to the ship and gone to bed.

'Sorry,' I gasped when I saw her wondering. 'Indigestion, that's all, Maggie.'

She spontaneously sang a little jingle:

'Alka-Seltzer.

Happy Alka-Seltzer.'

Then she took a bar of soap, grimaced at it as though it were of inferior standard, shrugged, and began to soap me carefully all over. My hands went down to the small cherry

21

breasts and I rubbed them fondly as she rubbed me. She seemed to be pleased and began to hum a quiet, almost whispered, tune. Her hands busily worked the soap into me a square inch at a time. She brought hot water in an enamel jug, also marked 'Canadian Pacific Railways', and washed me down with it. I had a feeling strange things were about to happen. They were.

If you ever have the misfortune to get acute appendicitis, try to ensure that you are not in Bodie's brothel in the Arctic at the time. Facilities for dealing with it there are limited.

Maggie had bathed me like a child, and dried me carefully six square inches at a time with a rough towel. The effect of this gentle operation was such that she was able to actually hang the towel on me, like a flag, while she went around the screen to what was apparently a set, hundred dollar, ritual.

'Captain,' she called. 'You come in now.'

I went around the screen and saw that she had prepared what in my not inconsiderable experience is the oddest oddity I have ever discovered. Even now I find it difficult to pick my words with enough care so as not to cause embarrassment to myself or to inconvenience others. It is difficult to know exactly why, because although what took place was exotic, it also had that certain domestic charm, which is something I have sought throughout all my life and travels. I have never chanced upon it since, even in the Orient, and when the memory now returns I am only sorry I was unable to stay, for the finish.

She had lit a small primus stove and upon it had placed a saucepan of water. Over this, if you please, she required me to sit, with part of me going into the pot to simmer gently. She was going to cook me!

At first I staggered away, blushing and laughing, at the very absurdity of the notion. I flustered and pushed my hands out, but she firmly led me to it and made me squat as she required.

'Water not hot,' she said. She was right. She was very serious, but I began to laugh at the very idiocy of it.

'No laugh,' she warned sternly. 'Very good for man to cook first. Make it very good for later.'

'How will I know when they're done?' I asked.

'You know,' she said. She obviously liked this bit herself and she wanted me to be serious. She came over and kissed me fully on the mouth, and then moved her small breast to my lips. The water was getting warm in the saucepan. My natural anxiety was overcome by curiosity. A delicious feeling began spreading upwards through my loins. I felt my blood running fast and my tension and desire becoming more with every moment. (Here I feel constrained to include a warning that this strange technique unknown to me before and since – embarrassment coupled with fear having prevented any lonely experiments – has possible dangers of which *I* know nothing and should only be attempted with extreme caution and with medical aid within reach.) Then the pain really got me. I don't know whether it had been waiting until I really was in the middle of everything, or whether this culinary sex had brought it on, but it went through me like a vengeful sword, streaking right up through my stomach and my breast. I howled and staggered, doubled up. I heard her cry out and over went the saucepan, but fortunately not the stove.

Staying there was no good. I had to get out and get help. I pulled the towel half about myself and stumbled to the door, spiked with agony, bile filling my mouth, eyes unable to focus. Right opposite was a room marked 'Service' which I had noticed before. Crying with the pain I lumbered across the empty landing and in through the door seeking someone to help.

As it was I burst in on my acquaintance, the small but truculent Neddy Shanks, riding naked on the biggest fattest girl of that day's import. She howled and he snorted with disbelief when he saw me. I had the impression of him sliding from her like a man slithering down a mountain. He was swinging his fists as he came towards me, but he didn't need to hit me. I collapsed and through the misty pain the shouts subsided. Then there were voices and steps all around me and I felt myself being borne away. I must have been muttering my excuse. 'Service, it said Service' because through it all I could hear the annoyed tones of Mr Bodie saying: 'There's a man who don't know poetry. Who'd think it? Who'd think it?'

Well, for God's sake, who would have thought of calling a room in a knock-house after Robert Service, Arctic poet though he was. Not much of a memorial for a man like that. They should have stuck to Big Bear and Poundmaker.

Apparently they sobered the doctor up sufficiently for him to give me some morphine and the next day they flew me out on the same ski-plane which had brought me in. On the landing strip as they were about to load me Maggie arrived and treated me to a sweet kiss. I whispered, 'Goodbye, Mrs Beaton,' in her little ear, but she didn't understand.

There was some commotion at the extreme edge of the airstrip and they told me that a man called Turk, who had a leg mauled by a bear and lived alone on Monro Mountain had been found dead among the trees.

'Must have been trying to get into town to see the new women,' said the pilot. 'Like they say, it's not just the women that kills you. It's the running after them.'

2

The McCanns, having emigrated to Wales from Ireland via Scotland, a classic compounding of errors, were a strange family, riven by rumours, suspicions and jealousies far more than most. There were individual pockets of love and regard and some temporary alliances were formed when appropriate, but, in general, we were a family wired together by our hatreds.

My father, Philip McCann, was a crewman on board a Bristol Channel pilot boat, but told everyone, even those who were in a position to know he was lying, that he was the actual pilot. It must have seemed strange to many people that such an exalted man as a marine pilot should live in a house like ours. To those who made this point, my father would reply that he was honourably paying off family debts accumulated over the years. He was a wide, gingery man, much given to uncontrolled laughter at his own jokes. From the moment when I was old enough to realize who he was I did not like him (for a start he built a sort of trick high chair for me when I was a baby, which collapsed when I sat in it; a poor basis for love).

The family guessing game revolved around trying to compute which of my mother's six sisters had not been bedded by my father. There was known to be one who had not had her Phil, as it were, just as surely as there were known to be five who most assuredly had.

Christmas was, predictably, never a happy time for us. There was a cloud of suspicion moving around the table; eyes getting smaller and imaginations getting larger and even when they were laughing they would all be looking sideways at each other. My father sailed through it all of course, the big shining bastard, and my mother was the most unhappy of all. Even the children, my cousins, as they grew to understand about sexual relations would join in the elimination game to try and put a fix on the untouched aunt. They would squint around the festive table with the rest and in a way it was interesting, I suppose, because once they got too old to believe in Santa Claus there was something else to occupy them and that void which other children know was conveniently filled.

Nobody ever *did* anything about my father. Not until Uncle Lewis managed it on his death bed; the best and foulest trick anybody has ever perpetrated with their last puff. But that was the trouble; we all left it too late.

I used to crouch in chapel on Sunday, with my old man's praying and singing voice many decibels louder than anyone's, looking at the necks of the famous seven sisters of Newport, my father's harem, in the long pew in front. Once,

25

when I was very young, I saw my Uncle Cess crying into his hymn book.

Floss, Daisy, Clementine, Ramona, Peggy, Nardine, and Josie, my mother; those were their names. Sometimes, even at the distance of all these years and miles, I have mentally ticked through the list and tried, without success, to eliminate one from my father's conquest. They were the daughters of a pork butcher in Dock Street, Newport, and they were a handsome family in those days. I used to think that my mother was probably the least beautiful of them, but this could have been familiarity, seeing her about the washing and gardening or carrying the coal; or sitting, her face clogged with unhappiness and doubt, waiting for my father to come home.

'He's got a perilous job, your father has, Arthur,' she used to say when I asked what was troubling her. 'Perilous.' She loved the word, with its sniff of religion and the sea. She would quietly moan through the late hours. 'He could be at the bottom of the Bristol Channel at this moment. Right down deep among all that black mud. That's why I worry, Arthur. That's why.'

Later when I grew to know things, I realized that if Phil McCann was deep down among anything it was more likely to be somebody's bedclothes than Bristol Channel mud. But she waited for him, sometimes keeping the light bleakly on till daybreak, screwed up in painful half-sleep, and always pitifully glad to see him when he arrived, fussing about making tea and grilling bacon and scolding me, saying it was time I was in bed because I was only a little child. This would be three or four in the morning. I had sat up all night because it had never occurred to her, until then, to tell me to go to bed. How I hated him even then. I was always so tired.

My mother and her sisters were all Welsh girls, of course, but unusually tall and stately, each with fine long hair mantling their backs or piled high above their faces. Each walked with her ovalled chest pushed forward in the manner of the distant Edwardians so that when they processed down Dock Street, as they sometimes did, the whole clutch of them, they looked like a flotilla of ships' figureheads. Even when they were all married-off they would still meet regularly at their father's shop and float down the street, making short squeaky calls to each other as they voyaged, laughing shrilly, or trying to compose their faces after some shared joke. Newport men would stand in the doorway of The Donkeyman Hotel and make jocular but complimentary remarks about the seven beautiful sisters, saying it was a shame the age of the bustle had gone because they would have suited the girls.

In those days, of course, Newport was a coaling town and the sisters were for ever wiping smuts of dust from each other as they walked towards the little black park that squatted forlornly among the dingy streets at the docks. At some sort of sensed signal they would stop and gather about each other wiping off grains of Ebbw Vale Number Six with lace handkerchiefs and spit. The clouds that puffed up from the loading ships at the wharves hung over the streets like gunpowder after a battle. Rain would force it to the pavements and smear the windows of the houses. The rivers, the Usk and the Ebbw, floated on cradles of coal.

There were always ships at the end of our street. The terrace houses stretched down to the dockside where they fused in a conglomeration of masts and funnels like some sort of fairground. The view was as natural to me as a child as factory chimneys or rising fields would have been to other children. Before the war all the ships would be lit at night with globular lights like big stars and I would lean from my bedroom window and watch them.

In that street husbands used to straggle up from the Newport docks, coal-faced like miners, the dust falling from their trousers and even trickling from their ears. On Fridays they would get drunk as they got paid.

'Who's that who's fallen down by the lamp, Arthur?' my mother would say, only half interested, trying to see from the window and through the only good privet hedge between the Cardiff Road and the Bristol Channel. 'Mr Griffiths or Mr Jenkins?'

Seeing men, their faces as black as gunners, lying in the gutter on Friday was no phenomenon. Children would sometimes gather around them and poke them with their toes, as though they were dead animals. Once the lump had been identified the interest was in witnessing the appropriate wife, summoned by the street grapevine, come to claim her man. I once saw Mrs Richards, a lard-coloured woman who for some reason always wore a black skullcap, arrive up the street to get a bundle she understood was her husband, only to find on arrival that it was Mr Jenkins. 'That pig,' she snorted, rolling him back into the gutter and going back to her house.

Most of the women were heavy and capable enough, or had sufficient bite in their voices, to either drag or rouse the men from their stupor. They looked strong but they didn't live long. Six women in our length of terrace died in their forties.

Mrs Figaro, who lived next door to us, was not only foreign but thin and weak as well. Her husband Will had brought her home like a prize from the Spanish Civil War. His name was Llewellyn but in her early days in the street she couldn't say it, so she called herself Mrs Figaro, which I suppose must have been her unmarried name, and it stuck. When he came home from the docks and fell down somewhere by the way, all the children in the street would rush to get there, because Mrs Figaro put on a show of weeping and wailing such as none of us had ever heard.

She was eloquent in her tears, to our delight actually lying across the prostrate body, crying, pleading, praying, beating him with her small olive fists, letting her long black hair fall across his uncaring back. Then she would offer us a half-penny each if we would help her to get him to the house and Mr Llewellyn would be borne down the street to number twelve by twenty triumphant children, the weeping wife holding his unconscious head as though fearful it might

28

topple off. Other children ran alongside screaming and hooting as he was taken home.

These were the men who stayed in the houses in the street. The others, who went to sea, came home infrequently but, usually, with equal spectacle. There was a ship's cook at the end of the terrace who would break nearly all the windows in his house, and some of those next door, to announce to his family and neighbours that he was safe home again. He spent all his leaves putting glass back in the windows. Mr Evans, across the road, used to play his accordion on his doorstep when he arrived in the middle of the night, and Mr Finnegan, an Irishman, would shin up the street lamp outside his wife's bedroom and try to look through the window, attempting to catch her with somebody else. Everybody knew he did this. My mother would say casually to my father: 'Mr Finnegan's home, Phil. I can see him up the lamp trying to look through Amy's window.'

There was the odd tragedy. Mr Owen, a donkeyman and a rare considerate husband for those parts, returned one night during the war and, not wishing to wake his family, stepped into the air raid shelter to sleep, not knowing that during his voyage the shelter had filled with water. The poor donkeyman was found floating and drowned the next day.

'You're not going to sea, Arthur,' my mother said when we had the news of this mishap. 'It's too perilous.' The fact that Mr Owen had survived mines and submarines in the Atlantic only to be drowned outside his own back door did not occur to her. She always said I must not go to sea. She did not even like me going to the docks to see the ships, or cycling down to the lighthouse to look at the immense Channel. 'The salt will give you catarrh, Arthur,' she told me. 'Your father's got catarrh from too much salt and the sea is so wet.' She would gaze at me with embarrassing concern, rock her head and mutter: 'Don't ever go foreign, boy. It's no good to anybody going to those parts.'

Not that I had felt any urge to go to sea. As a boy I liked to watch it from the anchorage of dry land, and I would go with the others in the street to see the ships, like helpless babies being led from the port to the open channel by the Newport tugs.

'If you want to travel,' she would suggest as a compromise, 'join the Company.' The Company was Great Western Railway. That's how she used to think, poor cow. But I suppose waiting for Phil McCann to come home year after year must have taken its toll. Besides which my sister Audrey, who had been confirmed in Christ and was a Sunday School teacher, had joined the Women's Air Force and when she came home on her first leave screamed dramatically from the top of our stairs: 'Where's my arse-holing toothbrush?' My mother had to cling to something.

Sometimes I used to think it must be Clemmie, Clementine, whom my father had failed to furgle. She was jolly and laughing and she used to snap the men's braces and put her hands in their trouser pockets, but she used to blush sometimes too, when someone made some untoward remark about God, or someone similar, and this made me think that beneath it all she was basically very good. Floss was going quietly but surely to fat; Ramona going at about the same pace and equal certainty to madness. Peggy went white and silent when my father appeared in a room and Nardine became flushed and chatty. Daisy always kissed him twice. The husbands all thought they knew who was the odd aunt out, their own wife, but each one, in his heart, doubted his judgement. Uncle Cess tried many times to get my father drunk, so he would tell him, but it was always my father who carried the sodden Cess home to his wife, returning at an early hour of the morning. I always thought that apart from my father and the particular aunt, my mother was the only one with the answer. And, for their separate reasons, none of them ever told.

It was Uncle Lewis who finally did for him. But for Uncle Lewis it *was* finally. His deathbed was in the Cardiff Marine Hospital, because he was one of the original Cape Horners and he was allowed to die in there. There was the customary phalanx of family around his pillows, sniffing, scraping their feet and looking at their watches as though there were a sweepstake on the time he would depart. His wife, Floss, was mumbling her grief into her scarf. Then my father burst in, new suit, trilby hat, smile; the harbour breeze still on his face.

Bouncing up to the candle-faced man in the bed he roared tactlessly: 'Anything you'll be wanting then, Lewis?'

'A decent burial,' stumbled my uncle, evoking a lost howl from Floss. 'And to shake your hand, Phil, that's all. I've been waiting for you, brother.'

He had too. My father strode up like some smartie getting a prize, hand shooting out briskly at the fading Lewis, whose poor paw trembled from beneath the Cardiff Marine Hospital bed covers. And (God be thanked, at least, for this sweet memory) into the bastard's healthy palm the dying man triumphantly pressed a turd he had been secreting in his bed.

A full, felicitous, and final grin, speared my uncle's face for a moment before jealous death wiped it off. My father stood suddenly drained and dreadful, transfixed by that brown, cemented handclasp, as though the death had been passed on to him like some disease. Auntie Floss flung herself in furious weeping across the corpse's bony knees, gathering them to her like someone collecting sticks. Never the most practical of people, my mother tentatively offered Phil the use of a small blue-embroidered handkerchief into which she had been gently crying, making little nervous wiping hints with it as she proffered it. This typical idiocy ignited my father and he furiously pulled his fingers from the chocolate shake. Hideously he began to berate the grey and moribund shell of Lewis propped up on its final pillows. A doctor came along and, showing no surprise whatever at the situation, told my father to cut the shouting.

'This is a dead man,' he said as though making a difficult diagnosis. 'He cannot answer back.'

'He's bloody well said enough!' hooted my father, holding that shitty dread hand out before him.

3

In my fifteenth year I became very frightened because I believed that Mr Winston Churchill, our popular prime minister, had personally sanctioned my execution and was dispatching a firing squad to Newport to carry out the deed. Today any lad of comparable age who thought he was imminently due for a similar end would be thought strange, if not entirely mad. But children are more difficult to fool now and in wartime at least three horrible things happened every day before breakfast. We heard about them on the radio. It was an odd and terrifying time and large and small disasters occurred everywhere. Bombs fell on the streets and ordinary people went out of their houses and never went back again. There were known to be spies everywhere (you were not allowed to tell anyone the time or lend them your bicycle) and the firing squads were busy shooting those who were apprehended. In any case it was my father who told me they were coming to execute me and if a boy cannot believe his father, who is there to believe?

'Sabotaging one of His Majesty's balloons!' he howled, after the police had been around to tell him what had happened. 'Leaving this town wide open to German air attack. Hitler must be pleased with you.' The next day he told me that Mr Churchill had written a nice letter to him at the docks (so my mother would not know) and had regretfully said that I had to be done away with. He said I ought to stay in my room and pray as much as possible and that I should on no account tell anybody that I was to be executed because it would only give the family a bad name. This, coming on top of the discovery that I was wearing my sister's knickers at school was almost more than my sanity could stand.

The saddest thought was that it was my own junior patriotism and my first clash with uncharted love and sex that brought on the tragedy. The barrage balloon, which arrived in Newport Park just after the war began, floated for days like a happy watchful elephant, silver above our dusty street, quite often above our very roof, in the prevailing South Wales wind. In my boyish way I came to be very fond of it (something I tried eventually, but in vain, to put forward in mitigation to the police and to my father) for it seemed to be the most peaceful and jolly weapon of war ever devised. When the sun shone it always had a smile on its fat face. We had a whole herd of them flying above the town, our silver guardians against the German bombers, keeping those devils so high they couldn't actually see where they were dropping their high explosive. Once, at school, I wrote a kindly poem about it (called 'My Chubby Friend') which my teacher read aloud to the class in a nasty derisory way and had all the other children rupturing themselves laughing over it. I found it difficult to get understanding anywhere.

But I found understanding in the park, at the barrage balloon site. The balloon looked big, calm and benevolent and tending it must have been the most agreeable way of fighting a war against Oppression. The young airmen in the unit looked after their silver bundle, blowing it up like children, letting it down, flying it, mooring it, generally tending to its wants; they kept the winch to which it was tethered in good order, painted their huts and latrines and planted geraniums and strawberries in their garden. They played tennis on the municipal courts in the park, and sometimes went on the swings in the playground with some of the older schoolgirls of the locality.

One day I saw some of the airmen, and the airwomen who were conveniently billeted alongside them, swimming in the black River Ebbw, shouting and laughing in the water under the coal-rooted trees. I was sitting openly on the bank, watching them, when one of the larky men pulled down the front of a young airwoman's bathing costume. In a blinding moment I saw the forbidden puddings, exposed, huge, luscious. (My father had said that if a boy under eighteen saw a naked woman he would turn to stone, and although I didn't believe him, I thought just then that this was happening).

The airwoman had huge ripe things. Memory may have inflated them over the years, but I don't think I have, even now, ever seen bigger. She shrieked a laugh and in an impromptu moment grabbed two handfuls of muddy Ebbw coal-dust from the bank and slapped them to her exposed front. It was my first erotic experience. Thinking about it that night (and many nights after) I wondered that she had not simply pulled up the front of her swimming costume again. Then I knew nothing about the strange perversity of women. But she was certainly big. So was Rose, for that matter, and the other girls there too. I think it might have been because they were specially chosen to help with pulling down the balloon in difficult windy weather.

In the evenings I was often in the park, by the thick inky river, watching the barrage balloon lying puffed out on the grass or floating happily miles up in the vacant late sky. It occurred to me that if the war went on long enough for me to become involved I would ask to go into the barrage balloon service, for what I saw I liked.

Sailors from our street kept on being drowned and the war in the municipal park seemed an attractive alternative, what with the swimming and one thing and another.

But patriotic I was. Wearing my scout uniform and with my stout scout pole in a military position I would stand, unrequested, for hours guarding our local doctor's car. People stared at me from buses and bikes, but I put on a stern face indicating that I alone knew the national importance of my duty. But one evening I heard the doctor's wife shout clearly from the house: 'Glynn! There's that mentally defective boy standing by your car again.'

This discouraged me somewhat from the self-imposed duty and I therefore transferred my decent enthusiasm to the park and the barrage balloon unit, and every evening I would run, walk and eventually stagger on innumerable half-mile journeys to the fish and chip shop on behalf of the balloon men and women. To do this I had to run the gauntlet of an army smoke-screen platoon which used to park its trucks along the main road with the duty of belching oily clouds over the town and the docks, thus further confusing the German bombers, already bemused by the barrage balloons.

It was, as can be imagined, a nasty, greasy job, manning the smoke screen trucks and I suppose they had selected a certain rough type of person to do it. Which is why I had to run the gauntlet with the fish and chips, for the smoke screen men would grab at my scout's shorts, pinch me and pull at my lanyard and my woggle, and try to steal the airmen's supper.

I was always terrified of that frantic run I was forced to make, but it had to be done for there was only the most circuitous of detours which would have rendered the fish and chips cold by the time I reached the park. So I had to brave it, head down, heart beating ribs, thin legs going like a frightened flamingo. The smoky men always made some sort of attack. It was usually less savage when they were attending to the burners which sent out the foul fumes, so I tried to time my run when they were thus occupied. Sometimes I got through with little hurt or annoyance and my cargo intact, but at others I was near to tears, clutching the almost empty wrapping of the South Wales Argus and, like as not, half a piece of hot cod fillet stuffed with boorish malevolence down my young trousers.

My scout shirt and neckerchief became so thick with grease that I was ashamed to show them to my mother and I was admonished at the scout meetings as the grubbiest boy in the troop. I told no one of my evening errands but, after the more desperate runs I would sit panting, and imagine with deadly satisfaction that I would one day be found expired in that spot of a junior heart attack, and that then the whole story would come out. It would be in the *Argus* and my father would tell everyone that I was a good boy after all.

The barrage balloon crew were occasionally grateful, sometimes less so, especially when their supper had been drastically mauled by the smoke men. I was thanked and rebuked in almost equal portions. For my trouble, they gave me a few pence which I put away, intending to make a major contribution to Newport's Buy-a-Bomber Week Fund.

Unfortunately my scout shirt, woggle and neckerchief had become so foul with grease that I reluctantly had to put replacements before a new parachute for a pilot. Otherwise, I was warned, I would be drummed out of the scouts.

On the first evening I wore my new shirt I had a terrible ten minutes getting by the smoke screen trucks. I tried creeping along, as close to the wheels as I could, but a sentry who was supposed to be guarding against German agents spotted me and at once the hunt was on. My only advantages were my swiftness of foot, my ability to turn and twist, and the fact that I was small. But they caught me, my parcels were ravaged, and when I arrived in the park the remaining fish and chips were mashed into what could easily have been taken for a thick soup. One of the balloon men was particularly annoyed and berated me. It was then that Rose came in.

She had been in the park for about a year, a large and pretty girl, with a pink face and stormy black hair. She typed in the orderly office every day and when she saw me she would call out cheerily and wave. Her smart blue uniform was very swollen at the top and I tried not to look at it too much, or think about it at night. She probably had a large bottom and fat knees too, but I don't remember. To me she was a formidable friendly and desirable balloon girl. She pushed aside the complaining airman, picking up one of his few remaining unmashed chips, dropping it casually into her mouth in the same movement, and then guarded me out of the hut.

'Your shirt, lad' she sighed when we were outside in the evening sun. 'What a terrible muck.' She had a Yorkshire voice, almost unknown to my ears.

'The chips get squashed against it,' I explained with more sorrow than I felt, for her large calico hand was on my shoulder and part of it touched my neck. 'It's a new one, as

36

well. I've even got a mess on my woggle.'

'Which is your woggle?' she asked quietly.

'This is,' I said pointing to the leather band holding my scout neckerchief at my throat. She touched it and I felt the backs of her fingers against my enlarging Adam's apple.

'How come they always get so mushed up?' she said. She took me by the hand and we reached the door of a hut. 'Just a tick,' she said. Pushing her head around the door she called violently, 'Get 'em on, girls. There's a man coming in.'

Some small commotion came from inside the hut and I backed away nervously. 'Don't worry, lad,' said Rose. 'It'll be a right treat for them to see a real man for once.' She giggled engagingly. 'I've got some stuff that might get the grease off.' She waited for a moment and then called: 'All clear?' It was and we went into the airwomen's hut with beds and little wardrobes lined down each side. There were about half a dozen women in there and I stood thin and embarrassed, while two of them let out wolf whistles at me. Two were dressed in their uniforms, a couple more were in woolly dressing gowns and two were in the same bed, their heads sticking out in curiosity mixed with mild annoyance, wet hair in curlers, blankets clutched up about their necks.

'You didn't tell me how the chips always get mushed up,' Rose repeated. She had sat me on the rough blanket of her bed and she was kneeling in front of me, rubbing something into the grease on my shirt. Her breasts were hanging forward heavily against my knees giving me agonies of happiness and fear.

'It's the smoke screen men,' I explained, wanting her to stay like that for ever. To my annoyance she backed away from my knees.

'What's it to do with them?' she asked.

'I have to run past them and they try to grab the chips from me,' I said resignedly. 'They do it all the time.'

She stared at me with speechless concern. Then, I thanked God, she leaned forward again, those great tender tits against my boy's bony knees, and began working again

37

on my shirt. 'Do you mean to say those men do that? Chase you and knock you about?' she said eventually. 'Have you told any of the boys here?'

'Yes,' I answered. 'I had to tell them because the chips kept getting in such a state. But they said I'd have to run faster, that's all.'

To my joyous embarrassment the other girls in the hut were gathering around now. It was like sitting in a forest of large and beautiful trees. One of those wearing a dressing gown leaned forward to touch my head sympathetically and as her body came forward and the robe opened I felt like a greedy boy looking into a bag of huge sweets. The two in the bed remained where they were but called out questions and sympathy. Eventually Rose took me to the park gate and with my head full of the smell of her powder and the chemical she had put on my shirt, I walked home like a small prince through the violet evening.

On the next fish and chip run I crept in my usual fearing Indian fashion to the edge of the smoke screen vehicles to be greeted with a shout of 'Hello Little Arthur!' It was the sentry. 'Come on, son. Nothing to be afraid of.' Nor was there. For the smoke screen men had suddenly become benevolent escorts, seeing me safely on my way, asking me, if I had time, to go for fish and chips for them and sending their love to Rose. For the first time I came through without a scratch or a bruise or a single crushed chip. I don't know what Rose did to them. Nor will I know.

I only know what she did to me.

My association with Aircraftwoman Rose Kirby is, I imagine, somewhere documented, written up, and filed in the archives that tell the detailed story of Britain's fight against Nazism from 1939 to 1945. It probably makes plum reading for any clerk who knows where it can be located. For me it is among the sweetest memories I have. I can even remember her number. 842912.

In that golden wartime summer nothing happened between us for a long time. I used to go down to the park and carry out my fish and chip run as before, but now with no danger of damage from the smoke screen men. She always behaved like a big rosy friend, smiling at me with her round and pretty face and touching me with her expansive chest; sometimes gently making fun at me. In the empty evenings, when nobody seemed to be about, and the vapour trails of the day's planes had faded from the sky, we would sit comfortably in the lee of the tethered balloon. She was reading *Gone With The Wind* and she was a slow reader. It took her half of July, all of August and into September. I would be reading *Wulf the Saxon* by Henty or Baden Powell's *Scouting For Boys*, for I was anxious to get several proficiency badges that summer.

We would read passages to each other, quite long pieces sometimes. I found it difficult to get unduly enthusiastic about the blighted love of Scarlett and Rhet, and I don't think she always followed what I was saying about following a spoor or lighting a fire without matches, although she used to help me to memorise the nature signs I had to learn for my woodcraft badge.

Very few people used to see us or bother us. When the balloon was not flying the others in the unit would go into their huts or disappear into the park or visit the picture house in town. She had a full-blown melodious laugh, like a sweetly played tuba. When she came to a description of a battle in her book she would put her wide plain hand on my thin arm to arrest my reading and in an almost comically flat Yorkshire voice she would relate the passage, supposing that, as a boy, I must be interested in battles and blood. I would wait patiently while she retold the slaughter and then I would enlist her aid in rehearsing the woodcraft signs; the signs which signified the presence of water or a mad dog, or the two stones which told the tracker that the quarry had gone home to tea.

'That looks like a cottage loaf,' she said, when I showed her how the stones were placed, the smaller sitting on top of the other. 'Gone home, is it? I think that's really neat,

Arthur, that is. Really neat. Much better than writing it down.'

'Well,' I said logically, 'in the forest you wouldn't be likely to have pencil and paper and even if you did the message would probably get blown away.' I looked up at her and saw she was regarding me with a potent, serious smile. 'Will you help me with some of the others?' I asked carefully. Something nervous began wriggling inside my chest. I hesitantly glanced again at her to make sure I wasn't mistaken, and my throat clogged with the sudden and powerful excitement.

'Come here Arthur, lad,' she said quietly, moving up closer to the balloon.

'I *am* here, Rose.' The sentence stumbled out like a man staggering from a fire.

'I mean here,' she urged, half laughing. 'Here. By me. A bit nearer.'

I shuffled towards her childishly, on my bottom, and sat there, stark with anticipation. Quickly I turned to look at her again and I saw that her peachy face was shiny with perspiration. Her lips seemed enormous and fruity and her eyes shone like lights.

'Move around to me a bit, love,' she muttered seriously. 'Round facing me.'

I felt my limbs do as she required. Then, abruptly, her head lolled forward as though with tiredness and, astounded, I felt the lovely, full, flow of her heavy hair against my face and my neck. My boy's face went into it, my nose burrowing into its luxury. Instinctively I rubbed myself against her face and I could feel it wet through the strands of her hair although I did not know whether it was tears or sweat. She made short little sobbing noises and I asked her helplessly: 'What's wrong? What's the matter, Rose?'

A moment later I knew for sure what was the matter. Her fingers were picking at the buttons of my shorts. I felt the cool evening air whistle through the front and her beautifully soft, big, comfortable, airwoman's hands dip inside. I would have had a choking fit but I fought it back in case I spoiled it all. My breath was popping out in plaintive gasps, I could feel my face burning, and my legs shuddered.

Her head was still against me, the hair still smothering me, so I could not see, only feel, what she was about. She had all my personal bits cupped in her wide-winged hands now and had taken them out, as though they were quite separate parts from the rest of my body. She did it with gentleness and concern, like Old Moses, the poacher who used to take rabbits from their burrows on the banks of the Ebbw, with the rabbit hardly moving or protesting at all.

(He was a very interesting man, Old Moses, which, needless to say wasn't his real name but just a nickname made up by the children of the district. But he had a marvellous way with animals and I had thought of trying to contact him with regard to the habits of the badger, which I was studying in connection with my woodcraft badge. A family of badgers had made a home a bit further up the river and Old Moses knew all about their habits and their mating and all that sort of thing.)

Well, anyway, she was holding me like that down there, like Old Moses, kneeling against me still so that I couldn't see, only feel, what was going on. I felt ashamed that my thing was so stiff, like a little signpost, but it was something I found I honestly could not prevent even when I became even mildly excited. There it was, the bloody nuisance, stuck up, impudent, disgraceful. I could feel it and, worse, I knew she could see it.

'I'm sorry, Rose,' I apologised. 'I'm very sorry.'

Then she did begin to cry. Her head was jogged with sobs and her large tears kept plopping on my bare knees.

'I'm wicked,' she sobbed. 'Wicked.'

I was just about to tell her she wasn't wicked when she did something to me, well, to mine, which indisputably was. I do not intend to enlarge on it here, since it still remains, despite all that has happened since, as the supreme shock of my life. At that age I did not even know that such things *could* be done. But she lowered her head and she did it right there and then. I fainted.

* * *

Young and artless though I was, I learned quickly and cleverly in those earliest days in the park. Shattered I might have been, and no one since the founder himself has ever repeated 'A scout is clean in thought, word and deed,' so assiduously as I, and pausing carefully between the last three nouns, but soon I was dragging my wretched, depraved young body from my bed at two in the morning, dressing like a thief and making off to the park.

Had I been an enemy agent I could so easily have blown up that balloon; well, not *blown it up*, but cut it to shreds or set it loose. Because no one ever challenged me when I went there in the dark. There was a guard on the balloon compound, propped in his little shed like a body in a coffin, but there was an entirely adequate entry through the park boundary hedge from the main road which no one bothered to block. The first time I went was on the same night as the unbelievable encounter I have just described. When I had fainted Rose parcelled away my private parts and pounded off for some smelling salts. When she returned on huge and anxious tiptoe I was sitting against the flank of the balloon desperately memorising my woodcraft knowledge, repeating the signs aloud to myself as a barrier against what I was convinced was rapidly approaching insanity. It could *not* have happened, I told myself. I was just going crazy. My mind was going to curds like the scoutmaster said it would if you did certain things that I could not resist doing.

But when Rose came back like a sweet-smelling cloud I knew that it was unbelievable reality. Neither of us mentioned it, but I could see by her overflowing expression that it had been and would be again. I said I ought to be going back home or my mother would start looking for me in the dark.

'You *will* come back, won't you, little Arthur?' she said with sincere anxiety, waving the smelling salts in front of my face. Then she smiled and said one word, one thrilling, adult, fantastic word – 'Lover'. As she said it my eyes began to spiral in my head and I thought I was going off into another faint. I grabbed the smelling salts and took a deep sniff. 'I'll come back – lover,' I gurgled through the invisible stranglehold around my throat. 'Tonight.'

I ran home like a berserk redskin, seething with jubilant boiling emotions. They escaped like steam jets from every joint and hole and seam of my body. I kicked over a dustbin, seized a harmless cat by the tail (since I was in uniform, a unique sight for any student of scouting,) and eventually ran into the school bully of whom I went in terror. I laid into him joyfully with both bony fists, reducing him to a blubbing heap on the pavement, and suggesting he should send his dad along next time he wanted trouble.

My elation was not sobered at home. As usual my mother was sitting with her eternal dejection, waiting for my father. I made her a pot of tea and washed the dishes for her, brought in some coal (she had a fire, winter and summer; a sort of symbol of her long vigils).

All the time I chattered like a South American parrot, about scouts, about school, about Mr Finnegan who had tumbled from a street lampost while trying to spy on his wife in bed, about the war, about Hitler, who, I confidently told my mother, would be finished in six months. She began laughing at me in a puzzled way. 'Never heard you go on like this, Arthur,' she giggled. 'You sure you haven't been drinking?'

'Never touch it, mum,' I assured her, breaking a fresh grin on her worried face. 'There's more to life than drinking.'

Suddenly serious she said: 'I'm glad you know it, son. It makes men and women do wild and wicked things.'

Christ, I thought. What would I be up to if I was hitting the bottle as well?

Although that night I was creeping out on a grown-up assignation, I was still barely more than a child. As I bent timidly through the darkness of the house and out into the street I felt like Wee Willie Winkie. It was two o'clock, an opaque summer night, close and still, with cats arched in the street and a policeman propped asleep beneath a lintel at the bottom of our road. I took fright when I thought I saw a face in a shop window and then realized it was the mirrored moon. For the occasion I had put on my best suit, brown shoes, white shirt, tie, and my Odeon Saturday Morning Club badge on my lapel.

I went like a shadow through shadows, gently avoiding the sniffing Home Guard sentry outside the off-licence, reaching the park, and letting myself in through the gap in the hedge. The balloon was lying like a fat woman asleep, rolling a little in the touch of night breeze. The excitement I had seething through my body left no room for any fear. I knew where she slept, the hut and the very bed. It occurred to me that the door might be locked, but it wasn't.

There was a short squeak as I turned the little brass door knob but the door swung without sound and I stepped in. It was close and scented in there. Suddenly I realized with a thrill of strange masculine power that I was in a room full of sleeping women. I could sense their breasts moving in the dark; I could see a white female face pinned beneath a column of moonlight coming in at a window.

Rose was snoring, a little lilt of a snore, lying on her front with her lovely big face buried in her pillows, her blankets kicked down the bed, a sheet half covering the moonlit breadth of her sweating back. I stood small by her bed, fighting down a sudden and urgent feeling that I ought to run, that everything was imagined. But I had her scent in my nose now and that made me stay. I knew that it was true, that her hair had been in my face, that she had done that extraordinary thing she did. It was true, and I knew it would be all right.

At first I thought I would rouse her with a kiss, and I hovered over her, lips pursed, trying to select a spot on which to put it, her cheek, her forehead, her shoulder, bare but for the single bridging strap of her nightdress, or the very middle of her fine large back. But my courage was only a lad's and I pulled away at the final instant. Instead I extended a worried finger and tapped her almost formally on the arm. She mumbled and stirred but did not wake. I put the finger into the nightdress strap and gave it a brief tug, letting the palm of my hand drop on to the shoulder. The sensation of her flesh went through me like a shock. I thought I was going to be taken short. I closed my hand over the warm skin I loved so much and felt her move and half wake. 'Fuck off,' she whispered.

I was transfixed. I pulled my hand away in some sort of terror. My whole body seemed to have dried up with those awful discouraging words. She stirred again and murmured: 'Fuck off, Danny, will you.'

Danny! I thought the top of my young head was going to fly off. Danny? Who was Danny? Who the hell was he to be told to fuck off? Jealousy and wrath flooded my interior, already well occupied with apprehension. I stood up and regarded her with indignation and tears. She opened one large eye, quickly followed by the other: 'It's you,' she breathed in immediately happy surprise. 'Little Arthur.'

'It's not Danny,' I muttered sullenly.

'Hush,' she warned sweetly. She propped herself up on one elbow to look around me at the others in the room. They still slept, but the action brought her half way from the sheet. The moon brushed her neck and flooded the indolent mounds inside the front of her nightdress. She saw my transfixion, reached for my hand and blatantly laid it against her skin. My sweat began to cascade inside my best suit. That lovely, swollen, soft, piece of Rose. And I was touching it.

She levered her feet from the bed. It was a long silk nightdress and big and statuesque as she was she reminded me of the picture of Britannia which we had on the wall at school. Or Boadicea, whichever it was. She took my hand, and glancing around the room again, made for the door. We went out into the soft night of the park and trod gleefully across the dewy grass to the somnolent barrage balloon.

We hardly bothered to look towards the sentry post. She pulled me down into the silver folds of the balloon and hugged me to her.

'You've got a collar and tie and long trousers on,' she whispered.

'It's my best suit,' I said. 'I thought I'd look nice if I was coming to see you.'

'Let's take it off,' she giggled. 'You'll get it all screwed up sitting down here.'

She helped me out of my clothes, just like my mother used to do when I was a few years younger, making the same little clucks as she did so, then folding the clothes up in a careful pile at our side. I had taken everything off except my underpants and I told her shyly I wanted to retain them, at least for a while. Underneath that wretched uncontrollable spike was up to its tricks again. Why wouldn't the bloody thing behave? I could see her looking at the tent it made in my underpants and felt myself blush.

'I don't know what to do,' I said because she was just kneeling and watching me.

'Come and have a rest down here,' she replied, turning and stretching herself out along the loose folds of the balloon. She was flat, laid out in her nightie, like Mrs Hughes was when she died and everybody in the street was allowed to go and have a look at her. Up to then Mrs Hughes was the only woman I had seen lying down in a nightie and she couldn't compare with Rose, not for a moment. Not only was she dead, she was a lot older.

I stood, for a moment, hesitating, not sure what to do, how to launch myself, just as I had once stood at the top of the slide in the park playground, childishly frozen before the first descent. Rose's confident fingers encouraged me. She crooked one from each hand mischievously towards me and then reached out and held me behind my trembling knee with her strong but exquisite hand.

I went to her, buckling at the knees, then going head first as I would into the Newport municipal swimming baths. She gave a short grunt as I landed on her and I muttered an apology. I had no time or room or words for anything else.

For in a moment I was involved in a situation so exotic,

so erotic, so incredible, that though I have known many women since, and varied positions and techniques, I have never again captured the pure joy of that first sensation. For me, ever since, it has been my sexual lost chord. All childhood vanished in a moment, my fears and barriers, my unawareness, my doubts, my joyless loneliness. I wallowed in her. That is the only word, *wallowed*. It was like swimming on a warm and wavy ocean. It was all I could do not to throw my arms into an exultant freestyle stroke. Her arms were hugging me with great, lovely enjoyment and, somewhat to my astonishment, she had my ear in her mouth. I've never had very attractive ears; they project and at school the others say they can see the light through them. But that's what Rose was doing. She *liked* my ears.

She began to groan and mumble while she was still doing this with my ear and I had to pull my head away from her and my ear out of her mouth before I could comprehend what she was saying, for the total effect was to render me half deaf and her half dumb. It was only my name: 'Arthur, Little Arthur.' Her forearms went around my sweating head and then I was all but smothered in her voluminous breasts. My face kept slipping all over the place for we were both very wet, up and down the slopes, into the middle and up and over again.

She steadied me strongly and more or less forced my mouth to the middle of her left breast until I had my lips around it, something I had not done since babyhood. I was conscious, despite all this, of my sharp knees sticking into the broad parts of her thighs, my hips tucked inside hers and my naked belly on the hot silk of the night dress. Several times I thought I was going to fall off, but she held me tight.

All this. But we had done nothing yet. That was coming. Rose, when roused, became excessively violent, as I learned from the beginning. Her hand swooped down and came away with my tattered underpants which, well washed and old as they were (underwear, like other clothes, was in short supply in wartime), more or less disintegrated at her powerful grab. I heard them rend and I made some forlorn move-

47

ment to save them, but they shattered before I got my hands even to their vicinity.

I don't know exactly how the next few minutes felt for her and much worse, I cannot now remember exactly how they felt for me. The years have worked on the edge of the memory and all I now know is that I *loved* it, by God how I did; loved it much more than anything I can ever remember either before or after. I was still scrabbling all over the place in my unaccustomed eagerness and once I actually did tumble off. She pulled me on again with eager tenderness and then, using those splendid hands, guided my body until it was going to and fro in some regular movement, like a steam iron.

Trying to recall it now is, of course, very difficult but I remember that I loved it and I loved her because although she was so powerful she was very kind to me. She even stopped for a few moments in her grown-up passion to let me get my breath back. I had a good idea, from my own experiments, conducted despite the scoutmaster's curdled brain warnings, what happened at the climax. But when it actually occurred I realized that I had only been a boy riding a rocking horse.

We lay quietly against the balloon afterwards, letting the night air cool our bodies. My bum began to get cold and I wished she had not ripped my pants like that. I began to worry about my pants, because my mother knew exactly how many pairs I had and one missing would soon be noticed.

'Rose,' I whispered.

'Yes, love?'

'I don't suppose there's any chance of you sewing my underpants together again is there?'

She was still lying beneath me and she began to laugh a breathless little laugh, turning her face away from me as though she realized I would not understand. She let her hand search about and she found my pants. She held the tatters up and even with my poor knowledge of sewing I knew that nothing could ever be done to renovate them.

'I'll buy you some more,' she said smacking my cold buttocks.

'That's no good,' I argued softly. 'She'll notice they're new and how will I tell her?'

What occurred because of this caused me all that pain and shame at school; so much that even now I feel myself shiver and blush at the recollection. After years I could not face my sister without burning with embarrassment and she, just like her, has never forgotten, even though she married and has boys of her own, who have probably tried on her knickers anyway.

But Rose and I were in the deepest love all that autumn. At least *I* was and I told myself that she felt the same, although I often wondered who Danny was. There were two Dannys on the camp and I didn't like the thought of either of them having been in the vicinity of the places I had been.

She taught me everything she knew, which was a lot, and of course I grew spiritually far out beyond the other boys of my age. They still talked unknowingly about it in the lavatories and went into war whoops when one had claimed to have had a full feel of Betty Pring, a half-mad, spotty girl at the post office. But I was aloof from all this. I kept silent, of course, but no one would have believed me in any case. I felt myself walking high above all of them, above all the people in the district, in the town, in the world.

I used to go down to the balloon in the middle of the night about three times a week and we nearly always did something or other. At that age I did not understand all the things she wanted me to do but I did them and learned and enjoyed every moment. And it was not all just bare sex. Sometimes she liked me to lie against her, my head on her shirt, the warm stuffing underneath comforting me, making me feel happier than I had ever known until then, and, in many ways, happier than I have been since.

The trouble was I was exhausted by these unexpected calls upon my untrained body. I had never been very big for my age (in fact until I was beyond my Mrs Nissenbaum period I grew very slowly, although I made up for it afterwards. I always felt that Mrs Nissenbaum must have triggered off something in my tardy growing cells and started them working energetically for the first time in my life). Often I staggered home like a drunk from my night meetings with Rose in the park. I frequently lolled off to sleep in class and once collapsed from exhaustion in the school lavatory, falling forward until my head rested against the door, only rousing when they were actually breaking in to get me. Since this was after the incident of my sister's knickers there were all manner of nasty interpretations put on it.

Naturally my mother worried over my fatigue. She took me to the doctor who looked at the pouches below my eyes, felt my scrotum and told me frankly that if I did not pack up what he said he knew I was doing then my brain would go to curds and I'd get a rupture as well. Fortunately he did this when my mother was not in the surgery. He told her that I ought to get more fresh air, that I should do some digging in the garden. Then I would sleep. My father, of course, agreed and I had to do a stint of digging in his lousy vegetable patch and as well as tending to my Rose, and this sapped my energy more than ever.

In late October I went to the park one night and found my Rose sitting alone in the little hut where the telephone switchboard was operated. When I crept up outside, standing in the big blotchy shadow of the balloon, I could see her comforting form, leaning a little forward over a magazine in the margarine coloured light. I gave my low Otter Patrol scout whistle and she saw me in the dark and laughed and called me over. That was the night we really ought to have left each other alone. She was replacing somebody on switchboard duty and it would have been better if I'd just kissed her a few times or fondled her breasts or did something, anyway, which did not interfere with the conduct of the war.

But she was much worse than I. I loved to explore all the large inches of her well-nourished body, but she went mad with desire over my bony, boyish frame and its minor appendages. Once she began to touch me, my trousers, the back of my legs, even my bum, there was nothing would stop her. She was overcome with need.

It was, as I have indicated, not a very well run camp, and nobody was ever moving at that time of the night. The sentry box and the guardhouse were at the extreme perimeter and the occupants were reliably asleep.

'Go through to the little room, darling,' she whispered to me. 'It's nice and warm in there. I'll just make sure that nobody is on the prowl, and then I'll be in.'

'But it's against orders, surely Rose,' I said in my worried way.

'It's bound to be,' she replied cheerfully. 'But never mind. Go through, love.'

I went into the little room behind the switchboard area. It was warm as a burrow, with a single bunk and a home made table with a kettle, a teapot and some cups squatting on it. I liked it in there. I lay on the bunk and waited for Rose to come to me. She wasn't long. 'I don't suppose England will miss me for half an hour,' she giggled. 'If the Germans invade they'll have to excuse me.'

'Are you sure you won't get into trouble, Rose?' I said anxiously. She was moving near to me and predictably unbuttoning her blouse. She always wanted me to do that first.

'I will if they find out,' she said vaguely. 'Shot at dawn. But they won't. And if the phone rings I'll hear it.' Then she came on to the bunk with me. She took up most of the room, but it did not stop us. Indeed because of our relative sizes, she formidable going on towards large, me thin and small, we were able to get up to a variety of tricks in many positions which would have been painful if not thoroughly dangerous for two people of matching proportions.

There was one thing, I remember, where I used to hang on to her like I have seen since a koala bear cling to the Australian gum tree. She would be standing, her soft but sturdy legs apart, and I would be hanging on in that fashion. Then she would gradually ease back until I was jockey style on her front. She liked this very much and so did I and we often performed it together. This, our last night, although, of course, we did not know it, was high-lighted, so I remember, by a protracted manoeuvre of this nature.

In its way I am certain it looked poetic as well as erotic for her movements were strong and controlled, like a weightlifter, and one hand, supporting me underneath, enjoyably massaged that tender section of my lad's anatomy.

Unfortunately, while we were thus immersed a fire was raging in the next room. In her hurry to get to me she had left a cigarette burning idly through her magazine – having folded over the cover on it. It ran quickly through the wooden furniture around the switchboard, but, as the dividing door was closed, we knew nothing about it apart from a decided rise in the temperature which, eventually, could not be attributed to our own exertions.

'It's very hot for October,' she murmured into my neck.

'Rose,' I whispered, staring over her shoulder. 'Rose, there's smoke coming under the door.'

She jumped with a movement that very nearly incapacitated me for life, and screamed when she saw the tongues of vapour oozing beneath the wood.

But she kept her head and did not open the door. There was a fragile window in the bunk room and she had it out of the frame with one frenzied pull and push of her north country hands.

'Grab your things, love,' she urged. 'Grab them quick.'

I caught up my clothes, being careful to include my underpants and like some circus performer, she hoisted me through the window. I fell on to the ground outside and heard and saw men running towards the fire. Naked, Rose came tumbling out like a bundle of laundry. She fell directly on top of me, knocking every whiff of breath from my thin body.

'Run, darling,' she said, kissing me briefly. 'Run like mad.'

I did. Bare and white as a nymph I made for the hole in the perimeter hedge. Out in the road I tried madly to get dressed but I had only put on my socks and my vest when the balloon exploded with a muffled woof, like a big dog, and a glow of light that lit the road like a stage. I fell over and when I picked myself up a policeman was regarding me with disbelief.

4

'Helping Hitler,' my father said. 'Oh God, that a son of mine should be helping Hitler!'

He was in my room and I was trapped in my bed.

'But I didn't,' I protested. 'I didn't know it was going to happen.'

'And with a woman! Big, fat cow. Old enough to be your mother.'

'She's not!' I howled. 'She's not fat and she's twenty-five.'

He came towards me and I thought he was going to hit me. I cautiously retreated in the bed.

'Women!' he snarled again. 'At your bloody age. *And,* mister, I heard about you at the institute tonight. Wearing girl's underwear to school! There's a sodding fine thing for me to be told at my club, I must say.'

'Who told you that?' I trembled. God, how I hated this bastard of a father. Who would tell him things like that? My face felt set and cold.

'Never mind who told me,' he said nastily. 'All I know is that your sexual oddities are being broadcast around this town. How do you think I feel being pointed out as the father of the kid who wears girl's knicks, has intercourse with airwomen, and sets a barrage balloon alight?'

'I didn't do that,' I protested. 'I didn't set it alight. It was an accident.'

'Well, it won't be an accident when they shoot you for it!' he shouted. 'That will be a nice disgrace, won't it. Having you shot for helping the Germans.'

He genuinely frightened me. 'They wouldn't do that,

would they?' I pleaded hoarsely. 'I'm only a boy. How could they shoot me?'

'Put you up against a wall and do it,' he said with malicious simplicity. 'The police and the balloon officer said that's what will probably happen. I'm expecting a letter about it tomorrow. You and that woman. Shot.'

'Rose,' I trembled. 'Oh, Jesus Christ.'

'Don't you "Jesus Christ" in this house, mister. And what about those woman's drawers you were wearing at school. What a fine little bugger you've turned out to be.'

'I was cold,' I said miserably. 'I took them from Audrey's bedroom.'

'Your sister,' he breathed. 'Your sister's personal knicks.'

'I was cold,' I repeated. 'Nobody would have known if the boys hadn't debagged me, the bleeders.'

'Watch your language, my boy.'

'Well, nobody would have known,' I whispered.

'Where were your own pants? Why didn't you have them on?'

'They got lost. Well, damaged. I wouldn't have worn anything at all, but it turned frosty, dad, and I was cold. They just picked on me that day for debagging. They're always doing it to somebody.'

It was no use telling him about it, of course; the hideous tribal attack on the lone boy, the throwing him down on the asphalt playground and the savage pulling away of his trousers. Looking up at all their primitive faces, terrified by their violence but much more by what I knew they would discover. On the outside of the ring girls were screaming and other kids were running from all directions to see the fun.

Oh, the bald terror of those few minutes. Fighting, fisting, wriggling, kicking, feeling the scratches and the blood on the mouth, ears full of the vicious laughter and the screams and the faces ringed over me. There was that girl, Mary Winters, who was supposed to be *my* girl in class (although we never did anything but wink and smile). She was there, looking down with the rest. Then they got my trousers away, just part of the way first and they saw the pea green of my sister's knicks. What a howl and a screech went up. They jumped on me again like hounds on a floored fox, tearing at me, pulling away the rest of my covering until there I lay shivering and crying in those ridiculous saggy things. They jumped and hooted, and then they pulled those from me too and went around the playground waving them like a flag, while I was left sobbing and bleeding against the school wall.

'I give up with you,' said my father. 'I've tried, God knows, but I think you're a bit potty in the head. Just stay in this room and don't come out. I'm going to try and save your life. It's not going to be easy, but the disgrace of having my son executed for treason is too much for me. I'll have to try and pull a few strings.'

I began to sob heavily. He went out of the door, the lousy swine, and I remember calling after him: 'Dad, please . . . please do your best.'

'Shut up,' he snarled from the landing.

'And, thanks,' I wept. 'Thanks ever so much.'

That day I wrote to Mr Winston Churchill, explaining my position, but I never did get a reply. I don't know what happened to Rose. We never saw each other again. My pending execution, naturally, occupied the whole of my mind. I could not see two soldiers walking together up our street, a common enough occurrence, without fearing that they were an escort come to take me away. My father, the bastard, nurtured this terror, and made a great show, each morning of going through the post to see if a reprieve had arrived from Mr Churchill. This, I know, seems ridiculous now, but I truly believed him. I played truant from school, I think to the relief of the school, and my days were spent creeping in the shadow of privet hedges, making hiding places in all parts of the district and planning to escape by running away. Audrey, my sister, who had always despised me, was stationed near Newport and came home every night. She told me she had seen a top secret report which said that I was going to be taken to the Barracks and shot. It seems unbelievable that I was fifteen and not for a moment did I suspect their lies. But fifteen then was not like fifteen is now; perhaps I was a late developer (in some matters); we lived with bombs and air raids and moments of death, and I knew that spies and traitors were executed every day. I didn't know at what age they began shooting them.

Then, in the middle of the night my father crept to my room and shook me. I thought they had come for me, at last, and I dived under the blankets and began gibbering my prayers for deliverance, mentioning to God that I truly loved my country and 'Our great leader, Mr Winston Churchill'. My father pulled me out and told me to shut up or they would hear me. I cowered before him.

'I've arranged it,' he said. 'Your escape from the country.'

'Oh, dad,' I breathed. 'Oh, darling dad.'

'Quiet,' he said. 'I've told you I couldn't stand the disgrace. Mr Churchill has refused a reprieve, so I've got to act.'

'You must, please,' I whimpered. 'They'll shoot me.'

Then he told me he had arranged for me to sail as a deck boy on a ship which was sailing for Panama the next day. I was so overcome by the news that, pressing my tear-swept face to his cheek I thanked him with all my heart.

'All right,' he said modestly. 'But it has cost money, you know. Just to get you aboard this ship. Have you got any money?'

I said I had two pounds and I got this from a hiding place in my room (while he gave a little knowing snort) and forced him to take it. At six o'clock that morning I was on my way.

My mother thought I was only going to see the ships for the day and all I took with me on that Atlantic trip was a packet of lemon curd sandwiches.

For the first week I was sea-sick and I did not observe that the first mate had his red eye on me. Not that it would have meant anything anyway. At fifteen such things were beyond my comprehension. I only knew about Rose and myself. Relations between other men and women were still remote, and men and men had never occurred to me. When Mister Gander, the first mate, invited me to his cabin for some boxing it only struck me as being an uncommonly friendly gesture from an experienced sailor to a young cabin boy.

I had never done any boxing, but the way I was able to knock Mr Gander about, so easily and with such power with no retaliation on his part – and he was a man of fifteen or sixteen stone and very tall – made me think that perhaps I should take it up as a vocation. It was the second best cabin on the SS *Queen of Atlantis*, the captain's being the best, of course, but even so there was not a great deal of room for boxing. The decor was strangely velvet and tassled. It reminded me of the small front room in my Auntie Clementine's house, when she used to tell fortunes with playing cards, apart from a framed newspaper headline above Mr Gander's bed which said boldly 'Coloured Seamen Discharged' and which puzzled me a good deal.

Mr Gander was there, in great white shorts, like a pair of flapping signal flags. His fleshy stomach and his wide, weak, chest, matted like a coconut, were surmounted by a red, breathless face. I thought he might have been warming up by shadow-boxing.

'Right, shipmate, get your shorts on,' he boomed jovially and he handed me a pair of dirty white knicks and I took my trousers off and put them on. That he was male and so was I made it seem perfectly proper, since this was a sporting occasion.

'You've got your little thing hanging down the wrong leg of your shorts,' the mate said pointing downwards. 'It should hang down the other leg.'

He made a helpful move forward, but fortunately I made the adjustment myself with a quick wriggle of my hips. He appeared a trifle dismayed and put his boxing gloves on sulkily. They looked big and dangerous, but I was anxious to prove my manhood now that I had become a sailor.

57

'I'm not much good at this, Mr Gander,' was all I said.

'Don't worry, son,' he mumbled. 'I won't hurt you. Hit me as hard as you like.'

I did.' I threw up my right glove and caught him spectacularly on the face. Now I realize that he must have been bending towards me. He went down with a theatrical topple, knocking over a chair and lying like a porpoise across the floor.

'Don't hit me,' he pleaded his gloves over his head. 'Please don't hit me.'

'I won't, Mr Gander,' I promised unable to believe what I had done. He turned and muttered 'Oh' in a strangely disappointed way. I was prancing about, in what would have been a neutral corner, smacking my gloves together with irrepressible elation. I had knocked down a grown man with one blow!

The blood surged through my arms, my face felt hot. He got to his feet and I went for him again, buffeting him across the cabin, his gloves flailing wildly but only succeeding in making contact with a chintzy lamp which fell softly. The terrible thing was, I really thought I could box. The revelation of this big man cowering at the end of my paralysing gloves and crying out agonizingly every time I managed to strike him! He seemed to fall so easily, and I would dance back snorting like a little dragon, while he squirmed and begged not to be hit again. Eventually he puffed, 'I've had enough,' and he folded me in an enormous, sweaty embrace, trembling above my head. 'You're a strong boy,' he sobbed. 'You're a really strong boy.'

It was all very exciting and unusual. Even I had to admit that to myself and when I told Hector, the ship's cook, he confirmed my misgivings.

'Don't you know about fruit?' he said. 'Pineapples?'

I was about to give him the benefit of my knowledge on pineapples when he stopped me by waving his hand and dropping his greasy face into a liquid scowl.

'No, I can see you don't,' he sighed. 'Can't fathom anyone putting a young lad like you on a merchant ship without warning him about the pineapples. The mines and the German submarines is bad enough, but we've always got the pineapples with us.'

'All right. What are they?' I asked bluntly throwing away my mental pre-war pictures of the laden barrows in Newport Arcade Market.

'They're men what fancies other men. Or boys. Like most men feels a yearning towards a woman so the pineapple feels a yearning towards other pineapples.'

The news flabbergasted me. I stared at him disbelievingly but I could see he was telling the truth.

'But I'm not a pineapple!' I shouted.

'Well . . . a lad doesn't have to be one of them . . . if you get me. They just hope he'll get the hang of it . . .'

'Well, I won't,' I said stoutly, manfully, but my mind racing through all sorts of questions. '*How* do they, anyway, Hector?'

He seemed miserably embarrassed. A gob of galley fat dripped from the end of his nose. He said he had to see to the custard in the galley. But I was almost in tears now and shouting. 'Come on, you bugger. Tell me how. Then I'll *know*, won't I?'

He couldn't bring himself to tell me. 'They find ways,' he shrugged and went off towards his custard. I followed him to the galley.

'But this was boxing. With gloves,' I insisted.

'And you kept knocking him down,' said Hector stirring the yellow pond in the big pan.

'That's right. How did you know?'

'And he kept snivelling and moaning. Right?'

'Right, Hector,' I admitted. I did not feel shocked now, just dull and hurt that my boxing match had not been what I thought.

'Well, Mr Gander just likes being hit, that's all,' shrugged Hector. 'It gets them in different ways. We used to have a bosun who was always putting mice down his trousers. It's just what they fancy.'

I walked from him stunned by this revelation of the

world's weakness and wickedness. The thought that my own father press-ganged me into it was even worse. For the next week I scuttled out of sight every time I saw the mate. Once I was told to go and help the crow's-nest lookout because his eyes weren't so good and as we stood together, close against each other, in the little barrel at the pitching mast-head, I was filled with terror in case this man too was a pineapple. He wasn't but he did lay his wooden hands on my young shoulder and we sang hymns together into the south Atlantic wind.

Two nights later, the ship was torpedoed. Naked, I ran around in panic, passing others doing the same on the dark, sinking deck. Their mouths all seemed to be open but I could not hear them because the explosion had deadened my ears. There were men slithering like carcasses of meat on the deck and others were floating in the sea. I saw a man on fire and two men throw him overboard. Then I found my-self, hunched and weeping, in a lifeboat jolting about in the dark ocean. I was so overcome I did not even see the *SS Queen of Atlantis* go down, taking with her my friend Hector and twenty-three more.

In the night and in my shock, I knew vaguely that there were three others in the boat. The dark drifted away and one man was dead at dawn. His friend, lolling next to him, had been trying to keep him warm by rubbing him. He had rubbed the skin from his left arm and his stomach, but the man still died and he went over the side. The man who had tried to keep his friend alive with rubbing was dying him-self. Even I could see that and I had no experience of death. His head went lower on his chest as the sun came up on the blue and peaceful ocean. He could not last long. And the other occupant of the boat, sitting at the tiller, unhurt, fat, naked also and with a lovely big smile on his face when he looked at me, was Mr Gander, the mate.

Even as he gazed at me I knew I must, somehow, keep the third man alive. He was my witness and my chaperone, and he was slipping away with every growing daylight minute. I found some brandy in the lifeboat locker and got it to his lips quickly in case the mate came the length of the boat to get the bottle from me.

'You're going to live,' I kept whispering to the man. 'Somebody will pick us up soon. You're going to live.'

He had to live. My virginity depended on it. Mr Gander didn't seem in a hurry. He sat smiling like a child as the sun got higher. There was food and water on board, and when I told the man he was going to survive, the mate shook his big smiling head and indicated that the man had no hope. In that case neither had I.

I shall always remember the joke Mr Gander told me while we were adrift in that lifeboat. We were both naked, and he was mad as well. I don't know whether it was the sun or the sinking or both. He was sitting at the stern all thick, red and obscene, drinking ship's rum from the boat's locker, and I was sitting at the bow watching him fearfully and he was watching me watching him too, because he realized, of course, by now that I knew all about pineapples and I knew he was not just a pineapple but a mad pineapple, and he might try to take a foul advantage of me out there in the lonely ocean, the bastard.

It wasn't long after he had pushed my friend, the guardian of my honour, over the side. I'd kept him alive for as long as I could because he was my witness, and my only hope. All the time I kept telling him: 'There's a ship coming. There's a ship coming, mate, an American ship. I can see it now. It won't be long.' His hooded eyes tried to open for a long time and sometimes his mouth moved and I poured in some brandy from the locker at my end of the boat. His eyes reminded me of the eyes of dying sparrows I had held in our street, flickering with some faint strength and hope, and then closing over for good.

Even after he'd died I pretended he was still with us, pouring dribbles of good brandy into one side of his mouth and hoping that the mate would not notice the stuff trickling out on the other side. I talked to him for an hour or more after he could no longer hear me or care, whispering

61

encouragement and lies close to his ear, taking his pulse and nodding to myself satisfactorily in a medical manner before looking up and seeing the fat, mad Gander watching me and smiling.

Eventually the mate said: 'You're wasting that brandy, darling, pouring it into a dead man. His fires are out for good. He can't hear what you're telling him. I know a dead 'un when I see him. Give me a hand, dear, and we'll put him over the side.'

'He's not dead, and I'm not darling,' I said defiantly. I was a lot smaller than the mate and I could feel my young tears pushing into my eyes.

'So sorry,' he returned with a polite, fat smile. 'Nevertheless he's gone and he won't be back. Over the side with him.'

'No!' I screamed hopelessly as he trundled forward. My voice emptied over the ocean. 'No, Mr Gander, he's not dead.'

'Only sleeping,' he said piously. The man was wearing a shirt. Mr Gander stripped it from him and tore it in half, giving half to me to put across my shoulders. I did and it felt like a balm after being naked under the sun. 'See,' he said. 'I'm a sportsman, lad, a sportsman.' Then he heaved the poor man over the side with one lift of his fat arms. A red sunburn was spreading on him but it didn't seem to hurt. When he came close to my end of the boat to throw the dead man over, his big, sweating tomato face came very close and I stumbled back to the bow. Under the seat was a spanner and I was going to hit him with that if he came at me. But he smiled alluringly once and then turned his gigantic white bare arse from me and went back to his stern. The actual arse was strange really, if the situation had not been so serious I would probably have thought it was funny. The red of his back continued down to where his buttocks began and then there was a white plank across them where he had been sitting on the stern seat.

I tried not to look at him sitting like a great lump of sealing wax thirty feet from me. I pulled my half of the dead man's shirt about my shoulders and Gander did the same. He was still swigging at the rum and I could see it oozing out of his pores as it went into his mouth.

The sun was high and hot now. I could feel it singeing my knees and belabouring my head. I put the piece of shirt over my head and let the rest dangle around my neck and back. He was still looking at me horribly and I modestly crossed my legs closing them over the top of my private parts.

'DO YOU WANT TO HEAR A JOKE?' he suddenly howled from his end of the lifeboat. My God, you ought to have seen him then, the bit of shirt clutched around his swollen shoulders with one hand, the bottle of Captain Morgan in the other, the maddest pineapple that you ever set eyes upon.

'A joke, Mr Gander?'

'YES, A JOKE. A FUNNY STORY.'

'Well, yes. All right.'

'REMINDED ME, US BEING HERE LIKE THIS, DARLING . . .'

'Don't call me darling.'

'IF YOU WANT TO HEAR IT, SHUT UP.'

I shut up and he told me the joke. To this moment I can see him lobster-red, bawling insanely at me from the far end of the boat, with the brilliant blue sea rising and shrugging away behind him, the sky bright, full of painful sun, and nobody but us in the aching ocean. I remember his feet were swollen horribly, like big red peppers.

'THERE WAS THIS SHIP'S PARROT,' he bawled. I couldn't see why he was shouting. The wind was hardly touching us, the sea's wash under the boat was only a mumble, and there was no one else's voice to overcome. I suppose it was the sun and the rum.

'Why are you shouting?'

'I WANT YOU TO HEAR THE BLOODY JOKE, DON'T I?' he bellowed. 'I'LL COME UP THERE AND TELL YOU THEN.'

'STAY THERE!' I howled back at him. 'STAY THERE, MR GANDER! TELL ME FROM THERE.'

'ALL RIGHT. SHUT YOUR MOUTH THEN. THIS SHIP'S PARROT, SEE. AND EVERY NIGHT A MAGICIAN USED TO GIVE A SHOW . . .'

His head dropped forward for a moment and I could see the drink dribbling out of his mouth and on to his chest. He lifted his huge face again, trembling with sweat now, like a man from a rugby scrum. It was in his eyes and rolling from his forehead, his nostrils and his sagging mouth.

'. . . A SHOW, A PERFORMANCE, SEE? TO THE PASSENGERS. AND EVERY NIGHT THIS PARROT USED TO SIT THERE . . . SIT AND GIVE THE FUCKING GAME AWAY SEE?. . .'

His head went down again and his chest began to heave as though he were crying. I sat still, terrified of him, and strangely, for him too. 'Wait a bit,' he whispered. 'Wait a minute, dear. It's a good story if you wait.'

He forced himself to go on. 'THE PARROT GAVE EVERY TRICK AWAY. EVERY TIME THE CONJURER DID SOMETHING THE PARROT WOULD SAY . . . "IT'S UP HIS SLEEVE" OR "IT'S BEHIND HIS BACK" . . . FOLLOW?'

'I follow,' I said. I was petrified, fascinated. I clutched the seat under me. He was rolling fatly from side to side.

'HE JUST GAVE THE GAME AWAY EVERY TIME. EVERY BLEEDING TIME. THEN ONE NIGHT THE SHIP'S BOILERS BLEW UP AND EVERYTHING WENT SKY FUCKING HIGH. AND THIS MAGICIAN AND THE PARROT ENDED UP EACH END OF A BOAT LIKE WE ARE. LOOKING AT EACH OTHER, SEE? THE MAN DIDN'T HAVE ANY CLOTHES, LIKE ME. AND THE BLOODY PARROT DIDN'T HAVE NO FEATHERS, LIKE YOU, DARLING . . .'

He looked at me strangely, almost pleadingly; 'Do you like it?'

I said 'It's not finished is it? That's not the end?'

'OF COURSE IT'S NOT FINISHED, YOU BLOODY LUNATIC!' he screamed. I thought for a moment he was going to rush me. He half got up but he sat down heavily, wearily, again. Then he continued.

'THERE THEY WAS, SHIPWRECKED, JUST STARING AT EACH OTHER, SAYING NOTHING. THEN AFTER THREE BLOODY DAYS . . . THIS IS THE END NOW . . . THE PARROT SAID TO THE MAN: "ALL RIGHT. YOU WIN. WHAT DID YOU DO WITH THE SHIP?"'

He went off into screams of sweaty laughter, holding himself and rolling about. His piece of shirt dropped from his neck and the light breeze took it over the side.

'Oooow!' he howled like a child. 'My bit of shirt.' He leaned over, that grotesque striped rump in the air, but it was gone, floating gaily away across the vivid waves. We both knew he would never get it back.

He remained staring after it for a while, as though he was watching some relative's departure for a foreign land. Then he turned and smiled his fulsome wet smile at me. 'I'll have to have yours,' he said as though it were logic. 'I've got more to cover up than you.'

'No you won't,' I whispered. I was crouched and terrified, but my hand still had the spanner hidden under the seat. 'This is my bit of shirt.'

'Come on, dear,' he said, staggering to his raw, swollen elephant feet, making the boat pitch. 'Let's have that shirt-tail.' Suddenly he shouted. 'LET'S HAVE YOUR TAIL! Ha! THAT'S ANOTHER JOKE!'

This time I bellowed with laughter in the hope that it would humour him. He looked at me with surprise that hardened to anger. 'I'm going to *have* you, lad,' he announced. 'You don't like my jokes.'

It was terrible the way he came towards me. I can't see a drawing of that Michelin Tyre Man without thinking of Gander; except he was red and he had a gigantic deep purple erection. Even under the sun I went cold. He plodded towards me over the rocking boards of the boat. His gross body was oozing sweat and this bilge was running from the corners of his mouth. His gingery hairs were stuck to his body. His tool and his toes were too terrible to contemplate. He was the most awful pineapple anyone could ever see.

'SEE IF YOU LIKE THIS JOKE!' he bawled as he came on. He put his hand around his member and advanced on me like a pirate pointing a thick, coloured, sword. There we were out on the ocean and he was doing that terrifying thing. He only needed a patch over one eye.

I don't know whether I remained still because I was frightened or calm. But I did not move from my seat at the bow of the boat.

'Go away, Mr Gander.' I said. 'I know you're a pineapple.'

A fearful howl blew out of him and he charged towards me over the last cross-seat then amazingly, he stopped and stood a yard away, swaying and dripping. 'Christ, it's hot, isn't it?' he said almost as an aside. Then his gleaming face looked with savage interest at me again and he moved a fraction more. I knew he was going to get me. I knew I had to do it then. I grabbed his tool with one hand and jerked him towards me; then I hit him on his red forehead with my tool; the spanner, that is. A big bloody star sprang up on his wet skin. He tipped forward at first and I thought he was going to land on top of me, but he somehow straightened and blank-faced began to topple back. I did nothing. I just watched him. The lifeboat heaved slightly as he fell and he went cleanly over the side.

I went to the gunwale and looked over into the bright sea. He was nowhere to be seen.

'Mr Gander,' I called fairly quietly. 'Mr Gander. Are you there?'

The only sound was the everlasting water slopping against the boat. I went back to my seat and, without looking at it, threw the spanner after Mr Gander. I felt suddenly very sorry for him. I thought about the joke and I laughed at it. Then I saw him again, or at least part of him. He was head and legs down in the water, his red and white striped bum floating daintily like a marker buoy.

After ten minutes he had gone altogether and I was glad because half an hour later I saw a ship.

5

She came from the horizon hysterically firing rockets and smoke flares, which puzzled me a bit because with the rescue of a shipwrecked mariner, it's supposed to be the other way around. I mean, *I* could see *her* easily enough, all three thousand tons of her, so the fireworks seemed superfluous. It was *I* who should have been signalling. So I let off the two Very lights from the pistol in the forward locker, pathetic little sparklers compared with their pyrotechnics. Then I watched with dismay and amazement while the ship, still a bouquet of smoke stems and bursting colours, sailed by me and went straight on, apparently not having seen me at all. When she was two miles or more away, and I was speechless from shouting at the fools, I found another Very light, a bit damp but a final hope. I loaded the pistol and pulled the trigger. It squelched pathetically from my hand and plopped over the side. I began to cry. What with having to kill Mr Gander and now this, the day had been altogether too much for a lad barely sixteen.

I looked up from my wet hands and saw that the ship had altered course. She curled in a wide loop, still firing off the occasional joyous rocket, and came back to me. An hour later I was aboard her and they were apologizing for not having seen me first time round. They were Argentinians and they had apparently been occupied for six weeks celebrating their country's entry into the war against Nazism. The rockets and flares had been in honour of this, but because of all the noise and colour they had engendered they had not noticed my flares. In fact I was only spotted at all because the first officer had gone aft to be sick over the side (everyone was drunk, too, by the way, because they had managed to elbow their way into the war) and saw my lifeboat.

At first, in his inane state, he thought I was fishing, and it wasn't until a fellow officer, less drunk than the rest, pointed out that I was six hundred miles from land that they had turned the ship around.

No one spoke much English, except the Captain and he was always asleep in his cabin, but I gathered they were bound from Buenos Aires to New York and were still delirious at being allowed into the war. They had obviously counted on being admitted because although she was a merchant vessel she had a little gun mounted forward of the bridge. With this they exultantly sank my lifeboat, explaining that it was to stop it falling into enemy hands, although why they couldn't have hoisted it up on to the deck I don't know.

In three days we were in the Hudson, sailing up towards the great piled city. Everybody on board took on a new surge of excitement, and people came out to us in small boats, all blind drunk and singing and waving flags. I went on deck in the morning and there they were all going crazy, fire floats in the river, spouting foam, all the ships' sirens sounding, and millions of people going berserk ashore.

I wondered if Argentina's entry into the war could be a bigger thing than I had thought. Then it suddenly hit me like a bucket of hot water that all this was for ME! New York's welcome for the little English cabin boy, the lad hero, taken from the wicked sea after his ship had gone down. I began to smile. I would probably get my picture in the newspapers, and be asked to tell my own heroic story. They might even give me a *woman* of my own! I had heard that the Americans were generous to a fault.

Nevertheless it seemed that the South American crew were taking less notice of me than a hero merited. They were busy letting off the remainder of their rockets and fire crackers, and shouting to the people in the boats. I waved shyly, befittingly I thought, but I could not detect anyone actually aiming their wave at me.

Then a port official came over the side from a launch and danced a little jig with the first officer. I stood and smiled manfully at him, my youthful hand at the ready so that I could thrust it straight into that generous American handshake at the first moment. But the port official in all his braid didn't seem to see me. He was standing quite near after his jig with the first officer, however, and I gave his sleeve a tug just to show him I was around.

'What d'ya want kid?' he asked, a bit truculently.

'I'm Arthur McCann,' I said believing the name would immediately switch on a smile of welcome.

68

'And I'm Adolf Hitler!' he exploded and careered around the deck laughing practically urinating over his joke. He ended up facing me again, however, and I said bravely: 'All right, what's all the excitement about?'

He gave me a jovial push that sent me staggering into the first officer, who pushed me back. 'Don't you know, the war's over, you dum-dum!'

'Over?' I blinked, and looking around at the capering Argentinians, 'That was bloody quick.'

'Maybe we fight too good,' shrugged the first officer.

It is very painful for me to describe the torment and embarrassment of that day. As soon as the ship got in the captain welcomed a beautiful lark-like young woman aboard and slammed his cabin door. Nobody would tell me what I should do. Everybody in the world seemed to be drunk or delirious. Eventually I went without formalities ashore and found a policeman, sitting on a crate on the jetty, who seemed to be reasonably sober and he told me to go to an office on the dockside. I went and found a boy about my own age jiving with a chair to some jazz music from a radio. There was nobody else to ask. He found a book and in between relapses when he gyrated about the room to the brass of Benny Goodman he discovered that as a distressed mariner I had to report to a department on the East Side.

He gave me a street map and then went back to his romance with the office chair. I went out nervously into the gigantic city walking faultily for the pavement felt strange after the lifeboat and the other ship, and the buildings reared over me. I walked through canyons filled with dancing people, ticker tape snowing down, faces miles up hanging from windows. The noise boomed and resounded from the frightening concrete walls. I walked on, head down now, amazed, numb and unbelieving. Soldiers and sailors were practically having free rapes of beautiful girls at every corner, legs and arms and mouths everywhere. And here was I, sixteen, a shipwrecked kid, sunk by the Germans, almost buggered by one of my own officers, walking unnoticed, uncared-about, through all this.

I saw a soldier disengage himself from a blonde girl, just behind a news stand. He moved away towards another female and, as the first one remained there stunned, arms open, body unoccupied, and as my disappointment and bitterness reached a pitch at that moment, I flung myself into her inviting embrace in his place.

We had a violent kiss, perfumed with bourbon, although I couldn't place the taste right then. I felt myself crushed into her breasts under a silk blouse, with the arms folding hungrily around me. Then, on second thoughts, she pulled away and looked at me with immediate stark horror. 'Aw, for Christ's sake!' she screamed. 'Get lost won't ya!' Then she flung me into the crowd and was immediately engaged in the foulest embrace by a bloody New York fireman who had never even seen a German or a Jap.

By the way they were celebrating you would have thought they had all escaped being massacred by a couple of hours. I saw a party of nuns singing on a little balcony and I went towards them, hoping to put my reasonable case to them. If I couldn't get hero-worship I wanted help. One of them saw me coming and lifted up her habit in a pretty un-nunly way. I turned and ran again into the awful crowd.

Like someone staggering from a rough sea I eventually cleared the masses and found myself in Washington Square. There were plenty of celebrations there too, but because everyone seemed to be standing and singing, dancing, hugging, and that sort of activity I found a seat and sat there miserably but gratefully.

At the other end of the bench was a man hung with rags, waking, moving his facial muscles sniffing into an empty bottle which he had retained in his hand throughout his sleep. He swung his feet to the ground and regarded all the celebrations, then looked at me.

'Why ain't you out there gettin' a handful o' some o' them wimmen,' he muttered like an accusation.

'I tried,' I admitted defensively. 'But I got chucked out. I'm too young, I s'pose.'

'Young,' he said. 'Then you're lucky ain't you? No more fightin'. Just think what you've gone and missed, boy. Guys gettin' killed, but you been too young to go.' He spat violently. 'It's us who's had the hardship o' the war. Now you got to make sure that you guys keep the peace what you ain't done nothing to earn.' He stretched himself and rose, the rags cascading down his body as he got up. 'Well, I guess I'll go an' try a handful o' some o' them wimmen myself.' He handed me the empty bottle as though it were my duty to take it and went unsteadily towards the throng at the fringe of the park.

I remained on the bench, puzzled and sullen, until I saw a group of four or five people standing a few yards off regarding me and the bottle with disgust. I didn't care now. I got up and threw the bottle behind a hedge, then walked on to where the map said I had to go.

On the opposite side of the city the celebrations were no less abandoned. I wondered how long, exactly, the war had been over and whether these people would drop from exhaustion before the sun went down. An Italian band was playing at one corner which I thought was strange because they'd started out on the other side. Some Chinese were burning an effigy of Hitler outside a restaurant, which also puzzled me because I'd never connected the Chinese with Hitler before. I took to creeping around corners whenever I saw a particularly violent celebration coming over my horizon, and by counting streets I came, at last, to the building where I was supposed to report as a shipwrecked sailor.

It was a poor-looking place with green walls and dusty corridors. The door was open but although I called out several times I could not get an answer. I imagined they must be all out in the streets. I was hot and tired and hungry, and without money. My legs were throbbing after the walk, after the lifeboat. The end of the war was getting me down.

I sat on a chair for a few minutes and then I heard a movement above me, so I went up some stairs and opened a door bearing a label ''The Welcome-Home Fund'. This seemed promising so I knocked and went in. It was a big, dreary office, and in a chair at one end was a man who was apparently welcoming home a young woman. He was sitting in the chair, and she was straddled across him, one leg each side. Pieces of clothing, his and hers, and a collection of champagne bottles were distributed about them. They were laughing and doing what they were doing as they laughed.

Naturally I knew exactly what was going on. Rose had once tried to sit on me like that but our combined weight had broken the chair in the telephone room. I wanted to back out, but I wanted to watch them. I remained there, my hand on the door, while she rode up and down to his jerky movements. Then he saw me. And the girl, who was very pretty, turned and saw me too.

'Jesus!' exclaimed the man, his face flowing from red to white.

'Christ,' whispered the girl putting her hands on her suspenders.

I felt I ought to say something. 'Excuse me,' I said nervously. 'I'm a distressed mariner.'

He was already picking up a bottle from the floor as I spoke and, considering his physical engagement, he threw it with amazing force and accuracy. It hit the wall above my head and I ducked out in fear with green glass falling all round me.

I ran down the stairs, to the entrance corridor again. They were not pursuing me. I heard the footsteps across the floor above my head again, and the door bolted loudly, then silence, so I presumed that they had gone back to their personal celebrations. Everyone was having a good time but me.

As I was about to go out into the street again I noticed a small glass door which I had not seen before. A shadow moved behind it and, since it was a single shadow and showed no signs of dancing or hopping about, I knocked on the door and went in. There was a grey man in a linen jacket putting away some papers in a file. He was the first normal person I had seen all day. He looked up.

'I'm looking for the Distressed Mariners Department,' I said quickly seeking to get in first.

'You've found it,' he said. 'Just arrived?'

'More or less,' I said. 'I've been trying to find the place.'

'English,' he said. 'Well, it's over now, son. That part of it, anyway. Only the Japs now.'

'They won't last,' I said confidently, glad of someone who was speaking instead of shouting.

'You're a bit of a kid for a DM.' he said.

'Torpedoed,' I said bravely. 'The Krauts don't care how old you are.'

'Well, it's all over,' he repeated softly. 'Unfortunately son, everybody's gone home or out celebrating. There's nothing I can do for you tonight. Come back tomorrow.'

'Tomorrow?' I cried. 'Christ, I've walked miles to get here.'

'No need to take His Name in vain, sonny,' he said politely. 'He's never done you no harm.'

I wasn't going to argue over that. 'What can I do?' I said. 'Where can I go?'

He began to write something on a form. 'What's your name?' he said.

'Arthur McCann.'

'What d'you call yourself, English or British?'

'Either,' I said. 'I just want somewhere to go.'

'I'm not the one to do this,' he explained looking closely at the form. 'I just clear up around here. But I've seen them do it.' He handed the form to me. 'Here now, take this to the Sailors' Home on West Forty-Second, and . . .'

'West?' I said. 'That's the West Side you mean?'

'Sure, son, that's where it is.'

'I've just walked from there. It took me hours.'

He nodded his head. 'Well, I guess I can lend a couple of bucks to a DM.,' he said. He took the money and handed it to me. I thanked him in a whisper. He told me where to get on the subway and I went out into the street again.

Standing on the corner was a coloured girl. She smiled and I smiled too. 'D'you wanna go to bed, honey?' she asked.

'I certainly do, miss,' I said innocently. 'I'm dead beat.'
I walked on down the street thinking that at last, and twice
in the space of five minutes I had met both friendship and
concern.

At the Sailors' Home my circumstances immediately improved. They gave everybody a tot of rum and two dollars
to celebrate Victory in Europe. I had never drunk rum so I
sold mine for fifteen cents and I began to feel more secure
in the world.

I was taken to a simple iron bed in a simple iron room, a
corrugated roof and sounding metal walls like the sides of a
ship, which I supposed at the time was to make the sailors
feel at home, at sea, as it were. It was like being in a tank or
a hold, with the men's talk booming and bouncing from the
green-painted walls and every burp and belch echoing like
a roll of thunder around the enclosed place.

A tottering man, a lame janitor, showed me to one bed,
but a sailor approached and, shaking a warning head, said:
'Don't put him next to Senga. Senga'll be crawling in with
him.' The tottering man nodded with bleak understanding
and beckoned me to the far side of the dormitory to another
bed. There was a striped mattress, a pile of folded blankets,
and a scratched wooden locker. The man who had prevented
me sleeping next to Senga strolled through the alley-ways
between the beds, and sat on the end of my bed.

'They should never stick anybody next to Senga,' he
sniffed, ' 'specially a young kid like you. They ought to
know that.'

'He's a pineapple, is he?' I said with the voice of experience.

'He'll be asking you over to his bed for a drink,' he agreed.

'It's a funny name,' I said. 'Senga. Where did he get
that?'

'Agnes backwards,' he explained. 'That's how he is, see.'

'What's your name?' I asked.

'My name's Sirod,' he said and his eyes dropped.

'Doris backwards?'

'You catch on quick, son. But you don't have to worry about me, mate. I'm sort of inactive. A smouldering volcano. You won't have any bother from me, in fact I'll look after you. Keep an eye on you just like your mother would. Did you get sunk?'

'Torpedoed,' I nodded. 'Must have been the last one of the war.'

'What ship?'

'*Queen of Atlantis*,' I said.

'Oh, aye, I've sailed in her. Old Gander still the mate?'

'He was.'

'Gone?'

'Gone.'

'Randy old pineapple he was. You probably know. He used to get the cook's boy to shoot at him with one of those guns that shoot off a rubber sucker. You know, the things kids have. He used to stand there, stark bollock naked, and get this kid to shoot these things at him. Downright disgusting.'

'With me it was boxing,' I said. 'But he's gone now.'

'Sporting day over, eh?'

'For good,' I said. A drooping man, thin and bent as a feather, not even glancing at us, shuffled between the beds and collapsed face down on to the bed next to mine. He was so light the springs hardly gave beneath him. He pushed his grey head into his elbows and began to weep.

'Who's that?' I asked.

'Nobody knows,' the sailor said. 'We call him Rider Haggard, for want of anything better. Greek or something. Don't speak to anybody and no soul speaks to him. Greek's a funny lingo. I've got a bit of German myself, and I've tried that on him but he just bursts into bleeding tears.'

'So you don't know what he's crying about?'

'No idea, mate.'

'It must be something big if he keeps on doing it.' I looked across at the man, who was sobbing heavily into his arms.

'I s'pose it must be, at that,' he agreed looking at the weeping neighbour as though seriously considering the phenomenon for the first time. 'But I don't s'pose we'll ever know.'

'What's your name? Your real one?' I asked.

'Billy Freeman,' he said. 'I'm Aussie.'

'My name's Arthur McCann,' I said. My outstretched hand was immersed in his huge soft paw. He was a big, hairy, powerful man. I could not understand how men like that could be pineapples. 'I'm from South Wales.'

'And I'm from *New* South Wales!' He roared a laugh worthy of a joke ten times as good.

'Why don't we ask him what's the matter?' I suggested.

'Who?'

'Him.'

'Rider Haggard? Well, I've tried. I've told you. I've tried German.'

'Have you tried English?' I said.

'Well, no I haven't tried that. Not myself. I mean he's Greek and I've tried German. I told you.'

I got up from my bed and moved the pace to the next bed. Nervously I put my hand on the heaving shoulderblade. It was as fragile as a bird's wing. I felt it wince at my touch.

'What . . . is . . . the . . . matter?' I asked as though I were attempting to speak Greek. Billy Freeman watched from the edge of the bed like someone witnessing an attempt at faith healing.

'What . . . is . . . the . . . matter?' I repeated.

'Arseholes,' whispered the man from his pit of tears.

'English,' I said.

'So he is,' breathed Billy. 'I never saw such a marvellous thing.'

I had retreated to the bed and with Billy watched the almost childish respiration of the shoulders as the man continued to weep. Billy shrugged again: 'Never saw such a thing,' he said again. He got up. 'Come an' meet some of the more sociable lot. You don't have to worry about any of them from the pineapple point of view, apart from Senga, that is. We're not sure about the Russian, because he's got those great big Russian, goo-goo eyes, and he rolls them and sings in a girl's voice. But even I can't tell, and I'm a veteran, but we call him Sivam, just to be on the safe side.'

'Mavis backwards,' I said.

'You're picking it up,' he said. We had moved from the bed. Billy glanced back. 'Fancy Rider Haggard being English. Never saw such a thing.'

We did a sort of ceremonial tour of the booming room. We met the others.

'Rumble Silkin. Got a bad belly.'

'John Pasco. He's a Mex.'

'Teddy.'

'Mr Cawling. Deaf.'

'Jones.'

'Sir Michael Mountley. English, like you see.'

'Arab.'

'William Little.'

'Flybutton.'

When I went back to my bed the feathery man was still sobbing. As I watched with concern and wonder his heaving increased and his sobs grew stronger. Then a trickle of water ran from his mattress, about half way down the length of the bed.

I was almost speechless at the phenomenon until I realised that he was weeping at one end and weeing at the other. I was very concerned and sad for him. But the others said he didn't matter.

That night I dreamed of Rose, her face, round and luminous with love, beaming at me from the front of a barrage balloon. Miles below my father, raging, was trying to pull the balloon down to the earth. Formed up around him was the firing squad sent by Winston Churchill to execute me. (By then, of course, in my awake life, I had realized that this was a fraud. I was growing up.)

In the morning an official came to see me, to take my particulars on a series of forms. He was a clean, young, man and he kept saying: 'It's only the Japanese now. It's only the Japanese.' It was as though he was waging a personal war and had to get it done. I was delighted and surprised when he gave me ten dollars, for which I signed. I asked him if he came from the Distressed Mariners Office and he said he did, so I gave him two dollars to return to the old man who had lent me the money the previous day. I thought he was the sort of person who would be honest about something like that. In addition I asked him if he knew the man in the Welcome Home Fund Office and he said he did and that this man did a fantastic job, something I readily acknowledged because I had seen him doing it.

The Australian Sirod came to my bed later and said that they were going to have an outing that night and that now I had some money I could join them if I liked.

'What are you going to do?' I asked.

'You'll see,' he winked. 'We have a great time where we go.'

'It's not pineapples, is it?' I asked nervously. 'I'm not going on any pineapple treat.'

'A different sort of fruit,' he said, and winked again. I began to look forward to it immediately because I was sure that at least some of them were going out after women in the city and after my dream of Rose and the Balloon I was feeling pent up in a young man's way. I had not wanted to be a sailor but since I had been shanghaied into the profession, and already shipwrecked, I was going to be a sailor in every way, including the women. I went for a walk through the long, tall city, now dazedly back to its normal self on this day after the victory, and saw that the women were very good and well dressed, not like ours at home tired with no stockings and wearing dresses made of blackout material and such stuff.

In the event the fruit that Sirod spoke about turned out to be coconuts. Six of us went to Coney Island for the evening, which surprised and disappointed me, because I had been to plenty of fairgrounds. The Englishman who called himself Sir Michael Mountley won three coconuts by bowling the ball overhand, cricket fashion, and we went to the beer tent to examine the prizes.

Notwithstanding my disappointment in the place for the outing, I felt my spirits welling and warming because I was a sailor among sailors, a man among men (give or take a few). Sivam the Russian was with us, and it was true he had huge eyes which always seemed to be brimming with sentimental tears. Sir Michael Mountley called everyone 'dear chap' even the woman at the coconut shy. Rumble Silkin was an Indian with dyspepsia and Mr Cawling was called 'I-can'ear-yer' Cawling.

In the beer tent everybody drank several bottles, with me anxiously keeping up, and then we all went on the big dipper, and after that had some more beer.

The lights of Coney Island seemed to be revolving about my head. Sivam wanted to fight with everybody, and was eventually taken by the others to a boxing booth where a mountainous Negro was challenging all comers to stay three rounds with him for thirty dollars. Sivam stripped to his huge Siberian waist, was in the ring, with our encouragement urging him on, and then out again almost immediately as the Negro uncompromisingly hit him on the jaw. He came back at us through the ropes like some huge projectile. We got him back into the fight again and this time the boxer hit him on the nose and in a minute we were carrying him bloodily through the fairground in much the same way as the children our street used to carry home the drunken men.

I think we took Sivam to a hospital but I've never been certain of this because I never saw my shipmates again after that night. The beer and the blood and the big dipper had all taken their toll of a callow youth. I reached the Sailors' Home and there collapsed spectacularly in front of reporters, photographers and a tall Jewish lady called Mrs Nissenbaum, who had been awaiting my return.

My story had been discovered. The Boy From The Lifeboat, they called me. New York in its victory frenzy was looking for a hero and they had found him. I was overwhelmingly glad it was me.

6

Her name was Rebecca Nissenbaum and she was a big and beautifully made woman. To me, at that young time of my life, she seemed about the size of the lady who was the Statue of Liberty, but, of course, much warmer.

Everything about her was large but perfectly kept. I've never seen such outsize, lovely, hands on a woman, the nails like sea shells, the fingers girded with thick rings, gold gems, the palms and the backs like the choicest white meat. Like Rose she had a heavy cloud of black hair, but whereas Rose's had been wild and hanging, or hurriedly pushed up into pins and combs, Mrs Nissenbaum's hair was built and *arranged*. It sat like a jet turban above the splendid contrast of her creamy face. Each eye was a portrait in itself, painted and shaded, embellished with streaks of black and purple, and at each centre a sumptuous pupil the size of an egg and a black centre so riveting that I felt no man could have the strength to turn his face from it. She had extravagant lips like a film star on a poster and her clothes, chosen to accentuate the superb white drum of her neck, her powerful breasts and hips, came from a leading dress designer for outsize women. Jewellery grew on her like fruit; her furs seemed to have kept their animal life. Her smell was such that you knew she was on the way even before she turned a corner; like an expensive breeze. She was thirty-five and she said she came from a poor Jewish family in the Bronx.

That, of course, even if it were true, was a long time before she met Mr Benny Nissenbaum, who was rich and had a house at Riverdale but was, at that time, missing presumed dead in Okinawa.

Only shadows remain from the first evening when she took me in her cavernous car from the Sailors' Home to her house. The stormy Coney Island beer within me gave me a shipwrecked appearance which went aptly alongside the story of my junior heroism as retold in the New York newspapers the following morning.

These were brought to me with my breakfast by a maid and I floated in the huge bed, watching the sun supported by the tops of the trees outside my window, like Oliver Twist on his first morning in Mr Brownlow's house.

Mrs Nissenbaum looked seven feet tall when she entered on elaborately platformed slippers, all clothed in fluffy pink and white garments like a brilliant ice cream sundae. Despite her size she seemed to float in the room. Her smile was magnificence itself.

'You're awake,' she said with a thrillingly deep tone. 'Better' are you?'

'Much better, thank you,' I said, staring at her.

She smashed a lovely fist into my pillows. 'Your picture's in the newspapers. Maybe you saw it already.' At her hem waddled a fussy toy dog. God, what happened to him afterwards! She called it Errol Flynn and she was always picking him up and cuddling him and pushing him inside her folding garments, next to her warm bosom.

I nodded when she said about the newspaper pictures and felt an uncertain smile grow on my face. Did she realize I had been drunk?

'Exhausted,' she said, sitting with astonishing lightness on the edge of the bed. 'Every bit exhausted – and little boy you sure looked it.' She picked up one of the papers and shook her head faintly at the spreadeagled figure of myself in the arms of my fellow sailors. 'For God's sakes,' she said unbelievingly. 'Imagine this city sending you to that dump when you had been sunk and shipwrecked. Imagine! It should have been the brass bands and the ticker tape even.'

'I didn't mind,' I muttered modestly. 'Everybody was busy celebrating the end of the war. I must have slipped by unnoticed.'

'Disgrace on America,' she said brushing my remarks aside with her words and my toast crumbs from the bed with a soft sweeping hand.

'Thank God, I have a friend who is the secretary of the

Distressed Mariners Committee, and she called up yesterday afternoon and told me all about the disgrace.' She leaned forward and enveloped my thin hand in hers. 'Arthur McCann,' she said sincerely, her black eyes like guns, 'I want to apologise for the City of New York and for the United States of America for failing in our duty. Even ignoring the rules of common hospitality.'

'That's all right, really it is,' I said, embarrassed and overwhelmed. 'I didn't expect anything.' I felt I had to make a more fulsome gesture. 'Plenty of others, younger than me, have gone and got killed in the war.'

To my surprise she began snivelling into the counterpane, picking it up like a big handkerchief and dabbing her eyes and her mouth with it. She was so large and she used it so elegantly that it hardly looked out of proportion.

'My husband, Benny David Nissenbaum,' she muttered. 'Captain Benny Nissenbaum. Missing believed killed, Okinawa.'

'Oh, I am sorry,' I said genuinely, patting her hand in return.

'Must be killed,' she continued mournfully. 'It's only a two bit place and I don't see how nobody, and surely not my Benny, could go missing without them noticing. Not Benny. He's the sort you'd notice anywhere, so he's not just *missing*. He's killed completely. Finished. Blown to bits, I say, because I think they'd have noticed him even if he was just dead like everybody else. Benny always stood out in a crowd.'

'I'm sorry,' I muttered inadequately once more.

'Arthur,' she said looking up dramatically. 'I am a Jewish person and we always make sure that our loved ones are commemorated in the way they would like. I don't think no stone tablet is good enough for my Benny, nor a million candles. He's worth something more than that.'

'Of course, Mrs Nissenbaum,' I agreed. 'I should think he is.'

She paused and her dark head dropped forward like a bison's. 'My husband deserves a *living* memorial, Arthur.

And I want you to consider yourself to be that memorial Will you do that? I want you to feel free to use this home as your home, and to feel that Benny Nissenbaum had got his hand on your shoulder. You'll be like a walking stone tablet to his memory.'

I sat stunned in the bed, not knowing what to say.

'You'll be my Benny's memorial, won't you, Arthur?' she said, those eyes filling her face again. 'His walking tablet?'

'Yes,' I said uncertainly. 'But what do I have to do? I've never thought of being anything like that.'

'Nothing,' she said. 'That's nothing you have to do, Arthur. Just be here and think of this lovely home as your lovely home.'

'It's very decent of you, Mrs Nissenbaum,' I said. 'And I'd love to walk around in memory of your husband, Benny. But I'll have to go back home, won't I? I've got to go home to my mum and dad.'

'But not yet,' she pleaded. 'Not yet Arthur. The war's only over just a couple of days. Let the sea settle down. You have some more bagels and coffee and be comfortable. The bathroom is right through there. Benny's toothbrush and his shaving things are still on the shelf and I know he would want you to feel free with them. And all I want you to do Arthur is to give a little thought to my Benny, in pieces like he is, when you are using his blades.'

'I will, of course I will.' I promised. 'I don't shave very often.'

At this she rolled her lovely head and whispered, 'So young.' Then stood up and went, strong, smooth, silent, like a big female machine, towards the door. She turned there hopefully: 'There's no Jewish in the family, is there Arthur?'

I said I didn't think so, although my father always said my grandfather Murky was like a Wandering Jew, something I could never comprehend because, at other times he always said the old man had never been anywhere. Poor

Murky, when I think of him now, and the killer roller skates.

She hardly seemed to hear. 'Ah, well, I suppose it was too much to expect a nice Jewish boy to get himself shipwrecked in a lifeboat just for my convenience. In this life you can't have everything.'

So there was I, who knew nothing of Jews or was even aware of Jews, in New York as a walking, talking memorial to a decimated man called Benny Nissenbaum. My lack of understanding of Judism was complete. When Mrs Nissenbaum told me that she and her husband had met at a barmitzvah I sincerely believed this to be some sophisticated drinking place in the city. For me, at that time, a Jew simply meant someone who had, more or less immediately, come from Jerusalem or appeared in The Bible. In the street we used to sing:

'*Nebuchadnezzar, the King of the Jews,*
Bought his wife a pair of shoes.'

My mother with stolid logic, declared that the Jews had the right religion because Jesus had been a Jew, so what was there to argue about.

The family Green, ten houses up our street, were said to be Jews and one evening when I was there, playing Jig-saws with Emrys Green, I innocently asked his father what it was like in Jerusalem.

He became suddenly and strangely ill-tempered at this and said that he had never been out of Newport in his life, and didn't want to, and if I wanted to know about Jerusalem I ought to ask my father because he went about making out that he knew God personally.

But that was all. Today a boy of sixteen would know everything about the racial distinctions in the same way as they know everything about every variety of sex. But then it was not so.

Mrs Nissenbaum bought me some new clothes and I went around to see her friends in her floating automobile. Until then I had never been in a car and to be drifting through the elongated city and its white suburbs in this

84

vehicle, sometimes driven by a Peruvian chauffeur and sometimes by the stately Rebecca, was like living in a daily dream.

Sometimes we went to restaurants and I could see she was very proud of me by the way she told the waiters and the people at the surrounding tables who I was, what maritime disasters I had braved and in which newspapers these adventures had been related. Once everyone in a restaurant put down their knives and forks and their wine glasses to applaud me until I had a nasty lump in my throat and a guilty technicolour (blue sea, blue sky, white boat, red and white mate) picture of Mr Gander toppling over the side of the lifeboat after I had clouted him with the spanner. People kept giving me money too and this collected in the pockets of my two suits and the drawer of my bedside table because I was never required to buy anything.

Everywhere I went with Mrs Nissenbaum, whether it was up the Empire State Building to the Central Park Zoo or to one of the stores on Fifth Avenue I tried to look as though *I* was escorting *her*. I walked on the outside when we were in the street, but although I stretched myself to my fullest height and even on to tiptoe, I never reached above her shoulder. When we were in a group of people I found myself almost permanently on the balls of my feet at her side, a difficult position to maintain especially since I was required to nod my head to the conversation at the same time. Once, when we were going down the wide steps by the fountains in Central Park together I asked her openly if she would mind if I walked a couple of elevations behind her, so that, at least viewed from the front, we looked as though we were of the same height. My face was very young too, of course, and this worried me. I stopped my weekly shave in an attempt to grow a beard but nothing happened. It was no good my pretending we were together because it was plain for all to see *I* was with *her* not she with me. I belonged to her.

Needless to say I was now grossly in love with Mrs Nissenbaum and her scented proximity was agony for someone so sensitive and impressionable as I was then. Her voice, the casual silk touches of those huge hands, her all-enveloping smile, her strong legs in her fine big, shapely shoes, her kiss on my cheek as I went each night burning to bed.

Sometimes in the day she went out alone and left me to wander, pent up with love and need, through the lovely home that she and the now fragmented Benny Nissenbaum had made together.

The maid, the housekeeper and the chauffeur seemed to melt into elegant wallpaper at these times of the day and I walked about touching things, looking behind doors, brimming with guilt and fear for her perfume was everywhere.

I went into Benny's study, where his moustached photograph smiled remote encouragement to me from the desk. It was here, to fend off my base emotions, that I began to write my novel, 'All the Coloured Lights Of The World by Arthur McCann', a saga of the sea and other things now nearing completion after more than twenty years. I picked at the opening chapter on Benny's typewriter, wondering, I must confess, where the fingers that last touched it were now located. But I was drawn out by the sweet, beckoning, emptiness of the house, and I would begin to perambulate again like a visitor to a small, scented museum.

It was full of old things I knew nothing about. Clocks and pieces of china and silver, displayed on shelves and in cases. The furniture was voluminous and the carpets like fields. I would play games, crouching in one corner of a settee and imagining myself again in the lifeboat, with Mrs Nissenbaum replacing Mr Gander, and a convenient air bed on the bottom boards. Or I would walk around and idly pull the curtains together by their gold-tassled cords, then open them again.

I looked through the late Benny's books but found nothing to interest me until, between the pages of a life of Abraham Lincoln, I discovered a wafer-sized volume called *The Red Light* which was a guide to American soldiers on how not to catch pox when they were away from their loved ones. I read this with arid mouth and pounding ribs. The things that were described! And how *easy* it all was. All over the world there were women willing, eager even, as Mrs Nissenbaum would say, to do these things. It said so.

My devilish excitement was accentuated because that evening we stayed at home and she lit the lamps and we sat on the cushions, on the floor, and listened to Jose Iturbi playing with the Hollywood Bowl Symphony Orchestra on the radio. Mrs Nissenbaum sat great and soft, her knees curling under her, her head laying back against the arm of the settee, her bosom rising to the music. She was like a lovely, tame, well-nourished creamy cow. I hardly dared to look at her. The combination of her presence, her perfume, and Iturbi clattering through Moonlight Sonata was almost more than sixteen-year-old flesh and blood could stand. Errol Flynn came in and with a little stiff legged–leap settled in her crutch, curled up in the enclosed intimacy of that erotic place.

'What you done today, my lovely boy?' she asked fondly when the commercials interrupted Chopin. 'You been busy?'

'Just resting,' I said. 'Walking about and that.'

'Good for you to have a rest,' she agreed. 'After all you been through on the sea.'

The next afternoon she went to the Jewish Committee for the Rehabilitation of the Slavs, or something, and I went to her bedroom. A dozen times I had stood outside the door, when she was in there or when she was away from the house.

Just stood, trying to imagine what was the other side of the pink barrier with its looped beading picked out in gold, with a sort of golden football cup at its centre. Once, when the maid was making the bed, I had walked slowly by, paused for as long as I dared and see, Mrs Nissenbaum's exciting pink sheets being changed.

Now I went in. I did a circuit of the house first. The sunlight coming through the delicate curtains only served to make the place more enclosed. It was like a perfumed prison. Then I stood outside her door, waited only a moment, opened it and stepped in.

I stood and looked at Rebecca's room, a low sneaky feeling

settling on me, making a layer of misery across my excitement. It was as I knew it would be, warm and light and rich; the bed like an altar covered with a drape, daylight coming muted through the lacy curtains, a photograph of the dismembered Benny on one side of the dressing table and, to my astonishment, one of me on the other. It was the original of one of the newspaper photographs. She must have sent for it. I felt so fearful there, and so ashamed, but thrilled that I was in the place where she rested that heavy, heavenly, body at night. I looked at the bed and imagined her in the dark, breathing at its centre, each sweet, deep-breasted snore sending out its own cloud of exclusive perfume. Stepping forward I touched the bed and pressed it with my hands, feeling its give. I warily pulled the quilt back and put my fingers against her pillows, looking at my fingers first to ensure their cleanliness.

There was another embroidered door leading to her bathroom and I went in there too, my excitement, shame and fear, hugging together in my chest. The heady sensation was accentuated as soon as I stepped through the arch. The bath was sunken and I stood and imagined her lying in it like some marvellous hippopotamus, the water lapping about her breasts, her pink nipples lying just on the surface like the noses of attendant creatures. I touched and then put my cheek against the towels that were waiting for her, smelled her pearly soap, and held her gilt-handled back-scrubber. How I would have delighted in scrubbing that wide and fabulous back, soaping those tremendous buttocks and watching the slow descent of suds down the turned trunks of her legs.

Then I did something quite despicable. I returned to the bedroom and, almost stifled by my guilt and exhilaration, I opened the drawers of her chests and dressing table. They were laid, like treasure trove, with coloured clothes, trinkets and handbags. I touched lace and silk and pulled erotically at elastic. Eventually, like the thief I was, I dipped into a drawer and came out with a magnificent pair of cami-knickers, emerald with lace about the waist and the legs. I let them run luxuriously through my hands, put them to my cheek and then, in a wild moment, stuffed them down the front of my trousers.

It is always at moments like that, at the ultimate of shame and guilt, that the key is heard to turn in the front door, and this is what happened. I could even hear her talking to someone in the hall. From there I knew they could see the bedroom door. My body went to ice. I left the drawer open and with her knickers still wedged in my crutch, I went like a shrike on to the landing almost materializing in front of their eyes. They were standing there with Errol Flynn yapping around their shoes.

'Arthur!' she exclaimed. 'Where did you come from?'

'Hello, Mrs Nissenbaum,' I muttered weakly. I felt that my body was full of cold water. With difficulty I walked down towards her.

'This is Mrs Rosnagel,' she said. 'She is the secretary of the Jewish Committee for the Rehabilitation of the Slavs. She's from Sutton Place. Come on down and say hello.'

I contrived a tight, deliberate, walk which more or less kept the knickers jammed in place, keeping my knees almost together and descending the stairs with an odd mincing step.

'He got something wrong with his legs?' inquired Mrs Rosnagel as I came down. Mrs Nissenbaum looked at her stonily. 'The lifeboat,' she said tersely. 'It's the lifeboat, can't you see? Maybe if you were in a lifeboat without food and water for . . . how many days Arthur . . . ?'

'Six,' I gasped continuing my crippled walk. 'I think.'

'Six!' she almost shouted at her guest. 'He *thinks*! You see, Sadie, he don't even *know*. The poor kid. And you go talking about the way he walks. It was the rowing that hurt his knees like that. It's only a wonder he can walk at all, after six days, or maybe more, even, in a lifeboat because of the filthy Germans. And you criticizing!'

'Rebecca,' the other lady said sharply. 'I am not criticizing your boy. I was only making a passing comment like I might say he's got nice eyes or ears.'

'He has,' said my hostess fondly. 'Thank God he didn't go blind in that lifeboat. With the sun he could just have gone blind.'

Hesitantly I shook hands with Mrs Rosnagel for I knew her eyes were on my legs. With a sort of doomed shuffle I allowed myself to be ushered into the drawing room with them. As I did so the cami-knickers moved and began to slide down my trouser leg. I grabbed at them in pitiful panic and managed to arrest their descent just above my right knee. Hurriedly I sat down on an edge of the settee, with my loaded leg away from the two women. Mrs Nissenbaum rang and told the maid to get some coffee.

'He's got a swelling on his leg,' said Mrs Rosnagel doggedly. 'Look – on that leg right there.'

'Sadie, will you leave his legs alone. He was in the lifeboat, like I told you.'

'He's gone very white,' said the visitor. Christ, I would have liked to strangle her then and there. Her eyes went from my trousers to my face and back to my trousers again.

'Who's to say he can't go white?' insisted Mrs Nissenbaum. 'With you going on about his legs.'

'He was red on the stairs just now.'

'I ... I have these turns,' I stumbled urgently. 'One minute red and the next minute white.'

'Like a street signal,' said Mrs Rosnagel.

'It's the lifeboat,' said Mrs Nissenbaum.

'Your leg, it hurts?' asked the guest.

'No. Not much.'

Shit on her. I was holding the bloody thing to stop them dropping right there on the carpet.

Then, inspired, I said: 'It *does* hurt a bit. It's not much. But I'll just go upstairs, if you don't mind.'

Mrs Nissenbaum, concern plastered right across her beautiful, large face, moved towards me, but I evaded her and holding my leg and her garment with my right hand I went towards the door like some suddenly afflicted hunchback. Both women were staring at me and Errol Flynn followed me. The hairy little insect began sniffing and snapping at my trouser turn-up.

Outside the door I tried to take a stride too wide and keep the dog away at the same time, and the cami-knickers slid down the chute of my trousers and on to my shoe. In the moment that I turned to see if the two women had rounded the door, Errol Flynn had the green garment and went off with it as though he had captured his first rabbit.

Mrs Nissenbaum came around the door and I dropped into my crippled pose again just in time. Mrs Rosnagel was just behind her. One all sympathy, one all suspicion. Fortunately neither of them noticed the dog and his capture. I repeated that I would be all right and staggered up the stairs.

Then Errol Flynn, with idiotic delight, flew into the hall with the cami-knickers in shreds, dangling from his jaw like limp lettuce.

Mrs Rosnagel bent to the dog. 'Looks like he's got a pair of your bloomers, Rebecca,' she growled.

'Naughty Errol Flynn,' said Mrs Nissenbaum. But I looked around and saw that she was still watching me limping up the stairs, the light of pity, and sweetness, in those outsize eyes.

7

That night it was hot, the curtains limp at the open window, the air like rubber, the darkness bearing down on me in my bed. I lay, damp with desire, wondering if Mrs Nissenbaum's big body was hot all over too. In intervals of sticky sleep my eyelids scarcely dropped. I wondered where it was possible to buy Spanish Fly, or if it were possible to make it and what were the ingredients? How was it administered to the victim? Or should I creep in and tie her up, do my terrible thing, and vanish into the torrid night? That would seem ungrateful after all her kindness to me, and, in any case I had a horribly logical vision of her breaking my knots with one powerful pull of those magnificent wrists. Or perhaps I should just present myself at her door and lean idly naked against the frame until she woke and knew why I had come.

The simplicity of this idea appealed to me and, after an hour of arguing with myself, working out the odds, and tossing heads or tails, the best of five, with a ten cent piece, I actually crawled out of bed and went out into the corridor. My heart seemed to be banging like a berserk pendulum against my ribs at either side. It had spent half its day swinging wildly. If this pressure continued I would have a seizure before I'd had a screw.

Naked as a stone I crept along the shadows of the corridor and stood outside the pink embellished door. The house was loaded with silence but through it I thought I could hear her profound breathing. Just a lad of sixteen, I stood, calm outside, trembling within, facing the door, my ridiculously outsized erection pointing forward and slightly up like an ambitious naval gun. If she had opened the door I am certain I would have fainted.

But nothing happened. I stood and stood. Then, sick with myself, I moved forward and let my forehead and the end of my willie touch the smooth paint of the door. I was there only for a second, in an upright dream. Then abruptly I realized what I was doing and in an embarrassed panic I scuttled back to my room. I sat on the bed and made up my mind to leave Mrs Nissenbaum and her lovely home. And it had to be right then.

I got into one of my new suits and put all my money in the back pocket of the trousers. It was my intention to leave a note, but I thought if I waited my resolution would dilute, so I decided instead to send her a telegram in the morning saying I had been suddenly called home because of a family illness. Now I was dressed I paused outside her door only to blow a faint sad kiss in the general direction of her bed.

A minute later I was looking up towards that same bedroom, its curtain flapping like a gentle farewell, from the dimness of the tree-hung road. As if to aid and abet my escape a taxi, going back to the city, came along the main highway and I stopped it and told the driver to take me to Times Square. I sat, tired and defeated now, in the back, felt in my pocket and touched the door key which she had given me.

Riverdale might have been sleeping, but it was only one-thirty and the centre of the city was full of lurid lights and people. I walked like a pasty ghost through them, not knowing where I was going, nor truly what I was seeking. Only that it was something sinful. I went into a place and had a hamburger, then I went into a taxidance, but none of the girls would take my money because they were too busy with soldiers, sailors and the like, still celebrating the end of the war.

Next I went into a gallery where you put a dime into a machine to see some illuminated pictures of women undressing and dancing in the nude. There were three or four other customers in there, bent against the machines, like experts examining some rare finds in a museum. They were intent and isolated from each other and the rest of New York. The place was presided over by an unkempt young man sitting in a sort of a pulpit at one end who was apparently there to see that propriety, as set down in the law of the State, was observed. His eyes were almost hooded but he obviously observed every nuance of the proceedings, because at one point he called wearily into a little microphone: 'Number Three, your clothing is too near the observation machine.' The man curled over peep-show Number Three shuffled back what I suppose was a regulation number of inches.

It was a joyless place, so I put three dimes in three separate machines, all in a line, and moved from one to the other, peeping from a bosom to a bum to a beguine, and then back the other way. I missed, of course, two thirds of each performance, so I inserted another three dimes, and then another three. On this third run I was dancing from one observation machine to the next when I collided with a greasy old man coming the other way. We disentangled and he leapt greedily at the eyepiece I had just vacated. Then the youth in the pulpit, who must have been watching all the time, droned into his microphone: 'Numbers Eight, Nine and Ten. No loitering on these premises.'

I went out into the warm two-thirty air, into the rudely flashing lights, wondering how I could have been loitering. Not that leaving that establishment worried me, anyway, for they were only moving pictures, ghastly ghosts compared to the living flesh of Mrs Nissenbaum.

Miserably I walked under the lights and among the people. What were all these persons doing in the middle of Times Square in the middle of the night? None of them were up to any good, that was certain. Except for hobos and vagabonds, who had nowhere to go, they were all seeking to find or to give something that was illicit. Why did they all ignore me? Why couldn't I join in? Did it have to be that my adventures would be confined to a mad, queer, mate in an open boat in an open ocean?

At the entrance to the Dime-a-Dance Palace, where I had already experienced rejection, was a Negro lady wearing a fur coat. The very fact that she had such an acquisition and was clad in it on a night when the temperature could not be below seventy Fahrenheit, drew me towards her.

Casually I stood at her side, two feet away, observing the people just as she was observing them. Every now and then she made a greeting to a man which was either returned or ignored. But none of the men approached her. After she had said 'Hello there' at least twenty times I swallowed hard and without looking at her said jauntily: 'You seem to know a lot of folks around here.'

'How old are you, honey?' she inquired lazily without even glancing at me.

'Nineteen,' I said brazenly.

'You're pretty fucking small for nineteen,' she rejoined.

'I'm from England,' I said quickly. 'We're small because of the war. Not getting enough to eat.'

'Nineteen?'

'Yes. I'm just small, that's all.'

'It's against the state law to screw minors,' she warned.

'I didn't come down here to buy a funny paper,' I said. I was overwhelmingly pleased with that and it seemed to impress her too.

'It's ten dollars, plain,' she said.

'I'll have you twice,' I boasted.

'Get a cab then,' she said. Then: 'No I'll get it. He maybe won't see you.'

In the cab I sat at her side sweating with excitement and embarrassment. I wondered whether I ought to hold her hand. Eventually she said: 'You sure you're how old you say? You don't look it.'

'I am,' I insisted in the dimness.

As though finally convinced of my qualifications she half-swung on the seat and pulling open the front of her fur coat she said: 'Want to take a look, honey?'

She was naked under the coat; black and naked. The lights of the streets, reds, yellows, blues, greens flashed across her stomach and her breasts. I stared at her as though I were staring into our coal cellar at home. Then my eyes travelled up to her face, split with a grin, seeking approval.

'That's very good,' I said inadequately.

'Sure is, honey,' she said. 'You got plenty of money?'

'Some,' I answered cautiously.

'Give me two dollars for the cab,' she said. 'And two more for me and you can get your little Limey head right in there.'

I gave her a five dollar note and waited for the change. None was forthcoming. But she reached out with slim black arms and pulled my head into that dark hothouse. She wrapped the fur coat about my ears as though protecting me from the world, and my mouth and my nose were thrust against the hot damp flesh of her upper body. The scent in there was sharp, overpowering, not like Mrs Nissenbaum's flowering perfumes around the rooms of the house. She forcibly rubbed my face into her breasts as though she were polishing them, her stiff nipples running across my cheeks and my nose, my mouth gasping open. Abruptly she pushed me out again into the open air and I was not entirely sorry for I thought I would have drowned or suffocated before long.

'Home sweet home, baby,' she said. She paid the taxi and we went into the entrance lobby of a block of apartments. A porter sat in a morose glass case, nodding towards sleep. He saw me and woke up.

'It's okay, Joe,' she called. 'Just a relative visiting.'

'He don't look like no relative to me,' grumbled the porter. 'He ain't even the same colour as you.'

'Poor guy's been sick,' she rejoined. 'Gone pale.' She was almost at the elevator door. She turned to me: 'Give Joe a dollar, uncle,' she suggested.

I gave Joe a dollar. 'Okay uncle,' he shrugged. 'Welcome home to the family.'

In the little box of the elevator she giggled and opened her coat for me to put my head inside again. When we reached her floor she gave my hair a little tug and said: 'You can come out now, baby.' She opened a door directly opposite the lift and standing directly inside in striped pyjamas was a small Negro boy. He stared at us with full but completely comprehending eyes.

'Another uncle to see you, Rufus,' she said patting him on the head.

'Sure, sure,' nodded the child with bored understanding. 'Another uncle. How come I got so many white uncles? I don't have no uncles the same as me at all.'

'Every family has its problems, honey,' she said. 'Ain't it time you was in your bed?'

'I was,' said Rufus. 'I just heard you and I came out to see what this uncle was like. And he don't look much good, mammy.'

'This uncle's a real nice uncle, honey. He's from England.'

Rufus regarded me critically. 'Gee,' he sniffed to his mother. 'You ain't tellin' me you been all the way to England and come back with *him*.'

She smiled fondly at him, but, to my relief, opened the

door to a bedroom and nodded to me to go in. It was all pink and black and gold and well used. Her clothes and shoes were on the floor and there was a mangy towel hanging like a rope over one side of a wash basin. I wanted to go back to Mrs Nissenbaum's lovely home.

But she stood in front of me and peeled back her coat, noting my eyes as she did so. 'I ain't told you my name,' she said. 'It's Judy. What you called?'

'Arthur,' I said hoarsely staring at the black, steaming body that had emerged from the coat. I could count her ribs, but the breasts above them were full and tight. 'Arthur McCann.'

'Take your clothes off, Arthur,' she invited. 'You and me, we're goin' to have a real cosy time. Just Judy and Arthur.' I began to rummage with the buttons of my shirt. 'Take it easy,' she smiled. 'Real easy.'

When I was standing undressed, she took one animal step towards me, her hand catching hold of me low down. She tugged and there immediately came the brisk ring of a bell almost as though her action had occasioned it. She stopped and apologised with a shrug. She went over to the telephone and picked it up.

'Christie!' she exclaimed joyfully, her breasts bouncing. 'Gee, great, honey! When did you get in?' She glanced at me intimately indicating that she would soon get rid of Christie, but she didn't. Christie went on and then she went on, one laughed, so did the other. Then they started talking about when they were going to meet up and the things they did in August, then what happened in September and October. As this was only May I thought I might have a long wait, standing there, nude, with a gradually dropping dick at the bottom of her bed.

Then the door was pushed timidly and in walked Rufus holding a bright yellow American football. He regarded my naked state with no surprise.

'Wanna play, uncle?' he inquired. He nodded towards his mother. 'She takes a long time.'

I gaped at him, but the next moment he had thrown the ball

and I caught it against my stomach. With a despairing look over my shoulder at that long seal-like woman, stretched out across the bed, her backside shining black in the lamplight, I tossed the ball back to the boy. He was delighted and made a little dodge across the floor before returning it. I threw it back again. The phone conversation stopped for a moment and she said: 'That's right, have a ball game for a coupla minutes. This friend, she just blew in from nowhere. I won't be long, honey.'

Into the phone she said: 'Sure he's playing a ball game with Rufus. Ain't that cute?'

Rarely have I felt so frustrated and utterly stupid as I did throwing that yellow object to and fro across the bedroom. Rufus was enjoying it and kept making dummy passes or going into a one-boy huddle and discussing the next tactic with imaginary team mates.

My penis had now predictably collapsed entirely and I was punting the ball to him with my bare toes. He laughed and I laughed dolefully too. Suddenly I was back in Wales again, in school, running through the mud along the wing with the ball under my arm, knowing that I would never reach that line before Hefty Edwards had me down. I could feel again his hot snorting behind me and the heavy grasp and tackle and over I crunched and everybody groaned and accused me of buggering it up again.

We dodged around the bedroom and then out into the hall, me stark, him pulling up the trousers of his striped pyjamas with one small dark hand while fielding the ball with the other. We didn't even hear her put the phone down. Then her head came around the door and she said: 'Okay Rufus, that's enough. Uncle has to rest now. You go and rest too.'

She led me into the room by the hand, and closed the door on the hurt black face of little Rufus, still plaintively holding his ball like a watermelon. She lay on her side on the bed and motioned me to go to her. I went to the opposite side and sidled across, my anticipation growing apace again. Her long arms moved out to meet me, caught me around the neck and guided me on the last knee-crawling part of the journey. My body was warm from the game with Rufus, but it felt cool against hers. She seemed to give out her own heat. I closed against her like a man hugging a hot water pipe.

'That fuckin' Christie,' she mumbled. 'She ain't no good anyhow. I sure don't care if I never sees the ugly face again. She double-crossed me in August and she double-crossed me in September, and in December she sure double-double-double crossed me. So I don't care whether she scrapes her ass on a rusty nail. No Sir.'

While this incantation was going on she was adroitly putting a contraceptive on me – my first fitting – and manoeuvring me between her legs. I was almost stifled with the excitement of it. She lay back with a sweet little groan and began to move beneath me. Then the phone rang again. The movement broke and she looked at me apologetically. Her slim arm went out to the receiver and she picked it up. Her face switched on with delight.

'Christie, honey!' she exclaimed. My soul became dark. 'Je-sus, Christie, that's great! I'm so glad for you, baby. Now you just listen to your Aunt Jemima. When that Leroy starts playing those tricks again, you do like I told you. Get it?'

Christie was getting it. But I wasn't. I lay dumb as a log. I made a few hopeful forlorn movements, but far from responding she shook her face at me indicating that she didn't want me to carry on without her.

I began to feel chilly. The night was cooling off, the window was open, and horizontal breeze was sliding into the room. Inevitably I began to think of Mrs Nissenbaum again, of her voluptuousness and her home comforts. The telephone conversation went on while I used one of Judy's breasts as a pillow and studied the topography of the other. It was like the slag-heaps in the valleys back home.

Eventually they had finished. The fond goodbyes took another couple of minutes, but then she replaced the phone and wheezed a happy giggle. 'Oh boy, that Christie,' she said. 'She ain't nothing but the greatest! Wow, what's going to happen now she's blown in!'

'I thought you didn't like her,' I spitefully pointed out.

She seemed amazed. 'How the hell do you know?' she demanded. 'You ain't even *seen* her. We're like lovin' sisters, Christie and me. I ain't never been one to keep a grudge . . . and what she gone and done to that Leroy . . .' Suddenly she seemed to come aware of our positions and my doleful expression.

'Aw, baby,' she apologised softly. 'I left you all on your ownsome. That woman would only call me because she knows I got a man here. She's just trying to ruin my technique and my reputation, boy, and she ain't getting away with it. Sly, idle, asshole of a horse that she is. You just come here to your mama, and she'll put you just right.'

Not in my most erotic and co-operative mood could I imagine her as my mother, but I let my sulkiness slide away as her hands lay flat on my buttocks again and she began to roll them with the practised finesse of an old-fashioned baker. The feeling flowed again and I groaned in chorus with her professional agony. Then the phone went again.

'Let it ring, darling,' she said. 'We'll just let it ring.'

Whoever it was they knew we would have to answer it no matter how long it took. Eventually its insistence had got us all out of time and pace. The enjoyment dwindled like a record running down. We stopped and she reached out and picked it up again.

'Leroy,' she breathed. 'Oh, Leroy just great! When did you get in from Big B.R. . . . And Christie! Sure she's here . . . right here in New York . . . and I want to tell you one thing baby, she's sure out to gun down that Clement. Boy, you should hear what she's got to say about him . . . What, he's going to call me? Clement? That shit. Oh, sweetie, you just wait until he hears what I've got to put into his mother-fuckin' ear . . . You tell him to call me right now . . . Just as soon as you've put down the phone. And I'll tell him what Christie said. Oh boy, that poor Christie. Leroy, can you just imagine . . .'

I could imagine no more. What was Big B.R.? My eyes were full of boyish tears and I longed for my bed in Mrs Nissenbaum's safe and scented house. I had shrivelled, within and without, and the wind was blowing cold on my rear. My body ached and my eyes drooped. While her telephone conspiracies went on close to my ear, I did not hear them because I had drifted to aching sleep.

She woke me with a nasty nudge of her stomach. I blinked at her. I felt stiff all over my body, except in one place. Her eyes glared at me in the half light.

'Jesus,' she said. 'You ain't gone off to sleep?'

'Just a nap,' I mumbled.

'A nap! Jesus Christ, nobody ever fell asleep on top of Judy Winton-Brown before. Nobody!'

'Well, you were talking on the phone.'

'Don't give me that crap!' she exclaimed. 'You just get out of here English boy, and don't you come places insultin' hard-working girls. This is a body not a fuckin' bed.'

'I haven't had it yet,' I complained.

'You ain't had what?'

'What I came for. In fact, I didn't come.'

'You came when you was asleep, buster. Real quiet. I know it even if you don't. And that means you got what you paid for.'

'I didn't have anything,' I insisted, but not caring anyway now.

I groped my way from the bed and she turned and buried her face in the pillow like the purest lover suddenly scorned. Getting some of my clothes on and carrying the rest I went to the door. Standing outside was Rufus, round eyes, pleadingly holding the ball in front of him.

'You wanna play, uncle?' he asked.

'Go and play with your mammy,' I said, a remark meant innocently enough but sufficient to arouse a terrible scream from the bedroom accompanied by accusations of encouraging incest and violation of innocent children. From the hall I heard her spring from the bed, so I got out quickly. The elevator was, thankfully, standing with its door open like an emergency exit. I stumbled in. She appeared at the apartment door and threw the yellow football at me. It was a good throw and it came into the elevator, beating the closing doors by a fraction. It struck me on the nose and bounced crazily from wall to wall as I descended. I could hear her screaming abuse from the top of the shaft.

I walked into the lobby with the ball under my arm causing the porter Joe to raise his tired head, then raise his eyebrows.

'Have a nice game, uncle?' he inquired.

I realised I was carrying the ball. Walking over to him I put it on his desk and went out without a word. I got a cab back to Riverdale and arrived at the end of the trees in the street when it was nearing daylight. Thank God I still had the key. I let myself in and went wounded to my room, pulling the sheet about my head to hide me from all the injuries the world would inflict upon me.

At nine o'clock Mrs Nissenbaum, wearing her pink robe and her lovely white smile came into the room, Errol Flynn running behind her. I peeped at her nervously over the hem of the sheet.

'It sure was a hot night, Arthur,' she observed.

'Yes, it was Mrs Nissenbaum,' I agreed. 'I couldn't sleep.'

'Nor me.' She sat in her familiar way on the side of my bed.

'It *was* hot,' I said again.

'I couldn't sleep at all,' she repeated. 'But I don't have any appointments today, so I think I'll lie-in this morning. Maybe you would like to lie-in as well.'

At that blinding instant I knew it was going to happen. I waited for it and she said: 'Maybe we could rest together.'

And Mrs Nissenbaum, lovely, big, sweet-smelling, Mrs Nissenbaum, put her strong arms under me, lifted me, and carried me like a joyful prize to her bedroom.

I was glad, in my boyish way, that I had saved myself for her.

8

From the summer the war ended, after I had returned from America, from the embrace of Mrs Nissenbaum (and the terrible and unique death of her little dog Errol Flynn,) until she left me on the municipal putting green last October, Pamela, my wife, was always somewhere in my heart. It was the very last day, the last hour, the last minute, that the putting green was open for that season. There was a tall, white old man (one of the tallest, whitest, oldest men I have ever seen) in charge of the putting green. He made it dramatically obvious that he was anxious to go because as Pamela and I putted each hole, he followed immediately behind us grumpily uprooting the little red flags and putting round stoppers like jam pot lids into the holes. All the time we were arguing and he was gummidging and the day was falling apart around us. He could not have realized, of course, that while all he was doing was wrapping up a harmless amusement for the winter we were wrapping up years of marriage. And, sorry as I was that he was injured in the ultimate painful scene, I cannot help thinking, even now, that if he had not been so anxious to bugger off I might be a securely married man today. It was the final ridiculous rowdy business that made Pamela turn and run out of the gate, more frightened over the immediate crisis than angry over the culmination of failures attached to our union. It was not our own divisions that broke it up for ever. It was an old fool's screams.

But in its way it was appropriate because years ago it was another aged man, my grandfather, Murky, who first brought us together. Two ancients like bent doorkeepers opening and shutting the doors at each end of our life together.

My grandfather was called Murky, for some distant reason which he would never discuss. He was a slate-coloured old man who contrived to look and converse like an ancient mariner, although my father swore that he was a filthy old liar who had never been west of the Bishop Light.

Murky came to live with us after my grandmother died during the war and he was the one member of the family who said firmly that it was Aunt Clementine who had never succumbed to my father's charms and persuasions. When she came to our house Murky would giggle into his carefully upturned miniature beard and repeat half a dozen times: 'Heh, heh. Here's the Dock Street virgin.' Clementine would fluster, grow red and look appealingly around to the other members of the family. If my father was there, and the old grandfather persisted, there would be a brief scuffle while Murky was taken out and locked in the outside lavatory which was unused because a bathroom had by then been interpolated into the house by the Newport Borough Council. When we were having tea we could hear the faint sounds of Murky banging on the wooden door and when he was eventually released he would come in, chastened, and spend the rest of the day sadly and quietly engrossed in getting the splinters out of his elderly fists.

I loved the old man because from my earliest childhood I was the listener to his stories of the oceans which my father swore were untrue. They sounded true to me and they still do.

'There's an island in the southern ocean, boy,' he would whisper, as though he alone had discovered it and was anxious to keep it secret. 'About eight south, fourteen west. Called Ascension. Comes out of the sea like one of them there ice cream cornets, turned up. And on the leeward side there's some tall, straight trees, like fingers on a man's hand . . .' He would hold his fingers up to show me. They were as brown and thin as an Indian's. 'Somebody planted those trees specially for sailing ships, like ours, that came in wrecked, demasted from a storm. Cut down a tree, boy, and you had a mast to get you home . . .'

Hearing this, or something like it, my father would laugh like a bursting boiler and call Murky a bloody old liar. 'Fancy telling the kid that,' he would snort in his big way.

'All you ever sailed in was a rotten dirty coaler.'

Murky would regard him with ancient hatred. 'I've been there,' he would say. 'What I'm telling the boy is right.'

'You!' mocked my father. 'Dressing up like you do. That cap and the beard. Wonder you don't cut your sodding leg off and get yourself a parrot.'

'No brains, let alone any memory,' returned Murky. 'That's you. Never did have. I've sailed before the mast and seen places you've never dreamed about.'

'Dream about them – that's all you've done,' said my father. 'Why don't you go down to the Hornpipe and drink with the rest of the old boys. Tell you why – because they'd find you out. They'd know it was a lot of made up tales. All you do is go to the James Street library. You get it all from books.'

One Monday morning they had a fist fight while my mother was doing the washing at the steaming boiler in the kitchen. It was about kodiak bears or the location of Quinn's Bar in Tahiti, or something like that. Normally old Murky would retreat from the argument under threats from my father to shut him in the outside lavatory, but he was particularly trenchant on this morning and it ended with a spontaneous brawl among the piles of laundry and the flying suds of the back kitchen.

'Buggering old liar!' bellowed my father.

'Conscientious Objector!' howled the old man. 'Cowardly bastard!'

'The child!' cried my mother. 'The boy!'

My grandfather was over seventy but he was as strong as he was brave. He rushed my father back to one end of the kitchen and it was then that the washing boiler tipped and poured its gallons of scalding water everywhere. My father was in his socks and he got the worse of it. He howled and danced out into the back yard, the blisters ballooning from his feet.

When I sailed to Ascension Island many years later, I saw the plantation of Norfolk pines at the side of the steep mountain. Some of them had been cut down for ships' masts and the rest stood slim and straight as my grandfather's fingers.

The Newport War Heroes Ball was held at Mandles Dance Hall in August 1945. I had, naturally, returned from my first eventful voyage to a great deal of praise and publicity, which gave my father even more to boast about than usual. After all, as he said every half-an-hour, was it not he who had sent me off to sea? Was it not he who had spotted the potential? Only I knew that his judgement had not only put me in danger of being drowned, but of being buggered as well.

Sadly now I remember the warm August night of the Heroes Ball. The moon and Mandles and Pamela.

In my grandfather's younger days Mandle's Dance Hall, overlooking the pebble beach at the end of the docks, had been a roller skating rink and the old man got seized with a bout of hysterical second childhood that night. All the week he had muttered and moped about wanting to celebrate the end of the war like anybody else, more, because he had seen more wars begun and ended, than anybody. Very strangely, I think he also got a bit jealous over all the publicity and the attention I got because of being sixteen and torpedoed. When the newspaper reporters and photographers were in the house he kept buttonholing them and saying: 'I once killed a giant sloth in South America.'

He began by whispering and, when no one took any notice, progressed to violent shouting, finally retiring to a defeated corner where he would moan to himself: 'Yes, a *real* giant sloth.' Over and over.

Then when they took the pictures he tried to edge his way into the lens, even nudging me from my place in front of the cameras. He nearly cried when he looked in the papers and found that he was not in any of them nor a single mention of the sloth. My father, naturally, got lots of space and his picture all over the place, although his part in the matter of the SS *Queen of Atlantis* was no matter for congratulation as far as I was concerned. Once, out of sheer pity, I looped my arm around Murky's old head to get him in the picture and this one did appear in two editions of the *South Wales Echo*. Unfortunately the photograph was so blurred that my grandfather's head could have been anything from a cannon ball to a Christmas pudding. The newspaper said I was embracing my dog.

This naturally upset Murky more than ever, so that when it was arranged that I would be one of the guests of honour at the ball, he demanded to be there too. My father told him to stop at home and mind the house in case the publicity attracted burglars, and the old man was having one of his cries when we left (he used to enjoy a sob towards the end of his life). The whole of South Wales society was at the Heroes Ball and they stamped, shouted and whistled as we marched through the ballroom to the band's version of 'The White Cliffs of Dover' (a difficult feat) led by a small sea scout in a gas mask.

This child had become a hero by offering another boy the use of his gas mask during a supposed gas attack on the town by German aircraft, which turned out to be a false alarm, a fact, it was felt which should not deter from his bravery. An assortment of soldiers, airmen, sailors and merchant seamen followed in ranks of four, and then an air raid warden carried by comrades on a stretcher, and the local women who had knitted three tons of sweaters, scarves, balaclava helmets, and gloves for the services. Three ladies who had served tea at the docks throughout hostilities followed, wheeling their scarred trolley. The squadron leader from the barrage balloon unit in the park marched just behind me and I could feel his hostile eyes on my neck as we paraded around the hall.

We halted raggedly, except one seaman who had been deafened by a foghorn when his ship was wrecked under a lighthouse in Scotland, and who marched resolutely on until pulled back by beckoning spectators. The Mayor inspected us and made a speech about us. All the time the small sea scout was wearing his gas mask, the window having now misted over.

It was during the mayor's oration that I first saw Pamela.

She was laughing into her hands and trying to keep it quiet. There seemed to be some sort of commotion going on near the door, although I could not see what was going on there because of the crowd around the floor.

At the conclusion of the ceremony the band swooped into 'The White Cliffs of Dover' again this time in foxtrot time, and I went to Pamela and asked her to dance.

'I saw you laughing,' I said.

'Couldn't help it,' she replied. 'Fancy making that kid wear a gas mask like that. And you all looked so funny. The man on the stretcher and the one who kept on marching when the rest of you stopped! God, I thought I was going to have a fit. And then there was some old boy about ninety trying to get in on *roller skates*! Did you see him?'

'No,' I said. I felt hurt that she should laugh at the Heroes' Parade.

'They were trying to chuck him out and he was trying to get in and his skates kept rolling from under him. It was just like a film. Funniest thing I ever saw. What's it all about anyway?'

'What's what all about?'

'Well, this,' she said. 'All this.'

'Didn't you know?' I frowned. 'It's the Heroes Ball. Everybody in the parade did something brave during the war.'

'Oh, I see. Even that little kid in the gas mask . . . ?' She began giggling again and her head dropped forward on to my chest as we danced. Suddenly below my chin, like a luxuriant beard was her dark hair. Eventually she straightened up. 'I shouldn't laugh,' she apologised. 'Not really. But it *was* ever so funny. All marching around like that. Out of step and everything, and that poor little bugger staring out of his steamed-up gas mask. And then the old man trying to keep his skates on the floor, while about six men tried to throw him out.'

'How did you get in?' I asked.

'Usual way. Through the door.'

'But you must have known what was going on,' I argued.

'It's a special all-ticket night. Did you have a ticket?'

'No, don't be silly.' She dropped her tone. 'I know the man at the door and he always lets me in to everything. Last week it was the Newport pets club, or something. They all had their dogs and cats and birds in cages with them. Somebody left a donkey outside. It was dead funny. Not as funny as tonight, though. Nothing like.'

'You just come in for a dance then?' I said.

'More or less. Not much else to do on a Thursday around here. Never know, you might meet somebody.'

She was seventeen then, her face sweet and assured, her eyes laughing at me, her body still with its puppy fat. Bravely I asked her if she wanted to go outside and she said she didn't mind going for a walk. I glanced around to see if I could see my father or mother. I saw him immediately dancing grandly with the mayoress, and then I saw my mother sitting alone in an alcove, a drooping fern over her like a sympathetic canopy, a bottle of orange squash on the table before her. Pamela was walking off the floor ahead of me. I followed her.

Outside a police van was just moving away and there were people standing around laughing about the old man on roller skates. We walked down to the broken beach, over the assorted pebbles, around the sheets and bars of rusty iron and tangles of barbed wire. Someone had seriously thought that the Germans might have invaded there. It was a close August night with the moon low over the coaly channel. She looked as though she had full breasts but they were flattened, oval, under her dance dress. Her figure was almost matronly in that immediate post-war moonlight.

'Heroes,' she ruminated. 'Christ, it was funny, wasn't it, Alan?'

'Arthur,' I said. 'And I didn't think it was *all* that funny. They didn't *have* to put the kid in his gas mask, I suppose. But it was pretty serious underneath.' I was waiting for her to ask me how I became a hero.

'I don't think it was serious,' she argued. 'That man on the stretcher, the one they were carrying like the Queen of

Sheba, he's no hero for a start, because he lives down our street. His name is Dodkinson and I know that he broke his leg falling down on a bombed site when he was drunk. Everybody in the street knows it. He's always plastered, running up and down the street in his tin hat, blowing his whistle in the middle of the night.'

We did not know it then, but that night was the last night of all the war. The Japanese surrendered and when we were kissing each other for the very first time all the sirens along the coast sounded off.

But before that, we were sitting on the grass above the short cliff, and the moon coming from the direction of Bristol made her silk dance dress shine where it was rounded over her body. The channel was a white streak under the moon, like a Newport workman's best silk muffler. The tide kept rolling a metal drum against the pebbles. Along the coast the lights shone freely and the lighthouse swung its arms like a gymnast.

'Just look at it,' I said pompously. 'It was really worth fighting for, you know.' I still wanted her to ask me about the lifeboat.

She was staring out to sea. 'My grandad looks through my keyhole and sees me dressing,' she said.

Stunned by the suddenness of the information I remained silent, torn between wanting to repeat my patriotic appreciation of this night of peace and a desire to hear what her grandad saw through the keyhole.

'Silly old devil,' she sighed. 'Still I suppose he's not got much to enjoy, and he's nice really. He makes me laugh. And if you can't do something for your own grandad who can you do anything for?'

'Quite,' I said inadequately. 'Who can you?'

'Do you know what my old grandmother looks like in the nude?'

Her bizarre twist of the conversation nonplussed me. She always did it; all through the years I knew her.

'No,' I said eventually as though I had been carefully considering it. 'No, I don't. What's she like?'

'Ghastly. Bloody ghastly,' she continued slowly, her eyes narrowed. 'I saw her in the bath one night and she looked just like a bit of old sacking held up with poles. Like one of those screens the men clearing the bombing used for a lav.'

'Sacking,' I repeated trying to nod wisely, wondering if she were playing a game.

'Just like,' she said. 'Sacking hanging between poles. So I thought there's not a lot there for my grandfather to look forward to, and so when I realised he was having a squint at me through the keyhole I let him get on with it. One day I'll probably go out and scare the daylights out of him. But that seems a bit unkind when I think about it. After all it doesn't cost me anything.'

Her odd conversation, naturally, gave me some hope for my personal ambitions. If she showed *that* to her old grandfather what might she do for me? I put my hand negligently on her shoulder and then let it slip down her side to her thigh. Without mentioning it she took it and replaced it on the shoulder.

'Mind you,' she said almost absently. 'I'm terrible sometimes. When I know he's got his eyes right up to the hole, right against it, I strip completely off and walk towards him. Slow as I can, wriggling as I walk. Then I hang my dressing gown on the door knob. It must drive him potty.'

I tried transferring my hand again from its companionable touch at the back of her neck down to her breast. She removed it again.

'Don't spoil it, Alan,' she said, dreamily.

'Arthur,' I grumbled.

'Well, Arthur,' she replied. 'I bet *you* don't remember what *I'm* called.'

'Of course I do. You're called Pamela.'

She appeared genuinely impressed at this. 'It is too,' she agreed. 'You must be serious about me.'

'But I *am* serious,' I said, jumping in. She was sitting primly, looking out to sea, so I had to curve my neck around to kiss her. She let me do it and responded a little.

Suddenly, and with dismay, I realized that I, who had

furgled Rose by the barrage balloon, who had spent half a steaming night with a Negress, and the entire next day with a six foot Jewish lady, I, Arthur McCann, sixteen-year-old international lover, was now faced with a *girl*. A girl with all the teenage corners still to be rubbed off, full of idiotic barriers and taboos, a chubby prick-teasing, seventeen-year-old who enjoyed telling me what she displayed for her grandad, but wouldn't let me shift my famished finger a quarter of an inch. After all the things I had done I was back at the beginning, back at the place where everybody else has to start. She wanted to be courted.

'I don't like it,' she sighed.

'What?' I felt helpless, drifting around in the flotsam of her conversation.

'Pamela, my name. Sounds like some sort of soap.'

'I think it's nice,' I assured her.

'Better than Alan,' she said.

'Arthur.'

'Well, Arthur. Better than that too. Not much, mind.'

I remembered a joke which somebody told on the SS *Queen of Atlantis*. 'Put this in your *palm Olive*,' I recited into her ear. 'Not on your *life boy*.'

'I don't like dirty jokes,' she said with no emphasis.

'Oh. Sorry.'

'It's all right. You couldn't know could you? I'm glad the war's over. Did you have to go?'

I choked over my annoyance. 'What d'you think I was doing marching with the Newport War Heroes tonight?' I demanded. 'I wasn't there to keep the buggers in line.'

'It *was* funny, though, wasn't it?' she giggled. 'That kid in his gas mask!' She gave me a friendly girlish shove with her hand. 'Go on, *admit* it. It *was* funny.'

My exasperation had curdled into a thick gloom. 'All right,' I nodded. 'We'll say it was funny.'

She moved closer as though she sensed my disappointment. 'You're quite nice, Alan,' she murmured.

'Arthur.'

'Oh, all right. Arthur. But you're still quite nice. Do you like me?'

'You're a bit strange,' I admitted, still sulking. 'But you're quite nice, too, I suppose.'

'Strange! A bit strange!' she exploded. 'What a bleeding nerve! How am I strange?'

I was saved from answering by the eruption of all the air raid sirens along the coast. I did not know why they sounded but I took advantage of her astonishment by kissing her again.

'It's the Germans,' she forecast dramatically when her lips were free. 'They tricked us, the bastards.'

A man was running along the rough beach below us, jumping on the sheets of rusty corrugated iron and making them sound. Some other people were chasing him and they all began to whoop and shout and run in and out of the sea in their shoes. They had come from the direction of Mandles and when they saw us one of the men shouted: 'Have you heard – it's all over! The Japs have packed it in. It's all over!'

Pamela and I got to our feet. 'Thank God,' I said like a grown man. 'I wouldn't like to be in that lifeboat again. It was hell.'

She turned tenderly to me and I thought that, at last, she had heard what I said. 'Watching war films won't be the same now, will it?' she said. 'You'll always have that feeling that they're only acting. Before it all seemed like it was real.'

'No,' I mumbled, defeated. 'I suppose there's that to it.'

'I'll have to go,' she said looking towards the lights of Mandles. 'There's the bus.' She glanced at me. 'Will you want to be seeing me again, or are you fed up with me?'

'How could I be fed up with you?' I said.

'People do. You'd be surprised. All right. Next Thursday, come down here. We can get in for nothing, because I know the man on the door and he always lets me in.'

'You mentioned it.'

She kissed me quickly and with only passing interest and then trotted towards the bus.

'Goodbye Pamela,' I said dejectedly, watching her go.

'Goodbye Alan,' she called cheerfully.

I went back to Mandles to see if there were any spare girls left for I was naturally reluctant to waste an evening on which I had been paraded as a hero. But everyone had gone home. Two men who were sweeping the floor with wide brooms said that people were dancing around bonfires in the town.

When I walked back through the streets everybody was up and celebrating the final, definite, end to the war. Some were taking the rare opportunity to embrace neighbours in their nightclothes, and there was a lot of berserk kissing and fondling going on, as though it had not been permitted during hostilities. There were also more fires burning in the town than there had been during all the air raids put to-gether. They were burning the tar in the middle of the streets and people were throwing shrubs and bushes from other people's gardens on to the blaze. One man was trying to retrieve his front door which had been thrown on to a roaring fire outside his house. Nearly everybody was having an unusually good time.

It was very odd, but my house was much quieter than the others. I went into the living room and there they were. My father was just pouring himself a whisky and not his first by the look of him.

'Here he is,' he said like an accusation. 'At last.' He eyed me sourly. 'I take it *you've* had a fine time,' he said.

'Yes, more or less,' I answered. 'The war's over.'

'I know. They're burning all the garden gates down the street.'

'I saw them,' I said.

'Your grandfather's dead,' said my mother sadly. 'He was dead when they got him to the police station. Your roller skates are over there.'

'Buggered up the end of the war for us,' grunted my father. 'Completely buggered it up.'

I walked out of the house and went down to the police station. 'Heart failure,' said the sergeant. 'You can hardly wonder putting up a fight like that at the door. And on roller skates! It's the roller skates I can't understand.'

I felt dull and hopeless as though I understood nothing. 'Mandles used to be a roller skating rink in his day,' I told him. 'He must have thought it still was. He just wanted to get into the Heroes' Bloody Ball, that's all.'

'That's no way to speak of Newport's returned heroes,' he said, sternly.

'No, I suppose not,' I agreed quietly. 'I'm a bit upset about Murky, that's all.'

'Murky?'

'The old boy. My grandad.'

'The attendants wouldn't have laid a hand on him if he hadn't tried to fight them out of the way,' said the sergeant. 'He wanted to take them all on, and on skates. No wonder his heart gave out.'

'Did he say anything?'

'Plenty. Effing something terrible he was. Kept on shouting about a giant sloth he'd seen, or something like that. It will all come out at the inquest.'

'He had,' I said.

'What?'

'Seen a giant sloth. In South America.'

He looked at me uncertainly as though thinking the whole family must be mad. 'I don't suppose there's many people seen one of those,' he agreed. He began to write in a large book as though it was important information. He looked up and seemed surprised that I was still there.

'No. Not many,' I said. 'Well, thanks very much for telling me about it.'

I went out. It was four o'clock and the people were more subdued, standing in groups about their gateless gardens, recalling the fine daring days of the war. The fires were low and glowering, sitting in big holes in the road. The council would have some filling-in to do the next day.

The war was over and as I walked I thought that, in a way, poor old Murky had been its last casualty.

Anyone who, before their seventeenth birthday, had been shipwrecked, murdered a man with a spanner, had voluptuous affairs with two large white women, and a traumatic experience with a thin black one, would have found working in the Newport Food Office far from enervating. That is where I found myself, counting millions of coupons and countless grubby ration books, filling in forms and deciphering plaintive, scrawled letters.

My courting, for that is what it formally was, of Pamela made life no more enjoyable. After all I had been through, and I choose the phrase carefully, it was painfully like going back to school. I kept with her for there was no other and because I was always in hope that one day, one night, I would slip around her podgy girlish defences and give her what I had given Rose and Mrs Nissenbaum with such obvious success. But my desirability for women of my own age was apparently far less than it had been for my seniors. The Americans, that all-embracing army, and the already returning British servicemen from the dead war were fighting it out, literally, for the presentable girls of the town. Few women wanted to listen to my story of the lifeboat and those who patiently heard it out did not believe it; not even my male colleagues at the Food Office believed it. I had Pamela. As far as she would let me.

We went to dances at Mandles and twice a week to the Pavilion, the Odeon, or the Super Cinema, frequently winding up a turgid evening stuffed into the corner of the gaseous fish and chip shop at the bottom of our street.

I, Arthur McCann, who had stood to be applauded at Sardi's and Club 21 in New York City, renewed my acquaintance with the sensation of vinegar leaking through the pages of the *South Wales Echo*.

Our goodnights were less than spectacular. While I was trying to get my fingers on her nipples she would be recalling Alan Ladd's excesses in the film we had just seen. Sometimes, but with decreasing incidence, I tried to compare the screen heroism with the real thing, as exampled in my own experiences in an open boat, but she always managed to head it off with one of her tangent remarks. She continued to bring her grandfather's senility to the boil by permitting him to view her through the keyhole, so she reported anyway; but when I suggested that her grandfather appeared to be doing rather better than I was, she brushed it away with the excuse of age deserving certain privileges.

This attitude apparently extended to take in my own father also, for when I took her home to tea one Sunday he quickly had his hands around her chubby waist and her protruding little bottom. After that he was always smacking his lips and asking: 'When are you bringing that lovely little Pamela home to us again, Arthur boy?' I liked the 'us'; my mother had less enthusiasm, for the obvious reason, and additionally because Pamela, who turned out to be an outstandingly clumsy girl, had toppled the teapot on to an entire plate of Welsh cakes which had been made, in those difficult rationed times, for the occasion.

Our goodnights were accomplished in a variety of dark slots and corners, and Newport has an abundance of these. The town might almost have been planned for lovers who had nowhere to go. Not that, with us, there was much to hide or to see. As each dull kiss succeeded the next my patience withered and eventually I asked her point blank what was the difference between my pressing her chest with my chest, which she permitted, and my putting my hands in the same vicinity.

'Skin,' she said. 'It's your skin, Arthur. You know very well. When you press your chest to my ... er ... chest ... you've got your coat and your waistcoat, shirt and vest, between you and me. Sometimes, if it's a nasty night, you've got your mackintosh as well. But if you put your *hands* there it would be your *skin*, and that would spoil it Arthur, honestly it would.'

On the following night I told her that I wouldn't be seeing her again because I was going to nightschool and I wouldn't have the time. Besides which there was a girl at the Food Office who wanted a partner for rumba and tango lessons and I thought I would like to learn the dances as a standby in case I ever went to South America.

I had the craft to tell her these tidings at the beginning of the evening so that she could dwell on them in the cinema or perhaps stalk off even before we got there, thus saving me the price of her seat. In those days I had to think of such practical things. To my disappointment she took it quietly, even agreeing that I ought to go to nightschool if I wanted to improve my prospects.

But during the course of *The Affairs of Susan* (Joan Fontaine and George Brent) the information worked into her and her head was noticeably drooping as we walked along my street towards her house at eleven o'clock. It was raining and the street lamplight was spread in the puddles.

'All right then, Arthur,' she said abruptly, her head coming up with decision. 'If you want to, very much. *That* much. Where shall we go?'

The breath in my body seemed to heat. 'Honest?' I said. 'You mean it?'

'I said all right, didn't I? Where do you want to go?'

It had to be done there and then. If we continued on to her street she might change her mind. Our street had as many sly corners as any of the others, but the rain was thickening.

There was an alley at the side of our house and an overhang of corrugated iron from the roof of a garden shed next door. But it was insufficient for two and as I faced her with businesslike romance the rain dripped drearily down the back of my collar. I took her by the reluctant hand and pulled her into our back garden.

'In there,' I said nodding to the old closet standing like a sentry box.

'There!' she exclaimed horrified. 'But that's a lav! Im not going in *there* with you!'

'It's not *used* now,' I urged pulling her on. 'We've got one inside, now. The council put it in. Come on, it's quite clean. And it's dry.'

The dual arguments half convinced her and with ill grace she went in as I gallantly opened the door. I closed it after us and then we were facing each other in the dark, the wooden rim of the bench toilet seat against the sides of our legs.

'I must say I expected better than this,' she sniffed sulkily.

'Just for tonight,' I pleaded. 'Just for now, Pamela.'

'You've got the chain dangling over your shoulder,' she observed. 'I can feel it.'

I pushed the thing away and then had to grab it in the dark to stop it swinging dangerously. Even I had to admit it wasn't the best place. The rain was rattling on the tin roof and a thin, evil draught came inquiringly under the door.

'Would you like to sit down?' I invited formally.

'I still don't want to let you do it,' she muttered, her chin down.

'Oh, for God's sake, Pamela. You promised.'

'I know. I just don't like the idea that's all. And I'm not sitting on *there*.'

We stood facing, not touching, hardly seeing each other in the rattling dark. Our silence was an ultimatum.

Then she mumbled: 'I'll let you have a *look*, instead, if you like. Just a look, mind.'

'All right,' I said controlling my anticipation. 'Fair enough.' If she showed them then the rest must surely follow.

She didn't move for a moment then she said firmly: 'All right then,' and began to fumble in the dimness. She undid her coat and then her cardigan, then a blouse. Her white flesh glowed, but indistinctly. She hesitated at several stages, but then made a movement which I knew meant she was slipping away her straps. Her breasts showed blurred white and tantalising.

'I can't see them,' I complained.

'Well *I'm* showing them. I've got them out.'

'But it's too dark. Go on, let me touch.'

She sensed my movement. She pushed me forcibly against the wall behind my back. 'Touch me, Arthur McCann,' she warned, 'and I scream this lav down.'

'Pamela,' I groaned. 'I can't see a thing. You might as well not be showing them.'

'You can get a bit closer,' she agreed like someone negotiating an armistice. 'Bend down a bit and have a look. But you touch me, Arthur, even with your nose . . .'

'All right,' I promised. 'I won't.' I bent forward, rather like the men in the Times Square peepshow had been bending. They were not allowed to touch either. My eyes were three inches above her fat flesh and I thought 'If I dip my nose in now, there's nothing she can do about it. Except scream.'

'I still can't see anything,' I sighed. 'I'm going mad not being able to see them like this, darling. When they're so close. It's more than flesh and blood can rightly stand. It's worse than not touching them.'

'Don't you dare lay a finger,' she muttered again. 'I meant what I said. The roof would come off this closet, believe me.'

'Well, that's that, then,' I said with a tone of finality. 'There's nothing more to be done, is there?'

'Have you got a light,' she suddenly suggested. 'You could have a proper look like that.'

She knew I didn't smoke, but with joy I remembered that a candle and a box of matches were kept, in the days of the outhouse's usefulness, on a little shelf by the cistern. When my father used to lock Murky in there as a punishment the old man, when he was fatigued with kicking the door, would light the mournful candle and sing to himself.

'Just the thing, a candle and matches,' I said, reaching up and finding the candle and the box with one open hand. I heard her sigh. 'Go on, sit down,' I said. 'It's clean. My mum still scrubs it.'

I could feel her sulking in the darkness. She sat down heavily on the wooden seat though, and I tried to strike the first match. They were damp. I tried three, then angrily rattled the box.

'They're wet through,' she said more cheerfully. 'We can't even keep newspaper in ours. Gets soaked.'

Then, delight, a match flared and I swooped it carefully to the candle and, turning, held the candle before her. She was sitting, a sort of condemned smile on her face now, her clothes pulled away from her neck and shoulders, down to her upper arms. Her breasts were only half way out. I moved forward but she said: 'Wait. I'll do it.' As though she were keeping to the strict rules of a game she pulled her garments lower down her puffy arms, and like two round heads coming over a wall they oozed up and out into my view, white and fatty, the nipples seeming to blink at the rosy light. I was transfixed by them in the candlelight.

'My darling,' I muttered. 'Pamela, my beautiful, lovely darling.'

I think she sensed the accident a moment before it happened because she jerked on the seat. But she was too late. As I bent with my love fervour, moving my lips down to her front, I let the candle tip and the hot liquid was streamed over the lip and splashed on to that tender bulging flesh. She screamed savagely and shot upright, knocking the candle out of my hand as she did so. She went on screaming for a full minute and at the end of that minute the door opened and there stood my father with a torch.

She must have been trying to scrape the candle grease off her because she was still exposed. When she saw him she pulled the front of her clothes up and began crying.

'I might have known,' growled my father after there was nothing left to see. 'I might have bloody known. Come on out, mister. I'm about fed up with your antics with women.'

At which Pamela howled again and ran off ponderously into the rainy night. All the neighbours were at their bedroom windows. The following day I decided to make the sea my life's work.

It was not just this incident, crucial as it was, which made me decide to return to the oceans. On the following morning I had good reason to believe that my father had been killed by a bus in Commerical Road. When I discovered he had, in fact, survived I thought the time had come for me to go.

I did not go to work in the Food Office that day. When I reached the bus stop I realised that I could not face another mound of grubby ration books, nor another million coupons, nor the strangled cabbage and chips of the canteen (for a Food Office the meals were horrific) nor the talk of motor bikes and compliant girls which filled my inky colleagues' conversation. So I walked up our street again and went up-stairs and lay on my bed. I wrote another chapter of 'All The Coloured Lights of the World by Arthur McCann', a gloomy episode this one, and stretched out again on the counterpane where I had once trembled at the thought of being dragged out for execution on the direct orders of Mr Winston Churchill. I thought of writing to Mrs Nissenbaum once more, but I rejected it for I had already written twice and there had been no reply. Poor Errol Flynn, stupid beast. She would never forgive me, I knew.

My mother was out shopping. Someone came to the front door and began ringing the bell – the only doorbell in the street, everybody else had knockers – with such urgency that I got up and went down. It was the greasy grocer, Mr Tyler, whose shop was down the street, on the opposite side.

I was astonished to see him for, not only did we make a point of never buying anything at his shop (my mother insisted that he got rich on the wartime black market, al-though he certainly never showed the least sign of this under-ground affluence), but we never even spoke to him.

'Arthur,' he said. 'You've got to come quickly. It's the telephone. It's your father. He says he's dying, Arthur.'

In a faintly confused way I wondered why, if my father were dying, he would tell Mr Tyler about it first. I went across to the shop and amid the bags of beans and tins of custard powder I saw the telephone lying like a dread hand.

I picked it up. 'Hello.'

'Hello, Arthur.' His voice sounded dusty.

'Yes, it's Arthur. Are you all right, dad?'

'Of course I'm not all right, you fool! I'm bloody dying. Didn't that twat Tyler tell you?'

'Yes, well he did mention it. But I thought he might be joking.'

'Joking! About somebody bleeding to death under a Newport Corporation bus?'

'Well, he didn't say anything about that. Nothing about a bus. Is that what's happened to you?'

'Shut up, for Christ's sake, you everlasting bugger. Just keep your wits about you and listen. I haven't got long left.'

'Can I ask you something first?'

'Shut up! All right. What? Hurry up.'

'If you're under a Newport Corporation bus, how can you be telephoning?'

'Initiative,' he said. 'We're not all like you, you know son. I am at present trapped under the counter of Lewis's the hardware shop, because I was in here and the bloody bus came off the road and crashed right through Mr Lewis's window. Now have you got the situation? I can only just move a finger and I've got every bone in my body broken and I'm spilling out my life's blood, but right next to my nose is Mr Lewis's telephone and the Newport directory. So I rang that fool Tyler and told him to go and get your mother, seeing as he's the only sod who can afford a phone in the street. Why ain't you at your bloody office anyway?'

'If you're dying,' I said evilly, 'don't you think you ought to moderate your language?'

'I'm *dying*,' he moaned sorrowfully as though the import had just come to him. 'Son, I'm *dying*. I've got my own blood on my hands.'

A strange calm, coldness came over me. I stood holding the phone, offering neither advice nor sympathy.

'Listen,' he croaked. 'And listen carefully.' His tone changed appeasingly. 'Just be a good boy and do a couple of things for your dying father.'

'What?'

'In my bedroom, in the middle of a book called *Babylon*

and its Environs remember that, *Babylon and its Environs.*
Can you remember it?'

'I'll write it down if you like,' I suggested nastily.

'No, there's no time. The weight of this Corporation bus
is pressing down on me, boy, and it's sodding heavy, I can
tell you. I'm in a very bad way. Bleeding. Now listen. In
the middle of that book is a Savings Bank Book with ninety-
four pounds in it. Your mother doesn't know about it, so
don't mention it to her because she won't be without,
and I know you'll always be good to her. So what I want you
to do is to put that bank book in an envelope and send it to
this address . . . Have you got a pencil and paper?'

'Yes,' I lied.

'It's Miss Gerda Peasbody, 109, Sutcliffe Gardens,
Bristol. Got that?'

'Yes,' I lied again.

He seemed to weaken, his voice whispered in the phone.
'I knew you'd understand, Arthur. We're men of the world,
you and me, son. You've had your little experiences, as we
well know, and I might as well tell you I've not been innocent all my life, although I've always been very good to your
mother. It's just that this lady, Miss Peasbody, lent me
some money a long time ago and I'd like to go now . . .
knowing that I've paid her back. And Arthur . . .'

'Yes.'

'Call me father.'

'Father.'

'There's one of your aunts I would like to send a last
message to.'

Inside I jumped eagerly. 'Yes, which one, father?'

'Your aunts are all nice, jolly, girls son. The most
beautiful sisters in Newport they used to call them, although,
you've got to admit, they're wearing a bit thin now. And
they've put poor Ramona away because she's bats. But one
has always stood out from the rest . . . just one . . .'

Oh Christ, why didn't he get on with it? Those double-
deckers were heavy. 'Yes, father,' I whispered encouragingly.

With the secret of the unfurgled aunt a syllable away there was a silence on the line, broken by brief groans and sobs. Then my mother rushed into the shop, knocking over a pile of tinned pineapple chunks – the staple Sunday luxury of the district – as she came in.

'Oh, Arthur, what's happened? Oh, my God, what's happened?' The street knew by now, of course, because the grapevine was ever lively. My mother had been told of my father's mishap as she alighted from a bus, informed by neighbours who were actually catching the same bus back into town in order to view the catastrophe. They were the same people who during the war used to go on outings to see the bomb damage.

'Arthur,' she moaned. 'Is he there? Is he speaking?'

'He's groaning,' I answered, unfeeling for him not her.

She pulled the receiver from me. 'Phil!' she howled into it. 'Phil! Are you there? Oh, my God, Phil, what's happened? Speak to me, Phil.'

I decided to go down to Commercial Road and take a look for myself. Even then I couldn't trust him. I got a bus quickly and from the front seat on the top deck I saw the crowd, and the fire engines, and the bus half buried in the shop. There was no pity in my heart for my father, only a cool void, and a suspicion that he would escape as he had always escaped. At the fringe of the crowd I stood, speaking to no one, watching the firemen moving the timbers and the bricks, watching the bus being carefully hoisted away.

Three people died in the rubble of Lewis (Hardware) Ltd., including Mr Lewis (Hardware) himself. My father, covered in red paint, was brought out with slight bruising. In the hospital they used three bottles of turpentine on him and sent him home. He had his picture and his courageous story in all the newspapers.

I went immediately back to the house, took the secret bank book from *Babylon and its Environs*, forged his signature and gave the ninety-four pounds to my mother as a parting present before I went away to sea. My father never mentioned it again. It was as though it had never been.

125

10

That night the wind got up while I was in bed and I could hear it leaping about the empty street. My bed, even if it were moored for ever alongside the Food Office, was stationary and warm, and I thought the sea would be a rough and lonely life. Which it is.

After Pamela's departure from our outside privy and my father's resurrection from the rubble of Lewis (Hardware) Ltd., I signed on for a six months voyage to Panama, through the Pacific to Suva, down to Australia, and back by way of New York.

There were no pineapples in the crew, at least no obvious and active pineapples, but there was an old sailor who prayed aloud in his bunk for hour upon hour, asking the benevolent God to save him from the sea. Between Suva and Brisbane he must have decided to put his faith to the test because he jumped overboard and wasn't missed for three hours until his watch came. The ship turned and went back three hours, as required by the hopeful regulations, looking forlornly into the enormous sea for one poor little man. The word of the law having been accomplished we continued on our way, and there were no more loud prayers to disturb our peace.

Propped in my bunk I continued to write 'All The Coloured Lights Of The World by Arthur McCann' and I would lie, too, and think of Mrs Nissenbaum and Rose, comparing their respective characters and anatomies. Sometimes I also included one layer of Pamela in this fantasy, but it was generally a disagreeable comparison, and I discontinued it after a few weeks at sea.

With the others I could see their faces and remember their warmth, although, naturally, Mrs Nissenbaum, being the later, somewhat obscured the accurate remembrance of Rose beneath the balloon. Against them the five minute experience of Pamela in the rain-rattled closet, the trembling breasts beneath the candlelight, and the terrifying conclusion of the romantic interlude, seemed sordid and all too real.

I told myself fiercely that if Mrs Nissenbaum was to remain a lovely memory, despite the bruising of it occasioned by the accident to Errol Flynn, then I must not see her again when I returned to New York. She had not written to me and for her it was obviously over. Then, I did not realize just how much it was over.

But as we went, day on day, climbing back up the Pacific, through the canal, and then moving up the eastern seaboard of the United States, my resolve to leave her untouched in my heart weakened. By the time we picked up the pilot at the mouth of the Hudson I was in the bath giving myself a shampoo and an energetic scrub underneath (there had been an incident with a casual girl at King's Cross, Sydney, which had worried me a little) and I came on to the deck in the winter sun to be greeted by that broad chested figure of Liberty, arms spread, gown folded over huge and welcoming body. By then I knew that I must find Rebecca again and take my chance with her memory.

As it happened her memory was never disturbed. As soon as I could get ashore I got a cab to Riverdale. The house in the winter seemed worn and when I got closer I immediately sensed that she no longer lived there. The lace curtains were still against the windows but, peering through, I saw that the elegant hall and the soft rooms were now empty boxes. The telephone was sitting like a spider in the middle of the floor and beside it was a New York directory. There was nothing else.

Riverdale was not like Newport, where it would have been easy and natural to knock on someone's door and ask what had happened to Mrs Nissenbaum, so I went back into the City. But the emptiness of that place, and the dumb telephone and directory on the bleak floor, was on my mind. Eventually it was the directory which prompted the thought of telephoning Mrs Rosnagel, the friend of Mrs Nissenbaum.

There were several people called that in the book, but I

asked each one if she or he knew Mrs Nissenbaum, and eventually the right Mrs Rosnagel said: 'Rebecca Nissenbaum. Sure I knew her.' I told her who I was and she sounded interested and suggested I went to her apartment on the south side of the Park right away. All the way in the taxi I kept wondering why she had used the past tense.

Mrs Rosnagel was not like Mrs Nissenbaum. She was a short, spare woman. Her corners seemed, somehow stapled together, pinched, including those at the edges of her mouth for she had a tight smile.

'Come in, come in, Arthur,' she invited. She was very well dressed, but I thought that it probably wasn't just for me. You could not imagine her having any old clothes. I went into one of those New York apartments that just close around you, warm, luxurious, so isolated, insulated from the city and the world that you wonder if those places are still outside the door.

'My, you've sure grown, Arthur,' she said measuring me from feet to head with her studded glasses held slightly away from her face. 'In just a few months. Will you have a drink?'

'Thank you,' I said. 'Whisky if you've got any.' I thought I would show her I had grown in all sorts of ways. 'I suppose I have got taller and put on some weight.'

'And how,' she said, getting the drinks. 'Boy, I certainly wouldn't like to try and lift you.'

I couldn't make up my mind whether that was just a chance apt remark, or whether Mrs Nissenbaum had told her that she had carried me from my bed. I watched her expression carefully as she turned from the drinks cabinet, but she was still wearing the same tight smile, so I couldn't tell.

I did not ask about Mrs Nissenbaum right away. Something made it difficult to introduce. I raised my glass and said a manly: 'Cheers'. It was bourbon which I had never tasted until then. It surprised my throat and I had a fight to stop choking. She said: 'It was clever of you to find me.'

'I tried nearly all the Rosnagels in the book. It's not all that much of a common name.'

'It's from the French Rosignol,' she smiled. 'Rosignol, the nightingale. We Rosnagels like to think of ourselves as singers.' To my surprise she sat down at a little white piano and began crooning 'Where the Blue of The Night Meets the Gold of the Day' while I stood wooden with embarrassment. 'The nightingale,' she shrugged again, getting up from the piano.

'How is Mrs Nissenbaum?' I asked at last.

'Not too good. She's dead,' she said bluntly.

I felt the whisky go cold in my stomach.

'Oh no, Mrs Rosnagel, not her.'

'Oh yes, Arthur. Her.'

I thought I was going to cry. I dropped my face away from her and drank deeply to hide my expression. This time I did choke and she came to me and gave me a sympathetic pound on the back.

'Oh, thank you,' I said. 'That's terrible.'

'It's strong stuff,' she said. 'Especially if you're not used to it.'

'I mean about Mrs Nissenbaum,' I said, marvelling at her stupidity. 'She was so . . . big . . . and alive.'

'She's small and dead,' she said. 'He came back.'

'He?'

'Benny Nissenbaum.'

'Her husband? But he was dead.'

She sighed: 'The same Benny Nissenbaum. The Japs didn't get him, the finks. No wonder they lost the war. The atom bomb's too good for them.'

I knew what the answer was going to be before I asked. 'And what happened to Rebecca?'

'She did what I would have done, honey, if Benny Nissenbaum had come back from the dead to me. She jumped off the Queensborough Bridge.'

'Christ.'

'Sure, Christ. Believe me, if a guy like Benny is dead then it's good to be alive. If he turns up alive, then you've got to be dead.'

'I thought she . . . loved him. She told me so. She even

said I was a sort of walking memorial to him.'

'Well, you ain't a memorial any more. So relax. And she loved him okay. But she loved him *dead*. Don't you get it? That's why she was so happy and bounding all around town like a great big bouncy ball while you were around. It was great, just great, to have Benny dead. Then he came back. They'd screwed it up. She sure would have liked to get her hands on those rat fink Japs.'

'And he was terrible to her.'

'To her? To everybody. And noisy and lousy. That guy's got a mouth like the Lincoln Tunnel, and he knows how to use it. It's a wonder you didn't hear him when you came up the Hudson.'

'Christ.'

'Christ, Schmist! Don't keep saying Christ. It ain't relevant. It was Benny Nissenbaum. Him coming back from the dead so soon after her dog going off to the Hereafter, if that's what dogs have. And you going away. She couldn't have had so many lousy things happen to her at once. So she took off from the bridge.'

She gave me another drink without asking and I sat on the edge of one of her deep chairs and stared into the pond of bourbon. 'Drowning,' I muttered. 'Nasty death.'

'She didn't,' said Mrs Rosnagel, decisively. 'She must have misjudged the wind speed. She went off course and hit Welfare Island. Welfare, farewell, Rebecca.' She spread her hands emphatically.

'I wrote to her,' I said stupidly. 'That's why I didn't get a reply.'

'Can you think of a better reason?' she said logically.

'I can't believe it. Not her.'

'I never can believe things about anybody,' she said philosophically. 'My own husband. Says he's in Europe on business. Tells me that. Sends me messages, flowers from Paris. And he's not a mile away at this minute. I could show you the apartment. Getting somebody else to send me love and roses. He didn't even go and fight the Japs. At least there was a chance of Benny Nissenbaum getting knocked off, but not mine. I can do without him. Say, Arthur why don't you have another drink and stay to dinner?'

I promised I would see her the next day, although I never intended to do so. I got a cab to the bridge and stood crying over the parapet, looking down to the ferocious river and to the hard bank of the cigar shaped island in the middle. I could imagine her lying there her pink nightdress spread all around her, her big feet sticking out. A policeman came along and told me it was illegal to jump. I said I wasn't going to jump. I was just weeping for somebody who had. He said they shouldn't have because it was illegal, but he seemed to understand because he nodded and walked on.

In the days after that all I could think about was my dear, big, dead Mrs Nissenbaum. The ship went south again to Maracaibo in Venezuela, stopping at Port de Loupe on the way. All the time, when I wasn't on deck, working, I was propped in my berth, staring at the porthole as though I expected her lovely head to be framed in it like a splendid portrait. To have had her die so near to the going of my grandfather, Murky, was a hard blow because they were two of the most unusual people I ever met in all my life.

I composed some doleful pages of 'All The Coloured Lights Of The World by Arthur McCann' which I have only to read now, to realize the fullness of my grief and loneliness following her launching herself over the bridge and on to the uncharitable ground of Welfare Island.

By the time we docked at Port de Loupe in the French Antilles I had made up my mind that I must set my life on a firm foundation. To do this, I realized, it was necessary, imperative, to marry as soon as possible. When we got ashore I went to the cable office in Port de Loupe and sent a telegram begging Pamela to be my wife. Then I sat down in the wooden bar of the Cockatoo Paradise Loungette and Bar, drank, and looked at the bitterly shining sea.

We were loading sugar cane and unseasonal rain had made the roads thick so the carts from the plantations were taking longer than usual. I went back to the cable office on the second day but they said there was nothing for me. By the next afternoon there was still no word from my beautiful, steady, Pamela, and the memory I had of her sitting in our outside lavatory, breasts bulging from her clothes, became hotter and more poignant as the hours went.

The loading of the cane was almost finished and we were to sail in the morning as soon as the pilot could be roused from his bed and sobered (such things were very unofficial in those days, especially in that part of the world). In the evening I asked at the cable office again. The old, patient woman there knew me, of course, by now, and she said I could stay there, sleeping on the floor, if I was so anxious to get the message as soon as it came in. She said she had never seen a young man so eager to get married before. Her daughter's fiancé had run away to Trinidad.

I went back to the Cockatoo Paradise Loungette and Bar and sat drinking again, watching the evening eating the hills at the back of the island. Lights buttoned our ship in the harbour. There was a girl called Monique in the bar, a Creole girl, who shuffled about serving drinks, swaying from her thin hips to the American jazz music coming from a wind-up gramophone. I had only heard her speak French so I had not spoken to her, just nodded when I wanted another drink, and sat trying to make the solid form of Pamela nudge out the pink memory of Mrs Nissenbaum from my poor congested mind.

This was Friday and quite a few people from the port came in, sitting around at the straw tables, drinking, talking loudly in French and jiving in the extraordinary way they did in those days. There was a fat planter flinging a coloured girl of about fifteen all over the place, through his legs, around his sweaty neck, showing her white knicks and brown legs to everyone and anyone who wanted to have a look. Some of the others from the ship arrived but they knew I was suffering from terrible melancholia so they did not even look at me.

The Creole girl, Monique, went over to my shipmates and asked them something about me. I knew this was so because all their faces came over in my direction at one moment. She was leaning right over their table, her skirt hoisted up the back of her legs. Then she came to me and, having put her tin tray on the bar, she opened her arms to me and invited me to dance. I stood up, unenthusiastically I suppose because my mind was still a conflict between the dead Mrs Nissenbaum and the live Pamela. Their images kept nudging each other out of the frame of my imagination like photographs in one of those bioscope things with slides on a screen. Still, common politeness made me stand and put my arms about her so that we could dance. So occupied had I been with my inward agony that now I realized that I had noticed nothing about this girl, not her hair, nor her eyes, nor the shape of her body, which was very unusual for me and still is. I had not even realized that the reason she shuffled everywhere was that she was wearing woolly bedroom slippers with pom-poms on them, like my mother and my aunts wore in the winter at home.

The wind-up gramophone was playing 'La Composita', a record so elderly and worn that the violins sounded like snores. I have always been quite a showy tango dancer and I ran her across the floor, swaying her over my knee, and unwinding her, so that her woolly bedroom slippers fairly skimmed across the floor. All the time I kept my melancholy face. We were the only ones dancing and quite a lot of the people were watching us and they must have noticed the tragedy in my expression.

One woman, wearing a sort of white hunting suit, watched me all the time. I could not help noticing as we swooped by. I suppose my glance must have got left behind once or twice, because she smiled and when the dance was finished she crooked her little finger and invited me across to the table.

You could tell that she was the sort of woman who called men to her like that. By crooking her little finger. And they went. I went. She was sitting next to a man in his thirties, dark and tired looking. He had a broken leg, the plaster cast thrust under the straw table, the mummified foot projected from the end. She said this was her husband, M. Jacques Grasse, but he spoke no English.

'I speak some English,' she recited. 'I am Annette Grasse. I am twenty-nine years. I have red hair and green eyes.'

I confirmed this for myself. She looked like Greer Garson, with whom I had been in almost demented love all through my childhood. After seeing *Random Harvest* I had gone down by my boyish bed and prayed that by some genetic miracle Miss Garson's age might be arrested until I could catch up with her and claim her as mine.

I used to imagine the headlines – 'Greer Garson Remains Twenty-two. Doctors Baffled.' And all the time I would be gloating and growing.

'My husband not dance because he fell from his 'orse,' she said. 'But we will dance.'

With no more preliminaries than that we were dancing. I had not said a word and neither had her husband. A waiter put a bottle of whisky and a glass in front of him and he poured an initial drink as though it were the fore-runner of many. He stared straight ahead and threw the spirit down his throat, then poured another. But this time we were whirling away from him.

'You are sad,' she observed. 'How old are you? Very young with black hair and brown eyes. And big hands. You have very big hands.'

'They're still growing I expect,' I said at last. 'I'm not eighteen yet.'

'I am just waiting for my 'usband to have his leg better – then phutt! I leave him,' she said frankly.

'Why don't you leave him now?' I suggested in my bravado. 'He won't be able to run after you.'

'Oh no,' she pouted. 'That would not be possible. For he is 'elpless, you understand. No, I stay. But I look for somebody younger. And with two good legs. And hands.'

'I'm leaving tomorrow,' I said blatantly. 'I'm on the ship.'

'I know. My 'usband owns all the sugar. It is his sugar you take. What is your name and why are you having a sad face?'

'Arthur,' I said. 'Arthur McCann. And I'm just sad, that's

all. A bit upset. A friend of mine died.'

'They do,' she nodded.

'And I'm just waiting for a telegram to come because I've asked a girl at home to marry me,' I went on.

'Marry?' She looked shocked, pulling her head back as we danced. 'That is worse than dying.'

'She's very nice,' I insisted. 'I need her.'

'At seventeen,' she shook her head. 'You don't need this girl. Not when you have such big hands. Come, we will go from here.'

She pulled me insistently towards the door, not even looking behind, and I staggered with her. 'What about him,' I said. 'Your old man?'

'He will love the bottle for a while,' she laughed. 'I will take you to the place where the little Josephine, who was the Empress of Napoleon, used to wash her feet in childhood. It is a lovely place for us. You will like it. It has history.'

She had a car outside. She said there were only four cars in the island and two of them belonged to her. One other belonged to a lover and the fourth to the chief of police with whom she was on good terms. I began to realize I was in the clutches of a powerful woman.

Outside the stars were looking low, mixing with the lights of the port. We sat in her car while a man from the Cockatoo Paradise brought out two bottles in ice buckets. I guessed they contained the champagne with which she was going to seduce me. It was quite a small car, nothing like as palatial as Mrs Nissenbaum's limousine in New York, but then that was hardly to be expected. It was strange, I thought, how many of my women had cars.

This one had a sliding sunshine roof and Annette pulled it back so that we could see the studded sky and feel the dark breeze.

'Voilà,' she said leaning across to me and making it a whisper. 'We have everything. Let me see them once more. Your hands.'

I did not know whether to feel happy or annoyed at her love for my hands. Somehow I felt it was a back-handed compliment; that there were better things about me than that. If I sound conceited, then I was. Not many lads of my age had experienced female admiration in its full mature form. I held out my hands as I not long before had held them out to show my schoolteacher that they were clean. She bent quickly and kissed each hard palm. I leapt forward to kiss her face, but she turned abruptly and started the car. I looked down cautiously at my hands, thinking they might have qualities I had hitherto missed. They looked the same. If her admiration was going to stop there it was not going to be much of a night.

We drove along roads meant for mules, bumping and banging in the dark. She sang under her breath, repeating the phrases of the music to which we had danced back at the Cockatoo Paradise Loungette and Bar. After twenty minutes she rattled the little car off the road and when she stopped the engine I could hear the cascading of water in the dark.

'The place where Josephine washed herself,' she whispered, as though the lady were still doing it. 'It has history.'

It also had a slab of rock, flat as a table, and big enough for two people to lie side by side. One edge, however, fringed a short but sheer drop into a pool into which the cascade was emptying. There was no moon then, but the water was ruffled with muted light as it flowed and we could see it from the rock. She opened the first bottle of champagne and let the frothy tongue drop over the little cliff. The barman had provided two glasses and we toasted each other.

'To you, mon chéri, and your beautiful hands.'

'To you, missus, and your husband's broken leg.'

She laughed, but the laugh dropped as though ashamed from her face, and she sighed: 'Poor Monsieur Grasse and his jambe. It is very sad. But soon it will be well and I will go from this place.'

'Don't you like it?'

'Phoo!' She blew out her cheeks. 'It is prison. I am a *pénitente*. I will go to Paris and Rome and London. Are you from London, mon chéri?'

'No, I'm from Newport,' I said honestly. 'But I know

136

New York pretty well. Riverdale, Times Square, Welfare Island. All over.'

She sighed and stretched herself out fully on the rock. 'Ah, what it is to be a sailor!'

'It's hard work,' I said practicably. The champagne was having a dispute in my gut with the native rum I had been drinking all the evening. I wanted to stop the talking and get her clothes off.

'The work is good,' she said. 'It gives to you those great hands.'

Without adding further to the conversation I took my clothes off. She did not even look at me, but continued lying out flat in her white suit, lifting her head slightly to drink the champagne (we were now on the second bottle) like a patient in bed sipping Lucozade. I felt like some ape man kneeling beside the planter's whiteclad wife. She did not move, nor look at me and although the air was tropic I felt it chill as I remained as though waiting for instructions.

'Put your hands on me,' she said eventually, and to my relief. 'Start from the top, from my fair hair, and put them on me all the way down.'

'Wouldn't you like to take your things off?' I invited cautiously.

'There is much time,' she assured me lazily. 'Do not be anxious, darling.'

Reassured, I did as she commanded, laying my fine big hands on her forehead and her soft springy hair. She closed her eyes as though I had applied a benison. Then she told me to commence the downward journey. It was very strange, I had to cover her eyes and nose, with my lower thumb against her lips. She kissed it then bit into it, so thoroughly that I quickly moved on to her neck. To my amazement she began to tremble. There was sweat on her neck. Well, with her, perspiration. Next I put my hands on her shoulders, on her white jacket, but eyes closed, she fumbled with the buttons and threw it open. Her shoulders were naked and her breasts tight balls in a white brassière. I misjudged her excitement. I took my hands away and put them under my thing, offering it to her like a gift parcel.

'Annette,' I croaked. 'I would like to give you this.'

Her eyes opened to slices, then closed again without interest. 'Non, non,' she almost whimpered. 'Take those magnificent hands from it. They make it look like a baby's.'

I felt my temper rise on a tide of champagne and Port de Loupe rum, but I made it ebb again, and continued with my laundry-like pressing of her body. My palms were across her breasts, still parcelled, down to her stomach, on top of her skirt across her thighs, and then down to the less interesting areas of her knees and below.

'Your hands,' she murmured when I had completed the journey. 'Encore, chéri, encore.'

It was like an encore too. I felt as if I were playing some prelude and fugue on an organ, my hands laid on and off, moving gradually down. I was at her waist this time, kneeling naked at her side, my palms rubbing the light skin when there came the unlikely sound of a bicycle bell from the road above us. Through the screen of trees a single light moved like a searching insect. She did not appear to hear anything because she wriggled with impatience for me to move my hands another stage down her trunk.

Then, through the heavy bushes came a young Creole in a grey jacket and peaked cap. He looked at me, in my nude posture, and silently handed me a telegram.

Annette half sat up. She pulled her jacket around her when she saw him and opened her mouth as though something powerful was about to come out. But the boy stopped her with a stream of French of his own. She jerked up as if she were on a sprung hinge, emitted a distressed cry, and tried to scramble to her feet. My hand went out to her and caught her around the leg. She screeched again and bellowed at me in French. She shouted something at the boy who stepped forward and gave me one powerful push which sent me tumbling off the rock slab and down the short, steep drop into the cold pool in which Josephine had washed her feet so many years ago.

I never saw my telegram again after that moment, I came

up among the ribbons of starlit water and floating rubbish, and splashed around among wrecked boxes and tin cans deposited by unromantic villagers unmoved by memories of Josephine. I flayed all over the nasty pool looking for my telegram, but I could not find it. Almost weeping with the frustration I crawled from the water and sat on the bank. Far in the distance I could hear her car going back towards the town.

Pamela! What was the answer? That word which had flown so far and crashed and drowned before I could see it. Would my uncomplicated Pamela marry me and save me from all the Josephine's pools of the world? Or had she found a returning soldier or a resident Yank? Naked as a caveman I crouched by the water, two empty bottles quarrelling in the stream at my feet; wondering, looking through the half light to see if I could see my lost message.

I knew that I had to go back to the town, to the cable station where they would have a copy, or, at least the old woman would know whether or not I was a prospective bridegroom. I climbed the incline again and picked up my clothes. Then I walked naked along the track for ten minutes, by which time I was dry and could get dressed.

When I reached Port de Loupe the cable office was locked and shuttered. A despairing panic caught me. We were sailing at six that morning, I had to know before then. The only lights in the town were in the Cockatoo Paradise Loungette and Bar, spilling orange, red and green into the street. The music from the wind-up gramophone was honking in the night air. Voices and laughter came from the open front.

I stumbled across the vacant street, weary from the weight of disappointment. I reached the step and immediately saw the boy who delivered the telegram. He was still wearing his official grey peaked cap. He saw me coming and backed away remembering the push he had delivered. Turning he spoke to the barman who was from Trinidad. The barman leaned over and said: 'Don't you hit him, man. Missus Grasse told him to do it. Everybody do what that woman says.'

'I wasn't going to,' I said. 'What was it all about anyway?'

'Monsieur Grasse,' answered the barman, putting a grimy glass of rum in front of me without my asking. Perhaps that was for not hitting the boy. 'Made a big row. Wanted to dance like the rest. And he got out there on the floor and fell down and bang! – broke the other leg, man. The other one!'

Monsieur Grasse's leg still wasn't so important to me as my telegram. I looked at the boy who eyed me distrustingly and shifted another pace up the bar. 'Will you ask him if he knew what was in the telegram,' I said to the barman. 'I lost it.'

'You lost it 'fore you read it?' inquired the barman.

'This bugger pushed me in the water.'

'Oh sure. Yes. I'll find out. Toulouse . . .' He motioned the lad nearer, but the boy said he did not know what the message was. He had not seen it. French cables he always opened and read but he couldn't understand English. The old lady from the cable station had gone home and he said he did not know where she lived, but he was probably lying. I sat, black and lost, over the bar.

'Man, what's your trouble?' asked the Trinidad barman. 'You got a face like somebody's crapped on your best shoes.'

'That cable,' I said slowly, drinking the rum he had given me. 'Was to say whether I'm going to get married or not. I proposed, but I don't know now whether she said yes or no.'

'Jesus! Is that all? Hell, you can pay me for the drink, man. Four francs.'

I gave him the money. 'It's not knowing,' I muttered. 'I don't know whether I'm engaged or not.' Over the grubby horizon of the glass I saw Monique in her bedroom slippers shuffling through the dancers on the floor. I had a feeling she was coming to get me.

'Listen,' said the barman confidingly. 'You listen, man. It's *got* to be right. She said "yes" that girl of yours.'

'How d'you know?' I said, but with some hope.

'Because she *answered*. You didn't pay for the answer did you? You didn't give them the money here?'

'No. She paid.'

'That's what I'm telling you, man. She ain't goin' to pay for no cable if she don't want you. She's saving for a new dress for some other fucker. You get me? If she sent back an answer, man, you got yourself a bride.'

'Christ! I think you're right!' I shouted jubilantly, the realization flowing through me. 'You're right. Have a drink!' Then I let out a sound that was half a burp half a yell of exultation. The drinks mixed inside me all reached combustion at the same moment. I heard the barman laughing and calling 'The man wants to get married!' and in a whirling moment I was locked with Monique in a wild waltz across the wooden floor. We turned and bounced and I could hear my shouting and her laughing squeals filling the tatty place. Round and round, like the dipper at Barry Island. Oh Christ, Mrs Nissenbaum, I'm going to get married! Wheee! Round and round. This Monique was a good sport. Now she's kissing me! She's so happy for me! Goodbye Mrs Nissenbaum, have a nice big rest up in Heaven. I'm getting married when I get home ... tra ... la ... la .... Ding dong the bells are going to ring.

Yes, more drinks. More for everybody! Rum on top of champagne – the *in* drink for the elite of Port de Loupe. My God, that's my hand on her little nipple. Have to watch it. And now she's got my leg caught in between hers! And we're still dancing around. I'm like a man with a wooden leg. A peg leg like old Murky would have liked to have had. Poor old Murky. Died on roller skates. Did he really see the giant sloth?

In the dizzy middle of it all I saw Madame Grasse come through the door. She came in like a ghost in her white suit. I couldn't see her properly but I could hear her crying through the whirling that was going on all around me.

'Deux jambes!' she was howling. 'Deux jambes.'

'Jambe today, jambe tomorrow!' I remember roaring and she seemed to stagger away from my screen. Out in the street I could hear her howling, the sound going from my mind as gradually as a dying wind.

It was terrible then. Rum by the pint is not good for any young man, especially after champagne. I felt I was caught up in a great rushing of laughter and tricks and faces, carried off on a shrieking wind above the trees of the island, and dropped upon somebody's bed. I imagined that Mrs Nissenbaum had come back to me, or that I had been taken to her through the trees and the sky and the stars. God, Mrs Nissenbaum, you've got so thin! I suppose that's what being dead does for you. Thins you down no end. And you smell different. Not full and sweet, but hot and bitter. That's being dead as well, I suppose. It makes you smell. This waist! It's not that lovely, wide, white, soft waist. It's narrow and brown. And your hair has got so tough. Like tin. I can't get my face into it now. It pushes my face away. But I do still love you, despite all this. And this dead intercourse is nice. It's lovely to be with you again, darling, and I'm sorry about what happened to your dog. Poor Errol Flynn. Do you see a lot of him now? Is he with you in Heaven? Has he got over that nasty choking? Oh why, oh why? Oh why did you make me wear that thing, Mrs Nissenbaum? I told you I didn't like it. Like going to bed in your socks. How you laughed at that. Oh, my large, lovely, lady, what has happened to yoooooooooou . . . ?

Even though I had not been at sea for very long I had already acquired the sailor's clock, that inward alarm which goes off to tell you that you're drunk and your ship is about to sail. Hollow and filled with a nasty dust I woke at four and lay in a stiff frenzy, fearing that I had missed my ship. Then I looked at my watch. There was time, but I had to go now.

I was lying in the middle of an extensive rough bed. I was naked and on one side of me Monique was lying naked also. It was necessary to lean closer in the dimness to make sure it was her. She slept quietly, her breasts poking their infant snouts over the single blanket we shared. On the other side of me, also sleeping, was a very old woman, face like a skull, hands behind head, a high pitched snore squeezing between two outpost teeth. I leaned closer to her but her breath caught me on the way down and I retreated quickly. There were other people in the room, all sleeping, propped against the walls or the bits of furniture, or stretched flat on the matting floor.

Carefully, in the half light I climbed over the old woman and immediately, thankfully, found my trousers and shirt at the side of the bed. My shoes were sitting neatly alongside the pom-pom bedroom slippers that Monique had been wearing the night before.

I got quickly into my clothes. The early air had a chill on it. My mouth felt foul and my eyes were gummed. As I was about to go from the room the old woman groaned and took her hands from behind her head. She said something in French without opening her eyes. I caught the word 'mer', which I knew, and I agreed quietly that I was going to sea.

There was a narrow stairway, steep as a chute, outside the room and there were more people all lying, sleeping, on that. Almost at the door, back propped against one thin post, plastered legs thrust out like a ship's loading derricks, was Monsieur Grasse, plastered too, a bottle clutched like a baby to his breast. I wondered however he had come to be there.

Out in the street I saw immediately, to my relief, the still lights of the ship. I ran towards her as though she were my mother, the violent and vivid dreams of the night coming back to me as I went. I boarded her with two minutes to spare and at the loss of two days' pay. An hour later we were picking our way into the mainstream of the channel that led from the harbour.

I was working on the hatches on deck. The ocean spread flat and sweet before us, our bow going through it like scissors through silk.

'La grande mer,' I said to the bosun cockily. 'The splendid sea.'

'It means your grandmother,' he said. 'Get on with the job.'

That's what she had said, the old woman. Grande mer. She meant the sea. Of course she meant the bloody sea.

What else. Not grandmere. Why didn't they teach us French at school? We ought to have done French. The sentence mumbled in the dark came back to my consciousness, almost easily. 'Bosun,' I said. 'Can I ask you something, please.'

'Look, McCann, you're here to work. What is it?'

I told him the sentence as I remembered it. He laughed and said: 'Something like "I'm the bride's grandmother." Now will you get on with your bloody work?'

11

One year two months and three and a half days later Pamela married me in St Chrisp's Church, overlooking the Bristol Channel. Wind and high rain beat about the church during the service so that to the ear it was like being at sea in a storm. The organist, carried away by the drama of the external sounds, played 'For Those In Peril On The Sea' while we were awaiting my bride. During the service my bastard father laughed so much he had to go outside and squat in the porch until he had quietened down.

At first I thought flatteringly it was one of the six aunts in a spasm of traditional crying. It came from just over my right shoulder as I trembled next to my bride at the chancel steps. The vicar, who was telling us that all this was for begetting children, glanced up and the little noise ceased, but then it started again and I realized that it was a man giggling. I closed my eyes as though that would shut it out. The sounds were like little hiccoughs, spaced at first, but then crowding together until the fool was gurgling for all he could. Pamela did not seem to notice. She was staring at the vicar, a lean and sexy young man, as if waiting to hear more about the begetting of children. Eventually the sounds behind became insistent, and people in the pews began to complain, so I turned and saw him with his face in his hands, his shoulders heaving to the unremitting giggles.

144

My mother, her face crumpled, forlorn, gave him a defeated push. He looked up face stained with hilarious tears, and then staggered, hooting like a drunk, down the aisle and out of the door. Then we got married.

The night before was very strange. My mother told me to go to bed early because of the big day and I went up to the small room I had known since early childhood. The wind from the Channel still agitated the window and, as it was Friday, men going home drunk from the dock pubs came up the street at intervals, singing bravely against the wind as though it were life itself.

I was eighteen then, but I had seen so much, done so much, done so much to so many women, that the childish room was too tiny for all my ghosts and memories. I tried to keep Mrs Nissenbaum firmly outside the door, but she came in with her spectre knock, floating on angelic pink chiffon, her hands reaching for me like clouds. Rose, sweet Rose of three years or a lifetime ago, seemed to sit bulkily on my bedside and read to me ponderously from *Gone With The Wind*. I heard the weeping of the sailor they called Rider Haggard in the Distressed Seamen's Home, and saw again the terrible red and white striped bottom of Mr Gander before it toppled beneath the sparkling sea. I even had a fleeting glimpse of Monique, shuffling on her pom-pom slippers about the Cockatoo Paradise Loungette and Bar, believing herself to be the wife of Arthur McCann. I still worried about that, but Port de Loupe was a long way across the world, and the Captain, an understanding sailor, to whom I confessed, a few days out, told me not to worry. He had heard that Creole women made bad wives anyway. 'Don't sign on any ship that's sailing for Port de Loupe, that's all,' he said. 'There's some places, lad, I dare not go myself.'

I had sailed the world in the year and two months since then. Pamela had said that if I was going to be a sailor for ever then I should go to sea looking nice, so I became a cadet with a blue uniform which that night was hanging pressed across my bedroom chair waiting for the wedding march.

The day I got the letter saying that I had been accepted as an officer cadet by the Blue Anchor Line I showed it to Pamela and she exclaimed: 'Oh, Alan, now you'll look really smart on our wedding day. I'll have the bridesmaids in pale blue to set it off.' We were getting married, and she still couldn't get my name right.

This night, the night before our wedding, I tried to sleep and I was nearly there when Mr Wynn-Griffiths, a new neighbour across the street, attacked his own front door with a garden hoe because Mrs Wynn-Griffiths had locked him out. Some men in that street spent more time outside their front doors than inside.

Hearing him choking and shouting frightened me in an ominous manner. I shivered in my single bed in the way I had once done as I waited for the firing squad sent by Winston Churchill to dispatch me. Even today I shudder at my imagination then of seeing my father showing them in and saying: 'Well, there he is gentlemen.'

Now it was Mr Wynn-Griffiths, a married man locked out in the blowy street, I sat up in bed and then I stood up and went to the window. The street was as empty as a drained canal. At the far end I could see the lights like flowers on the masts of the ships lying at the adjacent docks. Mr Wynn-Griffiths had stopped attacking his front door with the hoe and was sitting weeping on his doorstep.

When I went down the hoe was lying outside in the road where he had flung it, so I picked it up and carried it across to him. He glanced up from his wet forearms and looked half-pleased, half-surprised, but not shy or ashamed, even though he hardly knew me.

'Is this your garden hoe, Mr Wynn-Griffiths?' I asked casually, pretending it was not one o'clock of a deserted morning.

'Ah, so it is, boy,' he said wiping his wrists across his eyes and giving a quick sniff and snivel. 'That's my hoe.'

'Found it out there,' I said nodding towards the roadway.

'What, in the street? Wonder how it got in the street?'

'Can't think. Anyway here it is.'

'All right boy, thanks.' He seemed to think some explanation for his situation might be necessary. I could see that there were great bites out of the front door where the attacking hoe had been striking. 'Came out for a breather,' he said. 'These little houses get very stuffy, I find, don't you?'

'They do a bit,' I agreed. 'Mind I'm not in ours very much now.'

'At sea you are,' he said suddenly, very Welsh. 'Best place at sea, I think. You can breathe at sea. You can't breathe in these houses.' I was still looking at the door. 'Thought I'd scrape a bit of the paint off,' he explained casually. 'Could do with a new coat of paint. So I had a bit of a go at it. I'll have to finish it tomorrow. Or today, I suppose it is now.'

'I'm getting married tomorrow. That is, today,' I said.

He looked at me as though I had said I was volunteering for vivisection. 'Oh no, boy,' he groaned. 'Not married.'

'Yes,' I confirmed. 'St Chrisp's at three o'clock.'

'Don't do anything like that,' he whispered. 'It's a dreadful thing, you know. You don't realize until you've actually gone and committed it.'

'You make it sound like a crime,' I said wheezing an uncertain laugh.

'Oh, it is,' he moaned. 'It is. Crime against mankind. And I mean *man*kind. Run while you've got the chance, boy.'

As though to comfort me he shuffled along the doorstep making room for me to sit down. Hardly had I done so, however, than the door backed open to reveal Mrs Wynn-Griffiths in her nightgown holding a big brown teapot. For one moment of idiot optimism I thought she might be bringing us some refreshment, but instead she swung it violently. The lid was missing and a cold thick stream of tea looped through the air hitting me in the face and Mr Wynn-Griffiths in the back of the neck. She then shut the door firmly and quietly.

'That's Mrs Wynn-Griffiths,' said Mr Wynn-Griffiths, unnecessarily. 'I was a bit slow in turning round, or I'd have got it in the face as well as you.'

He became suddenly angry and was all for another attack

with the hoe supplemented by a spade, but I pulled him away and took him across to my house where we cleaned off the rash of tea leaves with the South Wales Echo and one of my mother's towels. He would not stay, but set off morosely down the draughty street to the house of a friend who, he said, would give him a bed.

'Goodbye Mr McCann,' he said sincerely before he went. 'May God protect you.' He paused, shook my hand passionately and added: 'We can always say we had tea together, I suppose.'

This thought seemed to revive him for he went quite jauntily towards the houses at the dockside. I turned the other way and began to walk towards the middle of the town. I did not know why.

There was a tight, small, feeling of truancy within me as I walked, like the excitement of the forbidden journeys I had known on those juvenile summer nights when, best-suited, I crept to my rendezvous with Rose Kirby at the barrage balloon.

I had no idea why I was walking now, or where, only that I required to be free from the trap of the pressing walls of my room. Waiting in there before a wedding night was like being a greyhound held in a trap for the race.

At every corner I turned in the town the wind turned with me, either pushing against my back, encouraging me to keep going, or hitting me in the face as it bent the other way. No one could be expected in the windowed streets at that hour and that weather and I went on an imaginary shopping journey inspecting carpets and staring at fifty-shilling suits, paints said to be the essential of every handyman, three-piece suites covered in cut flowers of uncut moquette. There were new daring colours in linoleum in the window of the Newport Floor Company and the little-boy-lost faces of the new nine-inch television sets in the South Wales Radio World Shop. Nursery furniture stood brightly waiting for babies; in blue and cream, embellished with cherubs and saucy-eyed deers. There were things on springs and strings like miniature pieces of gymnasium equipment and I

148

wondered at the changes since the days when I was given a raw carrot to chew in my home-made high chair, the contraption built by my father which, inevitably, meant that it had a sadistic habit of collapsing when I was strapped into it. Abruptly I realized that getting married meant that Pamela and I would have children. To think, I had never looked more than a night beyond the wedding day.

Then I arrived at a window full of postage stamps and I stood and gazed at them for half an hour. Seychelles, Fernando Po, Turks and Cocos, Ifni, Chad, Yemen, Gilbert and Ellice, Nauru, Somaliland Protectorate, and the Princely State of Negri Sembelan. Something wicked urged me to run then, to hurry down the narrow chutes of the streets to the docks and sail for Fernanado Po, Chad or even Milford Haven before the next daybreak. Anywhere distant from this place.

I had seen no one. It was too chilly for policemen and the wind was rattling my trouser legs, so I shrugged away from the world in that window and turned towards my room and my wedding. Then I saw, at the distant end of the shopping road, a person hopping in and out of the pavement squares. She was playing the game conscientiously because I could hear her saying instructions to herself and laughing when she made a mistake. She was very tall and I knew by the lightness of her voice that she was young.

Because she was intent on her game she did not see me until she was almost at the shop next to the stamps. Then she looked up and, unafraid, unsurprised, she smiled and said: 'It's Arthur McCann. You've grown!'

'Not as much as you,' I said.

'That would take some doing,' she laughed. 'God, if I'd known I was going to get like this I wouldn't have drunk all that milk they made us swallow at school.'

'That's years ago,' I said. 'Seems like it, anyway.'

'It's years,' she said.

We stood where the window light of the shop dropped on to the pavement, as though it were not the centre of a chill night, but that the townspeople were all around us and we had met at noon. She had a long face that looked all right on her because she was altogether long. Her hair was long and fair too, swooping over the collar of her coat.

'Listen,' she said. 'Do you remember Ruby Martin in our class?'

'Of course I do. There was that song about her.'

Spontaneously we began to chant:

> 'Ruby Martin
> Fell down fartin'
> Got up stinkin'
> Went home thinkin''.

When it was finished we stood, beamed at each other and laughed wildly at the idiocy of it. Immediately a window screeched open above us and an ugly man put his head out. 'Bugger off,' he ordered. 'Making all that row in the middle of the night. Go on, bugger off.'

'I think he wants us to bugger off,' she said.

'Is that what he's hinting at?' I said. I lifted my face to the gargoyle. 'Five past two,' I called to him. 'Time you were asleep.'

The sash came down with such anger that I thought the glass would be shivered out. Prudently we moved along the road. She was still making subdued laughing sounds but we did not talk again for a couple of minutes.

'Mary Winters,' I said at last. 'Fancy seeing you again.'

'Arthur McCann, fancy seeing you. What were you doing? Loitering with intent, I bet.'

'I suppose I was in a way. I was looking at the stamps in that window and thinking about the places, that's all. Wondering if I ought to get on a ship tonight and sail off.'

'You always were one of those,' she said. 'Dreaming of funny things. You go to sea anyway, don't you? Somebody told me.'

'That's right.'

'Everybody does around here,' she said. 'It's a wonder the girls don't end up climbing the masts or something. My father got killed last year. Fell into a dock at Marseilles. It was a dry dock too. And it was empty.'

'Oh, I *am* sorry,' I said. Then: 'Mary. Would you mind walking in the gutter and I'll walk on the pavement? We'd be about level then. You've really sprouted up.'

She giggled. 'All right, Shorty. If it makes you feel better. There's nobody to see us, anyway.'

'It hurts my neck, looking up,' I said.

'Hurts your pride more like it.' She smiled seriously and stepped daintily down into the gutter. We walked on, our heads now level.

'Where have you been anyway?' I asked. 'Tonight, I mean.' I saw that she wore no gloves and her hands were long and slim like her features. There was a bright little ring on the second finger of her left hand.

'Ruby Martin's,' she said. 'That's why I suddenly thought of the rude rhyme we used to sing about her. We sat there nagging and I missed the bus, so I went back and telephoned my mum and had a cup of coffee, then I walked. I don't mind walking.'

'You were playing hopscotch,' I said. 'I saw you.'

'I can still do it,' she said as though she had surprised herself. 'Not so good as I used to, but I can still do it.' Then she remarked: 'I'm getting married next week.'

I exclaimed: 'I'm getting married tomorrow! Well, to-day!'

'Really! What a thing! Let's shake on it!'

We were both laughing and we shook hands emphatically. But suddenly we stopped shaking and stood holding hands with mutual embarrassment.

'Mind you,' she said, taking her hand away and shuffling on. 'Everybody gets married around this time. It's the end of the tax year. They'll be queueing up and the papers will be full of pictures of three hundred honeymoon couples in one hotel in Guernsey or somewhere. It's a wonder to me they don't shake those places off their foundations.' She put her hands into the deep pockets of her coat and walked on.

'Three hundred simultaneous wedding nights is a bit of a risk, I would say,' I agreed. 'Anyone I know?'

'Who?'

'The person you're marrying.'

She smiled at once. 'No, he's not from round here. He's from Cardiff. Peter Phillips. I met him at a holiday camp last summer. Who's yours?'

I had a quick memory of her then, a moment of *déjà vu* a little girl and a boy comparing presents gained at the Sunday School Christmas Treat. The thought occupied me for a moment and she said: 'Did she go to our school?'

'Oh, sorry,' I said, shutting away the little girl and looking at her now. 'No. I don't reckon you'd know her. Pamela Dunn. She went to Dolphin Road Secondary, so you probably wouldn't.'

'No. She nice?'

'Naturally,' I laughed. 'She is to me, anyway.'

'It's a big thing,' she said moodily. 'Marriage.'

'You're a bit young, aren't you?' I said pompously. 'To get married.'

'What about you? You're the same. Eighteen. And you're at sea.'

'I'm doing my officer training.' I said. 'When I get on a bit I'll be able to take her to sea with me. They're going to allow that again soon.'

'Where's yours?' she asked.

'St Chrisp's,' I answered. 'Three o'clock.'

'St Michael and All Angels,' she recited. 'Twelve on Wednesday.'

'Nice, getting married on a Wednesday,' I said. 'Away from the rush. I'll think about you.'

'And I'll do the same. Promise.'

We walked quietly now, dolefully, our heads down against the pointed wind. 'Pity we didn't know,' I said eventually. 'We could have had a double wedding.'

She laughed at once, as she had done before. 'We could have invited all the old school gang,' she said. 'That would have been really funny.'

'That's if we could round them up.'

'I liked it at school,' she went on. 'Didn't you?'

'Not much,' I admitted.

'Do you remember they caught you wearing those ladies' knicks,' she giggled frankly. 'When they debagged you.'

Even in the chill air I felt my face redden. 'For goodness sake don't talk about that,' I pleaded.

'It was terrible,' she nodded. 'I tried to pull some of the boys away, but I couldn't. It was I who ran to get old Jones.'

'Fancy reminding me about that,' I said limply. 'God, it was like a nightmare. I only had them on because I was cold and my own pants had got torn and I didn't want to tell my mother. They belonged to my rotten bloody sister, and she kicked up murder too. The bastards had to choose *that* day to debag me. That day of all days. I only wore them once.'

'I cried about it,' she said slowly. 'I really did. I went into the girls' lav and I burst into tears. I'll tell you something – I was wearing my old man's itchy vest that day. It's a good job they didn't do that to the girls. Either I wore it or I didn't wear anything under my dress and I was cold too.'

'It's one of those odd things, I suppose,' I said. 'Afterwards you can see them as they really were; not all that important. But at the time it wasn't very funny.'

'I cried,' she repeated. 'It upset me.'

'You said,' I acknowledged. 'Thanks anyway.'

'It was so cruel the way they threw you down and all ganged up on you. I could see your face, like a ghost, with blood on it down among all those boys' legs.'

'We used to like each other, didn't we? You and me.'

She laughed. 'We used to "go" with each other, as they said.'

'We never actually "went" anywhere though, did we? We just passed those notes in class. "See you down the shops" or "see you in the park".'

'Or "by the dump",' she smiled. 'I remember that one because I was turning out some old things one day and I must have kept it. I had to laugh because I thought how romantic it was. By the dump!'

'Did you ever actually go to meet me?' I asked. 'Somehow I never used to believe those notes. It was just a bit of a game. Once I pinched two shillings from my mother's purse to take you to the Odeon, but I waited outside and you never came. So I didn't think you meant it and I didn't bother again.'

'Well I turned up at the dump once, I know,' she said. 'I remember being frightened because all the seagulls were flapping around over the rubbish. They seemed enormous to me. Like eagles. When you didn't come I ran home crying and I decided to give you up.'

'Give me up!' I exclaimed. 'That's rich, that is, when you think about it. We never *had* each other to give up. All there was were those notes.'

'And you used to wink at me. First one eye then the other.'

'Like this,' I said and I did it.

She laughed: 'That's right. Seeing you do it again is so funny. I used to think it was ever so clever. Winking with both eyes. Isn't it odd, Arthur, remembering it all?'

'Very odd,' I said. 'Do you still live in the same house?'

'That's right,' she said, sadly I thought, but I could have been mistaken. 'Just round the corner here.'

'We ought to be in bed with our big days coming up, me tomorrow, you on Wednesday,' I said.

'Don't say it like that!' she said putting her hand over her mouth. 'We ought to be in bed!'

'Sorry. I meant in our *beds*.'

'It's a bit late for the other thing,' she laughed.

'It certainly is. We should have kept sending those notes.'

'And not turning up,' she said. Then she asked: 'Do you mind if I ask you something?'

'No. Anything.'

'Well, are you looking forward to it? *Honestly* looking forward to it? Tomorrow and after?'

'Yes,' I said bravely. 'Yes, I suppose I am.'

'Why were you thinking about running off to sea tonight, then? Like you said.'

'Oh that. Oh, I only said that. Just a few last minute nerves, that's all.'

'I know,' she agreed. We had stopped now and I knew her house was only twenty yards up the street. 'It's a bit frightening isn't it?'

'It's bound to be,' I said as though I were wise. 'But it's probably one of those things that will be all right on the night.'

She laughed quietly. 'I expect so. Just think when we next meet up we might have half a dozen kids each.'

'That's what it's for, marriage,' I said. 'One of the things, anyway. It says in the service.'

'I know,' she said. 'I thought it sounded a bit personal when the clergyman went through it with us. I mean, people know that without having to be told by a vicar.'

'It *will* be all right,' I said reassuring both of us. I knew that she had to go now.

'Well, I must go,' she said. 'Have a happy marriage.'

'You too,' I mumbled. We were standing two feet apart, her feet still in the gutter.

'Let's have a quick kiss for old times' sake,' she said suddenly, cheerfully.

I swallowed and nodded.

We bent towards each other and kissed without our hands or anything touching. It was only a moment. Then she stood up on the pavement and went off towards her house. ''Bye, Arthur,' she called as I went the other way. 'Lovely seeing you again.'

''Bye Mary,' I returned. 'Have a good time.'

'And you.'

In the morning I listened early to the weather forecast for shipping. There was a force nine funnelling up the channel and no ships were leaving the South Wales ports because of the heavy seas. I would not have been able to run away anyway. The wind howled like a hooligan down the street and rain hit my window in handfuls.

St Chrisp's church is on a promontory overlooking the sea, its steeple used as a navigation marker by ships coming into the port. Many times since then I have watched it raise its point over the horizon and thought of that day, very clear to me, but now long ago.

The cars had to be left at the gate and it was a high exposed walk up through groggy gravestones to the church door. The entire wedding party climbed it angled like mountaineers into the wind. All my six aunts were gasping by the time they reached the top and Nardine had to be given a stiff mouthful of brandy in the very porch of the church. I can still remember my father pouring it into her with his sickening sexy concern, whispering: 'Never mind, girl, it's downhill when we go out and the wind's behind us.'

Mad Aunt Ramona, who was let out especially and who had about that time become of a religious disposition, dropped on apparently spent knees in the same porch and resisted helping hands who sought to help her to her feet, shouting that she was praying. This was all very fine, but she made a substantial mound in the doorway and this, combined with the space taken up by the semi-prostrate Nardine, meant that the remainder of us were kept outside in the windy rain, until both women could be removed.

Eventually they were all established inside the storm-caught building, coughing, spluttering and sneezing, Pamela's family one side, mine the other, all of them doing their share, as though to ensure that the others knew what sacrifices they had made to get to that height and occasion. One of Pamela's cousins, Rhoda, an extraordinary bell-shaped girl decorated in every variety of the then new-fashioned plastics, and in a myriad of wet hues and shining colours, began to wring the water from her galoshes. The resulting squirting sound took all the eyes from our side to theirs and she looked up from her under-pew squeezing to set the spark to the very first of the feuds between the families. I heard my Uncle Ned clearly say: 'God, I thought she was having a piss.'

Aunt Ramona had collapsed into prayer again, hands clutching the pious wood before her, making such a loud meal of it that the event might just as easily have been a funeral. To this was added the contribution of the organist who chose to run through 'For Those In Peril' with the rude gale banging at the stained-glass windows.

Pamela arrived in bridal tears after her ascent of the church path. She had to be more or less re-assembled in the porch and the tougher blossoms of her bouquet which had not been torn away by the wind needed to be arranged so that they concealed the empty stalks of those blooms which had been more exposed and were then scattering themselves along the blowy coast. Her father had been slightly injured when the umbrella with which he was gallantly trying to shield his daughter blew inside out and one of the spokes was thrust in his eye. The bride eventually came down the aisle weaving through the puddles left by all the guests. It was at about that moment that I felt soggy water inside my left sock and knew that my shoe had a hole in it.

The vicar, who naturally had good local knowledge, arrived covered in oil skins and wearing a sou'wester. At first many of those present thought that the coxswain of the Goldcliffe lifeboat had turned up, but with an almost mystic ritual the oilskins came off and the clergyman was revealed in his dry vestments.

I forget his name now after all this time; he was a beleaguered looking vicar, young, but slightly astounded. He stared at the congregation as though wondering what they were doing in his church. He was never seen in the town and people said he spent all his time in bed; more of a recumbent than an incumbent. But having a church stuck out there like a lighthouse I didn't blame him.

My bride looked lovely, her face as pale as her bridal gown, her train held by a couple of friends, dumb-faced as soaked mules. The rain which had caught her full-on as she scaled the climb to the church had struck her above the right eye and the black make-up from that lid was trickling idly down her cheek, but it did not bother her. She was a funny girl, that Pamela. I mean, she must have felt it running, and she must have known how unusual she looked, smiling at me and the vicar with that stuff wriggling down her cheek; but she didn't even give any sign that she knew. She was like that. She still is. I think. If something happens she can it happen and then close her mind to it. When we were choosing the hymns and the other music for the service she wrote down 'Persil's Trumpet Voluntary' on the paper the vicar gave her. Now I didn't know, and I still don't know after all these years, whether she really thought Purcell spelt his name like that or whether she did it out of her screwed up sense of humour.

Like anything else, if she did it by accident, she would never admit it. She just let it stand. I never asked her about it, although it bothered me, on and off, for years, because I knew she would just laugh and then I would feel the foolish one. She was just like that.

I don't think that St Chrisp's has ever had a noisier wedding. The organist had to pump his feet and bang his fingers down like fury before the wind inside out-sounded the wind outside. We had decided not to have the bell rung in the church on account of the expense, but throughout the service there came the miserable tolling of a rocking bell-buoy in the channel. From the pews issued every variety of cough, sneeze and snivel. One of her uncles had the most racking bronchial attack just as we were making our vows, and had to be belaboured about the shoulder blades by his adjacent relatives.

Remarks came from both families, too, sharp, sounding like random pistol shots penetrating all the other intrusions. When I knelt at the chancel steps and her followers saw that I had a hole in my shoe the shots became a fusilade. Then, as I said, my father started his idiot laugh, giggling and stopping and giggling again and finally guffawing so that he had to stagger out to the porch until the hilarious spasm had subsided. I never asked him why he had laughed. I hardly needed to. He was my father.

At the end of the service I led my wife between the iron smiles, to the porch, to the Trumpet Voluntary played on the organ. Pamela turned to me and with that confident challenge said: 'Persil's.' She said it as near to spelling it as she could and I nodded without argument. While we were in the doorway, crouched between gusts, before making a run for the cars, the organist shuffled around and gave us a little bow and said: 'It's Jeremiah Clarke, you know.' Somewhat stupidly, I realize now, I shook his hand and said I was pleased to meet him not realizing that he meant Clarke not Purcell wrote the music anyway.

The wedding party descended in short panicky bunches, each making a ragged dash for it, like soldiers under fire crossing an exposed place. The bridesmaids screamed as they ran. To add to the illusion, one of my aunts and Pamela's bronchial uncle fell over between the muddy gravestones during their particular rush and her uncle added unnecessary drama by crying out above the wind: 'Leave me! Just leave me!'

Pamela and I waited for our moment. The car was waiting two hundred yards down that violent hill. Then the clouds across the channel split at a seam and the cold sun briefly lit the disordered sea. I turned and saw a ship going out, a brave ship she must have been and a big one, pushing against the waves, dipping and bowing, but going on, going out to the ocean. The sun was cut off quickly as the clouds repaired the rent, and I turned guiltily and saw Pamela looking at me with something uncomfortably like amusement. It was as though I had been looking at another woman.

'Why don't you run?' she suggested. 'You might catch it.'

'Don't be silly,' I said. 'I was just looking at it that's all. It's a big one, isn't it?'

'Huge,' she said, still with that one-sided smile.

Someone from the bottom of the path whistled with their fingers which was the signal for us to run. I put my arm around her and was strangely and abruptly surprised to feel her quite substantial shoulders through the wedding dress.

'Don't hold me,' she wriggled. 'We can run faster without holding.'

We ran through the brown water toppling down the church path. About half a dozen of the remaining guests made the dash with us. Someone had gallantly suggested that if they grouped themselves in a sort of bodyguard against the weather they might shield the bride. It seemed a good idea, but half way down a dash of cold glassy rain struck us almost horizontally and scattered the escort like cowards. Everybody started running for themselves and it was all the bride and I could do to squeeze into the car, already full of wet, panting and complaining relatives.

As we were about to move off, there came an unmistakable clerical call, like a mild, high pitched bird, and immediately the door opened and the vicar, covered in his stiff dripping oilskins, projected himself into the centre of the crowd.

'Nearly forgot me,' he chortled. 'Fancy forgetting the vicar!'

I thought perhaps I had better stand up for him. He accepted the offer breezily and squeezed his waterproofs between the bride and one of her cousins. All the way to the reception I stood, bent as if caught by some sudden serious crippling, in the car while my new wife glared at me from beyond the nasty parish oilskins.

'Enough room everyone?' inquired the clergyman brightly, wriggling and sending rivers of rain down his hard creases on to the bride and the transfixed girl at his other side.

The reception had been arranged at the Hortense Rooms, Dock Road, and, from its earliest moments, never showed any signs of aspiring to anything higher than a sparring ground for family wars which are still being bitterly fought. My family had battled within itself for years but now it closed ranks to face this new, sharp and eager adversary, Pamela's family.

'Look at that old fool with a red pullover on,' I heard my Aunt Floss sneer. 'Is that her grandfather? And he's got a hole in it! Look, right in the front. Bloody cheek, going to a wedding like that.'

'He's got a bad chest,' I explained as I went by with a fizzing drink for my bride. 'That's why he's wearing a pullover.'

'No wonder he has,' retorted Floss who was never caught

without an answer. 'With the wind blowing through that bloody gaping great hole. No wonder he's got a bad chest.'

My father had cornered the two mulish bridesmaids and was filling their glasses from a bottle held by the neck in his right hand. His own glass was at his elbow and he good-naturedly held the hand of the marginally less ugly of the girls. His eyes were shining. My mother was sitting with a glass of brown ale talking to no one, her eyes going around with that defeated look of hers. She saw me and constructed a small jovial smile for me, waving a crisp at me as a sort of dry joke. I laughed much more than it was worth and pursed my lips in a stupid kiss.

Everyone was trying to get dry after the dash through the fierce rain and clothing was in great steaming piles on the radiators in the room. Some people had even taken their shoes off and put them under the appliances and were standing in their stockings and socks, drinking, chattering and keeping a guardian eye on their belongings. Pamela's father who had gone into a deep pool had taken off his soaked socks as well and was watching the steam writhe from them on the heater.

Fortunately the vicar did not stay. He circled the room, still like a sodden butterfly in his oilskins, but he could find no one to talk with him, so he left with a quick, wet, blessing just before we moved into the room where the wedding breakfast was laid.

I was wishing that, like my new father-in-law, I could have taken off at least my left sock since the rain had pene-trated the entire foot through the hole in the sole. This resulted in my walking about with a short, damp limp, which everyone who had not spotted it earlier, certainly noticed as I went into the banquet room with Pamela on my arm. Behind me I left a series of single smudges.

'You're limping,' my bride grumbled in my ear.

'I know. My foot is sopping wet.'

'You've got a hole in your shoe, haven't you?'

'Yes.'

'I know you have. My mother saw it. She nearly walked out of the church.'

I thought that once I got her alone it would be all right. The marriage could really begin; man and wife could love, honour and she could obey and, as it so erotically put words into her mouth in the service, with her body she could me worship. But until then we were marching between these rows of hideous relatives and I had a wet foot.

It is no use, even at this distance, pretending that the wedding feast was anything more than a failure. The food was a disaster for, although the war had been accomplished two years before, the country clung masochistically to war-time shortages and substitutes, and now even bread was rationed. I saw several guests stealing solid bread rolls and stuffing them into their pockets to take home. Recriminations were already beginning among my family and hers, and, as several people in both camps were now drunk, a number of catcalls were hurled across the table from one group to another. Although few of the people had ever met before they were already catching on to little deficiencies, deformities and infirmities and using them as hooks upon which to hang their insults.

'That one's got a funny eye.'

'Won't be long before she's dead. I wonder who's having her tiara.'

'Look at that kid, spitting his jelly out.'

'Had his flies undone all through the service.'

'Remember him, don't you? Always getting thrown out of the Donkeyman's Arms.'

'I didn't think you could buy dresses that size off the peg.'

'How can that woman guzzle sausage-meat and drink Guinness at the same time?'

The rabble was growing around three sides of the table when my father, for once timing his hypocrisy to my advantage, rose and bawled: 'Friends! Old friends and family, new friends and family, I would like to propose a toast to my boy Arthur and his lovely young bride.'

He got their attention that way, then launched himself into what appeared to be a spontaneous speech, but one which included such numerous quotations from Shakespeare and the classics that I knew he must have been swotting it for weeks. Some of the more familiar wisdom he acknowledged, especially the bits from the Bible which he identified by book, chapter and verse, but there was much he did not, indicating by his attitude that these subtle and brilliant thoughts had just come to his head. With a smirk he sat down to enraptured applause from his own side and grudging acknowledgement from the other.

Pamela's father, who had by now replaced his socks, stood up, swayed drunkenly, and slid beneath the table without a word. His own camp clapped loyally and loudly at this, glaring at our side, as though it were some kind of difficult ritualistic trick that we could not be expected to understand. Two strong male relations put their arms beneath the tablecloth and heaved him out as though they were rescuing him from some underground trap. They replaced him on his chair and retired to their own seats. The hubbub continued. I looked at Pamela and moving close to her ear I said: 'Having a good time?'

'What a mess,' she muttered, resting both hands on her dessert fork and sticking it hard through the cloth. 'What a bloody, buggering mess.'

'We'll be on our way soon, darling,' I assured her.

'Good,' she answered. 'Anything is better than this.'

But the nadir was yet to come. I had stood, trembling, to reply to the toast, and was stumbling through my prepared platitudes when one of her uncles rose and held up a hand like a policeman.

'Just a minute, son,' he said. 'Can you give us a break?'

I stood dumbly while two of them went into the other room and came back wheeling a battery radio set, a present from my family, on a tea trolley, a present from hers. At the centre of the room they switched it on and then, unbelievingly, I saw what was happening. Every man on her side, followed very quickly and appreciatively by many on mine, fiddled in his jacket and produced his football pools coupon. They were just in time. 'League, Division One,' said the announcer. 'Arsenal 2 Liverpool 1. . . .'

My speech was never given, but nobody noticed. We went off, after Scottish League, Division Two, was finished and began our honeymoon journey on the train from Newport station. She sat against the window and stared out as though trying to see the wind. I sat close to her, but, man and wife, we said nothing. It was then I realized why some people do actually throw themselves off bridges.

12

I suppose there are not a great many men who have committed adultery on their wedding night. I am not proud of it, but there is no doubt, it is unusual. Also, we went to Swindon for our honeymoon; gritty, bitty, shitty, Swindon, full of soot and railway engines.

Swindon, as our local newspaper account put it, was selected for the honeymoon. Selected, that is, by her parents who had a friend with a run-down railway hotel close by the renowned locomotive sheds and who needed the money at that thin time of the year. It was a smoky building on the corner of a downcast street. The windows looked out on the marshalling yards and their groaning engines. When we got to our room I pulled aside the flowered curtains and looked out over the mess of the railway lines and the hunched locomotives. It was like seeing cattle in a big stockyard, moving under the lights, moaning as though they were being prodded.

It was nine o'clock. Pamela sat on the bed while I arranged our suitcases so that they did not block our access to the washbasin. The landlady, Mrs Donelly, had said she called the room the bridal suite because it had the washbasin, but its romance was muted by a single orange bulb hanging from a tasselled shade, a mirror like a dirty pond, and a reproduction print of The Rape of The Sabine Women suspended hideously over the bed.

'What shall we do?' said Pamela eventually. She hunched her back and sighed.

'Well, it's our wedding night,' I answered. 'Why don't we go to bed?'

She said: 'It's only nine o'clock.'

'Is there some special time?' I said.

She shook her head. 'No. But I don't want to yet.'

'What do you want to do then?'

'Anything, Arthur. Anything,' she sighed. 'Just something to repair the day a bit.'

'Repair it?'

'Yes,' she nodded truculently. 'That's the only way to put it. Repair it. It's been bloody terrible, and you know it. Right from the start. And now look at this.'

'I wanted to go to Bournemouth,' I pointed out. 'This was an idea from your lot.'

'Christ, don't let's start putting the blame out to people,' she said. 'It's bad enough having a family like mine, but having yours added to it is a bloody sight worse. What a mess up it all was.'

I thought she was going to cry. I was standing before her. Our knees touched then she withdrew hers, from habit I suppose, but I located them again and put my knees against them once more. She looked at me and smiled.

'Sorry love,' she said thinly. I bent my head towards her and she kissed me on the cheek. 'It couldn't have been much fun for you either.'

'Oh, it was marvellous,' I said. 'Especially when they started marking their bleeding football coupons when I was making my speech.'

Pamela shrugged. 'What shall we do anyway? I don't want to stay in here. It's like a rabbit hutch.'

'Look,' I said taking her quietly by the shoulders. 'Why don't we clear out and go to a decent hotel somewhere else? There's bound to be one in the town. Even a place like this is certain to have a proper hotel. Somewhere where the railway directors stay. We'll stay there for tonight and then bugger off somewhere nice tomorrow. We could go to Weston-Super-Mare.'

'Not by the sea,' she said. 'Nowhere by the sea. I've said that all along. All you would do is look at the damn ships.'

'In the country, then,' I said with growing enthusiasm because I thought she had half accepted the idea. 'There's plenty of open country even around a mucky hole like this.'

'We can't,' she answered sharply. 'You *know* we can't. We can't upset Mrs Donelly because she lets my mum and dad stay here for a week of their holiday.'

'They ought to be bloody grateful if we got them out of that,' I said. 'The place is bad enough now, in the summer it must be even worse.'

'They go on coach trips,' she sulked. 'They say it's a good centre for going on coach trips. Cheddar Gorge. Places like that.'

'If you went to Hell for a day from here it would be a nice outing,' I grunted looking out of the window again.

'Look,' she snapped. 'If you want to start off with a row, we can. I'm fed up as it is. I just want to get out of here and go somewhere nice. Somewhere just a *bit* nice. Like a cocktail bar. So I'll have one decent hour to remember.'

'We could take a tour around the loco sheds,' I said putting my face back to the glass. 'It's probably the most exciting place in Swindon. We could throw stones at the engine drivers.'

'Funny, funny,' she grunted. She had eased her red patent shoes from her rounded feet. Now she started to push them on again. 'I'm going out,' she said decisively. 'Are you coming or not?'

'All right,' I said. 'I don't think I could think of anything to do in a bridal suite by myself.'

'Good,' she said, standing up and pushing her hair into clouds. 'Let's go somewhere nice, then, Arthur. Like a cocktail bar.'

I changed from my uniform into my brown honeymoon

suit because it was raining and we stumbled down the shadowed stairs. Mrs Donelly, a pepper-faced woman in a wrapped-around grey overall, appeared like a sentry at the bottom.

'Off out?' she exclaimed.

'Just for a walk,' I smiled.

'Walk? On your wedding night? Times *are* changing, I must say! You like the room, don't you?'

'Very nice,' confirmed Pamela.

'Lovely washbasin,' I added.

She looked at me narrowly in the dark. 'Don't scratch it whatever you do,' she said. 'It's almost new. You can't get them.'

'It looks it,' I said soothingly.

'Are you going for a *long* walk,' Mrs Donelly asked. 'A *very* long one?'

'We don't know,' I said. 'If we get to like it we might.'

'You'd better take a key, then,' she said. 'I'm not stopping up all night.'

She gave us the key and we went out into the damp, gritty evening. After the confining shadows of the house it was like walking into a meadow. I put my arm about my wife's coated waist and we walked along the sticky pavement while the Great Western Railway's engines whined and wheezed beyond the adjoining wall.

'There was no need to be rude to her, Arthur,' she said.

'Rude?'

'Yes, to Mrs Donelly. About the washbasin and that. I don't think it's the Westgate Hotel, Newport, myself, but we're only paying three pounds for the whole week. Remember that. What we save can go towards a bit more furniture.'

'I know, love,' I said squeezing her middle. 'I'm sorry. I just wish that we were in our own flat now. Right at this moment, so we could feel at home with each other.'

'Well we're not, and that's that,' she said. 'And it wouldn't be any good if we were there, because the place is full of greengrocery, sprouts and carrots and stuff, and it won't be cleared out until the end of the week.'

'Do you think it will smell?' I said conversationally.

'Smell?'

'Well, if it's been stuffed up with vegetables for years it's bound to smell of them isn't it?'

'We're lucky to get *anywhere*,' she sniffed. 'You know that, Arthur. It was very nice of my Uncle Ben to offer us the two rooms above the shop. At least we'll have a home. I'll have somewhere to live and you'll have somewhere to come back to. Other people have to muck in with their parents.'

'Yes, well done Uncle Ben,' I agreed. 'Where are we going?'

'There's buses at the top of the street,' she said. 'I just this moment saw one. They must go into the middle of the town and there's bound to be a hotel with a cocktail bar there.'

'You really want to go to a cocktail bar?'

'Yes, I do,' she said firmly. 'I want to sit down somewhere nice and have a nice, decent drink. Somewhere where it's warm and there's proper lights and decent people. Just something to make up for the rest of this bloody day.'

'Was it that bad?'

'Well, it wasn't good, was it?' She looked at me at first with a challenge, but she saw my expression and she looked sorry. 'You know it was terrible, Arthur,' she said more softly. 'A girl only has one wedding day. Only one *first* wedding day anyway.'

'If they're all like that, one's plenty,' I agreed.

'The vicar was a bit funny, though, wasn't he?'

'In his lifeboat outfit,' I agreed.

She began to giggle. 'I couldn't believe it,' she laughed. 'I still can't. They way he charged around the reception in that dripping stuff. He was like a big bat!'

'And what about my aunty slipping on her arse on the church path?' I said.

'Christ! And my lunatic Uncle Percy. Silly old fool. What was he shouting? "Leave me! Leave me behind"!'

'And your father taking his socks off to dry them at the reception.'

'And yours peeing himself laughing in the church.'

'Silly old cunt!'

'Arthur!'

'Well, he is. I could strangle that sod.'

'Has he always been like that?'

'Always. He despises me.' I paused: 'Can I ask you something, Pamela?'

'Of course. I won't say you'll get an answer. Wait a minute, let's run. There's a bus.'

We ran along the long, damp, pavement, and got the bus just as it was about to move. It was going into the centre of the town. We sat downstairs so that the conductor could tell us where to get off.

'We want a decent hotel,' announced Pamela. Several people looked around at her. She scratched her nose with her wedding ring finger. 'Somewhere where there's a decent cocktail bar.'

A fat woman across the middle aisle, peeping from under a hood like some massive pixie, snorted vividly at this and turned her face away.

The conductor intoned: 'Two tuppennies George and Dragon.' It was only a few stops. When we left the bus it began to rain heavily and we ran, hand in hand, towards the expansive doorway, glowing like a furnace in the dismal town. There were soft swing doors and in a moment the warmth of the place closed around us, our feet were on its good carpet, and there was a slow smile on the round, pretty face of my wife.

'Cocktail bar, please,' she said to the porter.

'To the left, madam,' he answered on cue. 'May I take your coats?'

He took them. She began to purr. It was a nice place, the sort of nice place she liked, with beams and pots of spring flowers, and big rocking spitoons for ashtrays about the floor. The cocktail bar had subdued coloured lights and a man playing a violin, sitting alone on a modestly raised platform at one end. He played softly but tediously, his nose apparently welded to the instrument. There were a few people in the place, but the music just covered their voices.

'I love a good violin,' she sighed impressively. 'When it's played properly it's better than anything else.'

'I didn't know you knew anything about music,' I said.

'Just shows how much we don't know about each other.' She wasn't looking at me, she was looking about the room. I held her hand. A waiter came over and Pamela asked for a double crème de menthe. At random I asked for a Drambuie. 'That's right,' she encouraged. 'Let's enjoy ourselves. Let's have a good time.' Abruptly she turned and squeezed my elbow. 'It's nice here isn't it, pet? It really is.'

'Very nice,' I agreed. 'It's like somewhere expensive in London.'

'We'll go to London as soon as we can.' She made it sound like a promise. 'The shops and everything. And we could go and see shows.'

'We ought to have gone this time,' I said.

'Don't start that again Arthur, there's a good boy. You know why we came to Swindon. And it *is* very nice here isn't it? In here, I mean.'

'I was going to ask you something,' I said.

'Ask me something? When was that?'

'When we were running for the bus. Just before.'

'Yes, I remember. What was it, pet?'

'It was about your grandfather.'

'Oh, did you just see him today! Just like him, the old silly. Hole in his pullover.'

'Yes, I did. But it wasn't that. As it happens it was another hole I was thinking about.'

'What hole?'

'*Your bedroom keyhole*. Does he still do his peeping tom act?'

She frowned. 'Fancy bringing that up,' she said.

'Well does he?'

She shrugged: 'Yes,' she said simply. 'He was there last night when I was trying on my wedding dress. I know he was. My mother caught him at it a few weeks ago and he pretended he was all bent up with indigestion.'

'And he *saw* you last night?'

'I expect so. It was the last time anyway. Unless I stay at home sometimes.'

I sat dumb. The waiter arrived with the drinks and I'd drunk half of mine before I pursued it. 'He saw you *naked*. With nothing on?'

'Well, yes.' She looked perplexed at the questions. 'I was in my undies and things, but I stripped right off as well. I expect he saw me then. He wouldn't have wanted to miss that.'

I drew in my breath then turned to her. 'I think that's bloody disgusting,' I said angrily. 'Nothing short of bloody disgusting!'

'Shush! You mustn't use language like that in here.' Her face had emptied of colour. 'We come to somewhere decent and you swear and shout like that.'

'Listen,' I snarled, but considerately lower. 'Don't *you* think it's disgusting? Don't you? That dirty old bugger looking through the keyhole at you. And you showing him everything. Christ, he's seen more of you than *I* have. And I'm your husband.'

'You're seen my bosoms,' she corrected severely. 'You've done more than just see them. You practically fried them in candle fat, if I remember rightly.'

'That's all I *have* seen,' I said nastily. I finished my drink and the waiter began to circle us. 'I'll have another,' said Pamela to both of us. 'Double crème de menthe, if you please.' I wanted to say I would have a beer, but in a strange way I was afraid of her so I asked for another Drambuie.

'Think what you've got to come. What a treat,' she said haughtily.

'It's only a Drambuie,' I grunted.

'I mean with *me*,' she sniffed. 'There's the rest of me. All my body. You can see what my grandad's seen.'

'Thanks,' I said but mollified because I really wanted us to be happy that night. 'I'll be looking forward to it.'

'I wonder if that man on the violin does requests,' she said abandoning the subject as easily as she always did. 'Do

171

you think he'll do the Persil's thing for us? I thought it sounded lovely on the organ. When you could hear it above the wind, that is.'

To my surprise she got up and threaded through the chairs and tables, around a group of half a dozen people who had just come in, and up to the violinist. He was deaf and he made her shout her request close to his ear. She returned laughing and one of the middle-aged men in the group caught her hand as she went by and made a joke to her. She laughed deliciously and I sat and groaned deep within myself, wondering if she would ever laugh like that with me.

The violinist couldn't play her request, or he did not hear properly, because he launched himself into a series of solitary waltzes. 'He's lovely,' sighed Pamela. 'I do like the violin. When it's well played.'

We left after about an hour. The half-dozen people in the group got up at about the same time and went by us into the hotel dining room. For one terrible moment I thought Pamela was going to suggest following them. But she gave an infinitesimal shrug and we went out into the town again. The porter pushed the swing door for us.

'You ought to have tipped him,' she said when we were in the street. The rain had stopped and there was a pasty moon coming up at the end of the road.

'Who? The violinist?'

'No, the porter. You always have to tip porters. Surely you know that. That's why they stand there like that.'

'But he only shoved the bleeding door for us. I didn't ask him to do it.'

'He told us the way to the cocktail bar,' she corrected, walking ahead in a tubby but dainty way, her superior nose sniffing at the air.

'I feel like doing something else,' she announced breezily.

So did I. But instead I said: 'Well, what?'

'Dancing,' she smiled. 'I really *would* like to go dancing, Arthur.' I felt my face set. We stood in the street, facing each other, on this the evening of our wedding day, her persuasive smile forming slowly. Her eyes had become coy. 'Come on,' she encouraged me. 'There must be somewhere where there's *decent* dancing. It's Saturday.'

'It's our wedding night,' I mumbled.

'I know,' she said. 'If you want to go back to Spooky Hollow right away, then I'll come with you. It's just I'd like to go somewhere first, just to sort of warm up.' She lowered the coy eyes again. 'To get me in the mood.'

We went. The place was proclaimed as The Roxy in coloured lights, but some joker who knew where the leads were located had blacked out the second leg of the letter R. I experienced a quick squirt of hope as we went in, for a man in a smutty dinner jacket advanced on us holding his hands like fenders.

'Too late, old lad,' he boomed. 'Place is jammed. It's half past ten.'

'Right,' I nodded thankfully and began to turn Pamela towards the door which had hardly stopped swinging from our entry.

But she smiled her fattest smile at him and caught hold of his purple hand. 'Go on, let us in,' she persuaded. 'It's our wedding day.'

I could not believe she was saying the words. Trading something as personal and private and embarrassing as that for an entry ticket to a sweaty dance hall. I stared at her, but she still had her hand on his and he was beaming back.

'Today?' he inquired unbelievingly. 'Married today? And you've come *here* tonight?' His glance, at once a nasty and pitying glance, shot my way. Then his face exploded into a laugh. 'Oh, you must come on in! Have the freedom of the house. This is really terrific! Terrific!'

Pamela swung jubilantly on me. 'There,' she exclaimed. 'I told you it would be all right.'

'Let me relieve you of your coats,' he said pompously. 'And then you must come and have a drink, a nuptial drink, with me in the office. Now, tell me your names.'

'Mr and Mrs McCann,' she volunteered immediately. 'Pamela and Arthur. From Newport.'

'My name is Digby Frost,' he boomed. 'I'm the manager.' He paused, then said: 'From Newport . . .?' The remote thought arrived. 'You're not in *Swindon* for your honeymoon are you?'

'We are,' gurgled Pamela triumphantly.

The news appeared to shatter even him. 'Swindon, on *honeymoon*,' he repeated and looked at me with that snide pity again, now mixed with the suspicion that anyone who honeymoons in Swindon deserves.

He took our coats to the cloakroom counter and threw them across with an extravagant cry: 'Hilda – these are on the house!'

'Nothing's spared,' I grunted.

Pamela glanced sulkily at me. 'Don't start,' she warned.

'I don't think I ever will,' I forecast bitterly. Then Mr Frost zoomed back and took us through the double doors into the ballroom. The heat, the music, the fetid air jostled each other to get out. Youths with their hands in their pockets and girls picking their teeth were thick around the walls. There were others crowded around the floor, their heads silhouetted against an explosion of purple light which was haloed around the band.

'Terrific!' Pamela howled in Mr Frost's ear as we pummelled our way through the mob. I saw that she now had hold of the elbow of his dinner jacket.

'Best band in Wiltshire!' the manager bellowed at her.

'And they've got their new stardust jackets on tonight,' he added, half turning to include me in the information.

'Terrific!' responded Pamela.

'Terrific,' I groaned.

He poured us two double scotches, poured a lemonade for himself and toasted our future. Pamela sipped hers to the bottom of the glass. I am sure that *this* was the drink that did it. That *this* was the moment when the rot began, when our marriage began to go wrong. On top of the crème de menthe it was too much. As I watched her streaking towards the dance floor with the manager I knew that I had as good as lost her for that night, and, in a way, forever.

I stood in the ranks of Swindon's youth, my fists as clenched, my eyes as bored, my jaw working on the same non-existent gum as any of them, while my wife, happy-faced, hands like half-hung wings, performed the stuttering steps of a tango with the sweating manager.

'Now I don't reckon that's right,' muttered the youth next to me.

'What?' I asked miserably.

He had a yawning West Country voice: 'That soddin' Frostie takin' the girls on the floor. There ain't a bloody nuff to go around anyway.' He turned on me challengingly: 'Ain't you got one then?'

'Well I have and I haven't,' I said. 'That's mine poncing around with Frostie.'

He looked at them and then back at me again. 'Yours?' he said. 'Now, I wouldn't stand for that, boy. If you like I'll get some of my mates and we could duff him up a bit. We been wanting to give that bastard a duffing up for months.'

I might have gone gladly with this suggestion, but Pamela and her partner, after a shouted conversation during their Latin American advances and retreats across the floor, broke up and came towards me. Pamela was gushing with enthusiasm: 'Come on Arthur, pet. Come with us.'

Stiffly I moved forward, towards her outstretched hands. Her modest engagement ring was flashing like a signal in the light reflected from the revolving globe above the middle of that great hole.

'Go on, Arthur, pet,' mimicked the youth who had talked to me. 'Go on, pet.'

I was so sick and low with it all, the drink curdling inside me, the raging noise hitting my ears, that I was tempted to turn, give the tormentor one good punch, then run from the hideous place and vanish forever. Even back to Port de Loupe.

But Pamela had taken hold of me with more enthusiasm and tenderness than she had shown all through what should have been that most enthusiastic and tender of days. I was disconcerted by the knowledge of Mr Frost's podgy hand urging me forward with pats on the bottom. Then I realized what they were going to do. We were mounting the steps to the stage, among the musicians in their dazzling new stardust jackets. The bandleader, a moribund-looking man, who wore a gold jacket to contrast with the silver garments of his musicians, held up one hand and the music stopped except for one sleepy saxophone which went on wailing alone until nudged by a neighbouring performer, whereupon he ceased and looked about froggily.

The manager threw a whisper to the bandleader, who looked at me accusingly and then smiled a starved smile at my wife. Evidently the musicians had already summed up the situation and they bored into the palais arrangement of the wedding march. On the floor below the activity slowed and stopped and the white faces of the youth of Swindon and surrounding districts were lifted up to us. I shivered with the shame of that moment (I still do) but I looked across to Pamela and I could see her glowing.

'Ladies and gentlemen, boys and girls,' bellowed Mr Frost into the microphone when the band had finished its introduction. 'I want a big cheer for Mr and Mrs Mc-Cann . . .' He turned to us and hand over the mike inquired, 'That's right, McCann?' I nodded woodenly. He uncovered the instrument again. 'Mr and Mrs McCann . . . Pamela and . . . and . . .'

'Arthur,' helped out Pamela. 'Pamela and Arthur.'

'And Arthur,' continued the moron. 'Who come from Newport and were *married* only this afternoon!'

There was an astonishing chorus of female oooooohs and aaaaahs, like wind echoing in a tuneful mountain hole. There followed some spontaneous rudery from the youths yawning against the walls, but over this the manager flung his trump: 'And they are spending their honeymoon . . . guess where?'

'Bed!' a young man bellowed from the rear.

'In Swindon!' bellowed Mr Frost and this was apparently even funnier because he had to shout over the uproar: 'Three cheers for Pamela and Alan.'

'Arthur,' I whispered and nobody heard. The band

started up again and glasses of West Country champagne were poured out on the rostrum. We were toasted and we drank. Everybody cheered. Pamela screwed up her nose at the bubbles as though she were advertising the stuff. Then Mr Frost patted me on the shoulder and said: 'I think that was all right don't you? We didn't leave anything out.'

'Nothing,' I answered wearily, sadly. 'Nothing at all. Unless you'd like us to do a demonstration fuck.'

13

Even after this distance of years I keenly recall how embarrassing and difficult it was to get Pamela back to The Shunter's Arms Hotel that night. The amount and variety of the drinks she had swallowed made her noisy, violent and very truculent. At The Roxy the manager and what seemed to be relays of other men, who kept appearing from the noisy shadows, bought her drinks and she kept drinking them. It had all the appearances of a one-person wedding because I was completely ignored while she laughed and danced and made an exhibition of herself. I bought an ice-cream cone and sat quietly and licked it. It failed to mix with the Drambuie and West Country champagne and I went out of the hall and was sick. I felt much emptier, cooler and better after that. When I returned Pamela was in the centre of a sweating chorus line doing the Palais Glide (God, was it that long ago?), hooting her head off. She had not noticed my exit, and neither had anyone else. For all my bride knew I might have gone out to cut my throat. I certainly felt like it.

We were the last to leave the dance hall. By this time she had been reduced from a bride to an encumbrance. She hung on to my neck like a murdered albatross as I stood on the cold steps outside. The manager had, at last, gone home, not without giving me a final pitying handshake and Pamela a passionate embrace. 'Mr McCann,' he said, one encouraging arm on my shoulder. 'Or I think by now I can call you Alan . . .'

'Try Arthur,' I suggested.

'Arthur,' he agreed as though conceding a fifty-fifty point. 'I just want to tell you that you've got a great woman, there.'

'I think you're right, Mr Frost,' I nodded holding up my heavy bride. I shivered in the Swindon damp and tried to hold my face away from hers for the alcoholic fumes were thick. Eventually a taxi came patrolling down the street and we went back to the hotel.

No bridegroom has ever been more miserably tired on his wedding night. I heaved her up the stairs, not caring whether we woke Mrs Donelly or anyone else who was sheltering in The Shunter's Arms that night. But, unchallenged, we reached our wretched bridal suite and I rolled her out upon the counterpane that should have been covering our night of love. She was out cold, her hair sticking across her forehead, her face pallid, her knee staring through a hole in her stocking, the result of a fall during one of her tribal dances.

I was hunched at the side of the bed for half an hour as though keeping religious vigil on a corpse. The thought crossed my mind that I ought to undress her and put her into the bed, but as I leaned forward to touch her coat she emitted a grisly little snore and instead of touching her I turned and walked angrily from the room. Without hiding my footsteps I went down the stairs and out into the void street. I seemed to be spending a lot of my time walking in the dark at that period of my life.

The street was as comforting as a sewer pipe. Over the tall wall the engines were still stirring; trucks and wagons butted each other metallically in the dank distance. I trudged the length of the dumb houses and then turned a dark corner and another, without object, without thought. I felt almost weightless. Around the third corner, half way up the street, was one wall square with lights, music and noise squeezing out of its open windows and above that the sound of a girl singing with careless verve. There were three cars parked against the kerb and a herd of bicycles and motor cycles in the little patch of front garden beyond the privet hedge.

The pavement and the front path to the open door were spotted with damp confetti. The house seemed piled up with people. I stood for a moment looking into the door and, hardly crediting what I knew I was doing, I casually walked in.

There were three or four couples grappling romantically in the narrow hall. I smiled as though I knew everyone and nodded left and right and then turned craftily into a front parlour full of people shuffling in each other's arms. There was no musical accompaniment at that moment and I saw that the record on the radiogram near the door needed changing. It was revolving impotently, moaning to itself. I lifted the arm and turned it over, then thinking they might have played that side just previously, I took another record from the bottom of a heavy pile and put it on. Fortunately it was a slow tune and they continued with their minimal movements, lips against ears and cheeks, damp happy smiles, full arms. I saw some bottles on a table and poured myself a thick brown ale. I took a swallow and sat back on the edge of the table surveying them, trying to look as though I had been there for hours. At last I had found myself a wedding.

'What time is it, then?'

'Ten past one,' I answered. I turned to see who she was. She was leaning against the table, looking at the dancers through the bottom of her empty glass.

'Do they look any better through there?' I asked.

'Different,' she said. 'I wouldn't say "better". Here, you can have a look if you like, my dear.'

The elderly endearment did not sound odd because she was young, for her voice was undisguised rural West Country.

She handed me the glass with the air of a good child who doesn't mind sharing her toys. I held it up cooperatively and squinted through at the people.

'It looks even more crowded,' I said. I returned the glass to her. She was thin and a bit gaunt, but with strong eyes

179

and straight dark hair, long over her shoulders. She wore some sort of gipsy dress and, remembering her now, I realize that she was before her time because she looked like the girls you see around today. But in those days she was a rarity. If I did not know it then, I knew it later.

'Did you put this record on? You did didn't you? I saw you from the door.'

'Yes,' I admitted. 'It's all right, isn't it?' She nodded. I wondered if she had seen me come in. I said: 'Are you having a good time?'

'Oh aye, I always do,' she said. 'Haven't seen you around before. Been here all the time?'

'Oh, I came a bit late,' I said truthfully.

'Ah, you missed the performance then.'

'The performance? Oh, the wedding. Yes, I had to go to another wedding, and I said I'd just drop in as soon as I could.'

'You're not from around here, are you? You sound a bit Welsh.'

'I'm from Newport.' I thought the conversation was becoming dangerous. 'Want to dance?'

She did not say anything, but leaned logically against me, looping casual arms around my neck, and moved me gently back among the other dancers.

'Suppose you knew Ken, did you? When he was in Wales?'

'Ken,' I said. 'Yes, I knew him. Yes, in Wales.'

'Just think of them now,' she sighed. 'Making love.'

She glanced around the corner of my face and laughed at my expression. 'Well, they are,' she insisted. 'Down there in Bournemouth between the sheets. Ken will have fixed it all nice. Grand Hotel, champagne in the room. All that sort of thing. He's got a bit of style Ken, even if he's got no money. And I think you need a bit of style on a wedding night, don't you?'

'Definitely,' I said.

'You married?'

'Well, sort of.'

'Not getting on?' She sounded concerned more than just

interested, as though she might be able to help.

'I suppose you could say that.'

'Is she here then, your wife?'

The suggestion made me jerk guiltily. 'Oh no,' I said, nevertheless glancing around. 'She's not here. We're sort of . . . apart . . . temporarily.'

'That's how marriages should always be,' she sighed. 'Apart. It's better for a lot of people that way.'

'And you're one?'

'I'm one of two,' she agreed. 'Now, when you're married you can't do the things you want to do, can you?'

'You can say that again,' I agreed. How did it come about that on my wedding night my bride was drunk and unconscious in The Shunter's Arms, Swindon, and I was groping around a strange room with a strange girl who spoke with a voice like a farmyard.

'You sound like Lorna Doone,' I said. 'You've got that voice.'

'Not as far west as that,' she responded close to my ear. 'But far enough west. My old man says that with this voice I ought to be carrying a yoke and a couple of churns.'

'I'm not really supposed to be here,' I heard myself confessing, 'I don't really know Ken or anybody. I just walked in just now. I gate-crashed. It was just that I happened to be going by.'

'I know,' she said.

'You saw me come in?'

'Aye, because I walked in just before you. I don't know a bloody soul here either.'

'You're kidding! How about Ken?'

'Who's Ken?'

'The bridegroom, isn't he? You said so. You said he's gone to Bournemouth with the bride.'

'I made it up,' she said flatly. 'I knew you wouldn't know, so I just made it up. I could tell that you were sneaking in the way you came through the door. You looked like one of them spies.' I heard her laugh privately next to my ear.

'I saw the lights,' I said. 'So I took the chance.'

'There's no risk,' she assured. 'Not if it's as late as this. I do it all the time.'

'All the time? Walking into people's parties?'

'Every Saturday. I've been to more parties in Swindon than anybody in the town. Some people even recognize me from party to party. If they ask you how you came to be there it's easy to say that you came with George or Ronnie or Beryl, but they've gone home and left you.'

'You must like parties a lot,' I said. 'You must be keen. I wouldn't have the guts.'

'It's better than being by yourself.' We were shuffling, facing each other now. I looked closely at her. Her thin face was serious, her eyes still.

'You're by yourself a lot then?' I said.

'A fair amount. When you come to think about it, it's a bit strange that when you get married you start being by yourself.'

I said I knew what she meant. 'Where is he then, your husband?'

'He just goes away. He's working. You won't believe this, but the council here send him all over the place.'

'Swindon Council?'

'Yes, he's a dustman.'

'And he travels about? That's a new sort of dustman, isn't it?'

'Well, he's not just your ordinary, common or garden, pig-swill-humping dustman. He's one of the few who knows how to operate the new automatic refuse disposal machines. Or he says he is. That's what he tells me. They're very dangerous if they're not worked properly. Apparently they can just swallow up a dustman whole, and when they've finished all that's left is his flybuttons.'

I laughed, but she continued to look serious. 'It's the truth,' she said. 'And Bertram is one of the few in the country who knows all about them. So the council lend him out all over the place. Otherwise there would be hardly any dustmen left.'

Somehow, with my set ideas about women in those days,

I could not reconcile the way she talked, her accent, with the things she said. Until the record finished we said nothing then I said: 'Why don't you let me take you home?' I had been thinking of asking her for some time, but I had hesitated because, after all, it *was* my wedding night.

Even then, at the moment I said it, I had a thought that I ought to get away from her and from that place, and creep back to The Shunter's Arms and my snoring bride. But she said 'All right.'

'I'll get my coat,' she said. 'I shoved it in that hall cupboard when I came in. Is yours in there too?'

I did not have a coat and I waited for her and helped her on with hers while she smiled convincing and familiar goodnights to everyone around. Then, from the door, she called to a girl who was pressed close to a youth on the stairs: 'See you at the clinic, then. 'Bye.'

'I thought you didn't know anyone,' I said when we were in the drizzling street again.

'I didn't. Only you.'

'What about the girl you're going to see at the clinic?'

'I don't know her either,' she said shaking her rope of hair. 'I only said that on the spur of the moment.'

I laughed with surprise. 'He backed away from her very quickly,' I said.

'His expression changed a bit,' she agreed. 'But I didn't like her anyway. Accused me of drinking her gin when I first went into the place.'

'And you did.'

'Accident. You have to have a drink in your hand or you don't look as if you belong at the party. That's one of the secrets of being accepted.'

'Being accepted,' I repeated. 'That's a bit of a job anywhere.'

'Half life is being accepted. Look at us. My old man doesn't accept me, and your wife doesn't accept you. And we're married to the bastards.'

I did not like her calling Pamela a bastard, because, after all they had never met. But I stopped myself saying anything about it. Instead I said: 'But we accepted each other right away. You and I, I mean.'

'A thief to know a thief,' she laughed.

'How far do you live?' I put my arm around her small waist. It felt strange and starved after Pamela's.

'Just here,' she said. 'Be a bit quiet because that's a pet shop underneath and if I make the slightest row coming in it wakes up a crazy parrot they've got and he starts to scream and it wakes all the other things, so before you know what's happening it's like Noah's Ark.'

We sidled up the stairs. My guilt was now effectively engulfed by my excitement. She went ahead of me and put a light on at the top, just within the door. On the stairs she had pulled up the skirt of the long coloured gipsy garment she was wearing, and I looked up to see it drawn tight across her slim backside. From behind the wall to my right I heard a clucking and put my head to the wallpaper.

'Poultry,' she said. 'Ducks, chickens. You can smell them. It's supposed to be a pet shop, but it's more like an indoor farm sometimes.'

I went through the entrance. Two brand new metal dustbins were parked behind the door and another was a few feet up the short passage. 'My husband brings home his work,' she explained tapping the lid of the first one with her finger tips. 'He steals the good ones and sells them again. He couldn't be a jeweller or something like that and bring home diamonds or emeralds, worse luck.'

We went into a room furnished in such a haphazard fashion that everything looked as though it had been dumped anywhere. Books, hundreds of books, were in piles on the floor, while a line of bookshelves stood empty as the rungs of a ladder. A small table was lying on its side in one corner and casual chairs were standing around like loiterers.

'You haven't been in long?' I concluded looking around.

'Two years in June,' she shrugged. 'Like a drink?'

'Yes, I will have one, thanks. What's your name? You didn't tell me.'

'Belinda,' she said. 'Belinda Storey-Stroud. No, that's

terrible. Belinda Brown. Does that sound better?'

'The first one sounded all right to me,' I said.

'I made it up. I'm a terrible liar, you'll have to realize that. I do it all the time.'

'Well, I'm Arthur,' I said. 'Arthur McCann and that's the honest truth.'

'I don't care if it isn't,' she said. 'Now, drinks.' She put her thin fingers to her mouth. 'Christ, darling, we've only got elderberry wine. My father sends it up from Somerset. I call it Parishes Food, because he's a vicar. Do you know any clergymen?'

'I was with one this afternoon,' I admitted.

'Mine's enough to put you off vicars, the Archbishop, the Pope, the Holy Ghost, Jesus, God himself. When I was a little girl I found him urinating against the tombstone of a churchwarden he had disliked. Rotten bugger. Don't you think that's a low thing to do?'

'Well, for a vicar, I suppose so,' I said. 'But it couldn't have hurt a dead churchwarden.'

She looked thoughtful. She poured the pale elderberry wine from a stone bottle into two dusty glasses. 'Well it hurt me,' she said. 'I was only a kid, and I'd liked that man very much, the churchwarden. I used to stay with him a lot of the time and I thought it was my fault he was dead.'

I sat on the edge of a divan covered with a large, red check tablecloth. The wine tasted like syrup. She sat next to me, nursing her drink in her lap, looking far away beyond the walls.

'Why was that?' I asked.

'Why was what?' She shook her head, rousing herself.

'What you said. That you thought it was your fault he was dead.'

'Oh, that. Well, I used to have this funny idea when I was a little girl. I really thought I *killed* people. Just by *being* with them. First my mother. I loved her, of course, and she died, and I went to live with my grandparents, and they were both under the ground in a year. Then we had a house-keeper who committed suicide by tipping herself into the rain butt, and then Mr Jenkins, the churchwarden, who was a dear friend. If you ever thought of doing yourself in, by the way, the rain butt is the thing. Once you've tipped over there's no getting out because your legs stick straight up into the air. I can still see poor Mrs Powell's legs standing up out of the barrel. Even now.' She made the point seriously and in her yokel's voice it sounded all the more serious. 'They all went, one after the other,' she went on, 'and I truthfully thought that it was me who was knocking them off, that I was having this effect on them. You can probably understand that I was very upset about this and I couldn't tell anybody because I was only a child and thought you could be put to death for killing people like that. Anyway I asked my father if I could live with him and nobody else and, of course, he kept on living and that made me think that I wasn't really to blame after all. Either that or I'd lost the gift.'

'You don't feel that you do that now, do you?'

'Oh no,' she smiled. 'Don't worry. You're safe with me.'

'I didn't mean that.'

I felt that in the normal order of things I ought to kiss her or throw her on the bed or do something similarly masculine but, for once, my instincts played fair, I held back, and it was right.

'Why did you come to live here?' I asked. Then I realized she might have thought I meant that particular slovenly room, so I said: 'In Swindon.'

'Bertram thought the streets might be paved with gold,' she laughed. She sat down on the divan and patted the quilt-tablecloth at her side and I sat down beside her. We conversed sitting upright like strangers in a railway compartment.

'That's London, I always thought,' I said.

'Where the streets are paved with gold?' she asked, absent from me again. 'Yes, I know now. But we only had enough fare to get here. Poor Bertram. All he found in the streets of Swindon was garbage. And it's his job to pick it up. He's too good for that, really. Bertram's got brains, but he never seems to find a job where they need them. When we first came he worked in the new crematorium. He used to call himself the "crème de la crematorium". He's clever, you see. But he lost that. Some mix up with the bodies, as though it matters who's next.'

She revolved the elderberry wine in her glass reflectively and said: 'Still, I don't mind. I like towns. They're nice and hugging all around you. It's the country that scares me. All those trees and manglewurzles and men in the fields with bare chests calling after little girls, and all that singing over marrows in the church at harvest time. All is safely gathered in. Christ, I couldn't stand it! Every time I heard my father preaching to those people and telling them to live better lives I could see him pissing up against that churchwarden's headstone. And he was wearing his cassock. It must have been quite difficult in that because he had to lift it up like some old lady.'

Slowly I said: 'I don't think I've ever met anyone like you, before.' I meant it.

'Probably you haven't,' she agreed glumly. 'But I'll do for tonight, won't I?'

The bald honesty of the statement stunned me. I sat holding my drink down by my knees as though it were some sort of ticket that someone would be collecting soon. I felt urged to say something equally honest in return.

'Actually,' I said, looking down at the floor through the glass. 'This is my wedding night.'

Even that did not shake her. 'I had an idea it was,' she said. 'That suit you're wearing is a wedding suit if I ever saw one. It's a wonder it's not embroidered with bells. Those creases! If you crossed your legs you'd cut one off just above the knee.'

I examined my trouser creases. She was right.

'Has she gone home to mum?'

'No, not that. Pamela wouldn't do that. She'd be sure we stayed away for the week even if we never even passed a civil word. Just for the appearance of the thing, you see. No,

I'm afraid she got herself well plastered this evening and she's flat out at the hotel.'

'And you didn't stay with her like a good bridegroom should?'

'No. No, I didn't. I was fed up. There's other things ...'

She nodded. 'There's always "other things",' she said. 'As soon as you get married you start opening up little cubby holes in the other person and seeing things you never knew about before.'

'I don't think I can say it was quite like that,' I said, defending Pamela. 'But I was just fed up. I only meant to go out for a walk tonight. I didn't mean to get involved, or anything.'

'Go on with you,' she admonished, her voice deep and rural again. 'Nobody goes out at this time of night not meaning to get into trouble. Not half-hoping to meet somebody. They might not even admit it to themselves. But you haven't even got the excuse of a dog to walk.'

'Well, I'm here anyway,' I shrugged.

'And I am too,' she said, all at once with tenderness added to her practical observation. She had remained sitting formally at my side, but now she rose and turned and sank almost with relief down in front of me, kneeling and laying her thin body against my trembling legs and her head in my lap. Her hair sprawled out between my thighs like a black sporran. I was still holding my glass and I tried to reach for a side table with it but it was minutely out of reach. I plunged my left hand gently into her hair and swung around carefully but helplessly with the elderberry wine in my right.

Finding no solution and fearful less the magic opportunity should be broken by such a stupid inconvenience, I swigged back the rest of the wine, and tossed the glass gently so that it landed on the only rug in the place, a few feet away. For once I did not miss.

Both of my hands now searched through her mass of hair and ran down to the soft plank of her neck. Then I rubbed her shoulders and finally let both hands loop beneath her armpits with the palms against the flanks of her breasts. Her face came up to me and she said: 'I'll give you a wedding night, Arnold.'

'Arthur,' I said, but not caring this time.

'I can usually cry at this stage,' she said frankly. 'I can do it to order. If I just squeeze my eyes in a certain way the tears just ooze out. It's a very good technique, but I don't seem to want to do it with you. While my head's been down there I've been squeezing away like buggery and I can't get one drip out of them.'

'Do you want to have another go?' I said. 'Put your head back there if you like and try again.'

'No, we'll do without the tears. Perhaps it's a good omen. Perhaps it will be more like the real thing.'

'It will be the real thing,' I promised. When I remember saying that I feel embarrassed for myself because I did not know what I was saying. Her idea of the real thing and mine were so distant that I have to laugh.

Perversion had hardly entered my young life. My only experience of those frightening shadows had been with the bloated Mr Gander and I had remained triumphant, unsullied, and without shame. Apart, of course, from the fact that I murdered him. Before that my only remembrance of anything the least murky and exotic was in an early childhood dream in which I saw myself pushing my protesting mother up our chimney. For some reason it gave me a thrill of infantile sexual pleasure to be shoving her up the flue and to hear her bleating through the cascading soot.

My guilt over this absurdity had long before evaporated and, in any case, at that period, my lifelong efforts to get the maximum of ordinary sex, sufficient for the day without needing the evil, had left little time or room or, truthfully, desire for anything more complicated. Although at eighteen, I had experienced more women and quixotic situations than most men enjoy, or fail to enjoy throughout their life, I had been, in fact, building up a balance of normal unexotic experience. I had sought numbers not variations.

Now, this long faced girl with the black hair, asked me to undo the small toadstool buttons down her back and I did so carefully, savouring the widening gap in her gipsy dress at every moment. The bamboo bumps of her neckbone, gently curved towards me, increased in number with each released button. She remained bent in front of me and when my fingers had finished the buttons and had reached her tail, she dropped her hands to her sides and in three almost petulant wriggles had the dress lying about her knees.

That first time she was quiet and very slow, almost dream-like in her disinterest, merely laying her thin, white form across the divan and waiting for me to go to her. I folded my wedding suit carefully, those crackling creases sneering at me, telling me all the terrible things I was telling myself. Truthfully I think that I could have gone out then were it not for the embarrassment and upset of replacing my clothes. She lay slim and stiff as an ironing board, eyes closed, taper-ing arms at her sides, more like someone awaiting a doctor than a lover.

To relieve my conscience a little, and this is while I was still aware that I possessed the formidable combination of a conscience and a wife, I allowed myself a quick mental sound of Pamela's pungent snore. This assured me and I went to Belinda on her bed and made love to her.

It is pointless my pretending that this first amalgamation was not slightly dull. It had neither warmth nor movement. I even found myself wishing for Pamela's lumpy body, for this girl lay like a lath, eyes dead, body flaccid. At one point my shuttle movement caused my eyes to travel over the drop of the divan and on the floor I saw the yellow cover of a lurid book which she must have been reading in bed at some time. Its purple-lettered title was *Ruined by A Mad Secretary* and it was embellished with a crude, but I have to admit intriguing, photograph of a naked female hanging from some chains.

My present occupation was at such a slow pace that with each forward movement I was able to discern more detail in the picture and eventually to turn over to the first page and begin to read. The woman to whom I was making love showed no sign that she knew what I was doing.

It was a badly written book, but baldly exciting, and very dirty from the first paragraph. There was a multiple whipping going on in some ancient kingdom, administered (the whipping, not the kingdom) by small, strong, men who rode on miniature donkeys and belaboured beautiful female captives as they trotted by.

'It's very wicked, isn't it?' murmured Belinda without opening her eyes.

'What? Being here like this?'

'The book,' she sighed. 'The dirty book.'

'The book? Oh, the one on the floor? Well, I must say it did catch my eye.'

'Don't lie,' she reproved but still sleepily. 'You're reading the bloody thing. I can tell even without looking because you've improved all round in the last couple of minutes.'

I stopped with embarrassment. 'Don't be worried,' she continued quietly. 'That's why I left it there. Wouldn't you like to do some of those awful things, Arthur?'

'I can't ride a donkey,' I said, all at once afraid. 'I've not been on one since I was a kid at Barry Island.'

'Stop dodging it.' It was amazing how that farmyard voice could sound so evil. She was moving her thighs much more easily now and her lips were wet on my cheek.

'What were you thinking of doing?' I asked.

'Just imagine,' she whispered. 'Just picture, if you can, that I had my hands tied or chained above me . . . How would you like me, Arthur, tied or chained?'

She paused for the answer, far less embarrassed and worried than I was. 'Whichever's more comfortable,' I muttered.

'*Less* comfortable,' she corrected. 'Don't go and mess it up. It's only a game.'

'Yes,' I agreed. 'I understand that.'

'But it's a serious game. It's no use playing it if it's not.'

'All right,' I said, hiding my face in her neck. 'Tied.'

'Thick rope or thin?'

'Christ,' I groaned. 'Thin. Will that be all right? Which have we got the most of?'

'Stop it,' she warned. 'You've got to do it properly.'

'Well, thin. That will cut into your wrists.'

'You dirty beast,' she sighed.

She gravely extended her arms above her head and linked her hands as though they were secured.

'There,' she said. 'I'm tied with thin rope. Now what are you going to do with me?'

I didn't know. After all it was her game. 'Tie your feet?' I suggested.

'Good, very good. You're learning. But you tie my feet, my ankles, with something soft. Like a piece torn from my clothing.'

Hardly was the cue out than I made a realistic ripping sound and felt her react beneath me. 'Where did you tear that from?' she inquired with splendidly acted dread.

'Your dress,' I volunteered. My God, she felt different now. I thought she was going to burst and me with her.

'Not yet, not just yet,' she asked. She took three or four deep breaths, which apparently levelled her off. 'You tore it from my dress, you swine. My lovely summer dress. My silk dress with the pretty yellow and red flowers on the bodice . . .'

These fashion notes went on for some time and included the information that the dress had been given to her by her father, which may have been significant or not. Freud would know, but I didn't. And I must confess that despite the oddity of it all and the embarrassment, felt by me if not by her, I was dropping almost mesmerized into the charade. I felt like iron inside despite my prudish inclination to pull myself out of the fantasy and observe it for what it was. Jesus, I was enjoying myself! Now, on top of all my troubles, I was a sadist as well!

'Now you have torn my dress what are you going to do?' she asked. I got the feeling she would have been happier if she had not had to prompt her tormentor so much and had been freer to wallow in her own role. I ventured: 'I am going to tear away the rest of your clothes.'

'Garments,' she muttered.

'Garments,' I agreed, wondering at the nuances of the

pastime. 'I am going to tear them away. Your garments.'

'You're *not* going to tear my nice silk summer dress, are you?' she pleaded. 'Oh, please don't do that.'

Since the business now appeared inevitable I thought I should lean forward and enjoy it. 'I am,' I growled. 'Like this. I am tearing it off, strip by strip. Like this! Like this! Like this!'

'My lovely summer dress,' she squeaked. 'Silk and with pretty yellow and red flowers on the bodice . . .'

'Yes, your lovely summer dress,' I repeated faithfully. 'Your silk dress . . .'

' . . . with the pretty yellow and red flowers on the bodice,' she finished. Then: 'Oh, my bodice,' she howled, with an underdone howl. 'You've torn my lovely bodice!'

With all these arguments going on I suppose a real-life torturer would have shoved a lump of the dress in the victim's mouth and shut her up. But the dialogue was everything.

'Now my other things,' she suggested. 'My things underneath.'

'Your vest!' I snarled wickedly.

'Vest?' Her face screwed up and she opened her eyes in annoyance. 'Vest?'

'Yes,' I mumbled. 'Well, I thought . . .'

She looked at me oddly, as though I were perverted, but then seemed to have second thoughts and sank back, eyes fluttering closed again, and smiled: 'All right, then, if that's what you like. Vest.' She fell into the play again. 'Oh, no, please don't tear my vest.'

'Now, you're sure?' I asked solicitously.

'Yes, yes,' she nodded impatiently. 'It was unexpected that's all. I'd never thought of a vest before. But perhaps it's winter.'

'You've got a summer dress on,' I pointed out.

'Don't quibble,' she said. 'Get on with it, you cruel bastard.'

I treated her to a realistic growl and decimated the vest. Our sex had stopped now, unfinished, almost incidental, and we were entirely concerned with the plot.

'The brassière,' she said quickly, apparently fearful that I would think up some other unacceptable garment. 'Please don't expose my bosom.'

With a fierce lustful grab and a brief twanging of elastic it was broken and torn aside. 'Oh, my bosom!' she cried sotto voce. 'Inhuman monster! No man has ever seen my bosom!'

To be truthful she didn't have much. They were small, undernourished, just details. I had hardly given them more than a touch of my lips and the odd passing flick with the leading edge of my hand. But now I began to make a meal of them, kneading, rolling and pulling, even blowing violently on them. She writhed with the pleasure of acted agony and in the middle of it I came with a flourish and a moment later so did she.

I found I was running with sweat, sprawled exhausted across her. 'God, I'm tired,' I said, my nose in her hair.

'Tired?' she complained. 'Tired? You can't be tired yet. Not yet. You've hardly touched me.'

Wearily I nodded my obligation. We were still joined and I turned my imagination back to our dream sequence with the rags lying about her as though a million moths had enjoyed a tea party.

'I know your sort,' she immediately declared. 'You're the sort of filthy devil who enjoys beating a young girl across her knicks.' This suggestion sounded somewhat incongruous coming, as it was apparently supposed to come, in the context of the drama, from a maid who had howled, a moment before, that no man had ever seen her bosom. She had obviously picked up the information on what to expect from somewhere. I growled: 'How did you know?'

'I just *know*,' she answered uncertainly, the same logic obviously occurring to her. 'You like to pull them half way down over a girl's bottom and then do your cruel, beastly things.'

She came out of her trance, and asked, like a producer discussing a point with an actor: 'Is it to be the cane or the whip or the birch thongs, or what?'

'What would you like?' I asked hopelessly.

'The cane.'

'All right, it's a cane.'

'*The* cane,' she prompted firmly.

Again nonplussed by the importance of the terminology I sighed. 'Yes, *the* cane.'

'Your *special* cane, you swine.'

Her eyes had closed to narrow channels once more.

'Yes, my *special* one!'

'Is it thick or thin?'

'Christ. Thin.'

'Oh, no! Not the thin and bendy one?'

'The thin and bendy one,' I confirmed grimly.

'Oh, God. Here you go, torturer of young girls! You've got it in your hand, haven't you? And you're coming towards me. You've got that cane in your hand.' Her voice was a croak.

To my astonishment I felt my hand clench. There was sweat between my fingers.

'I'm coming,' I repeated, a remark which turned out to be something of a prophecy, for we again failed to reach the climax of one thing because of the climax of another. We lay there for a long time after that until eventually she said coolly: 'You must have a mind like a cesspool to think up things like that.'

There was no point in argument. 'Would you *really* like someone to do that sort of thing to you?' I asked. It was a genuine inquiry, for I was drained and deflated. My heart fell when I sensed her stiffen at my flank and in a single writhing movement she was away from the bed. She went to the piled books in the corner and bent over feeling for something. I watched her globular backside with a sinking feeling.

She turned quickly to face me, hiding something behind her back, a child's mischievous expression on her face. 'I've never experienced it,' she said. 'Bertram will have nothing to do with it. He's a masochist as well, which is a bit like one person having two right feet. Nobody else has ever asked me.

Nobody.' I stared with a strangely excited horror as she produced a school cane from behind her back. 'There's no time like the present,' she said.

'Oh, for God's sake, Belinda!' I protested. 'I didn't mean it. I'm flaked out, for a start, and it's one thing playing games and another doing the real thing. I might hurt you.'

'That's more or less the idea, Adrian,' she pointed out. 'Go on. Just once. Just to see what it's like. If I don't like it I'll tell you. It's been my ambition and I hate to let an opportunity slip past.' She held out the implement. 'Just once.'

I staggered up from the bed and took the cane from her. It made me feel sick with excitement and apprehension just to feel it. 'Only a tap, then,' I promised. 'And I'm not Adrian.'

I could see her eyes were savage with anticipation and her lips were wet in the lamplight. The challenge made her face shine. It was I who was the victim not her. I was sagging with disgust and fear of what she wanted me to do. Dear Jesus, if my bride could have seen me then.

'Where do you want me?' she asked.

'Where do you want yourself?' I asked wretchedly.

She looked around. 'Across this chair,' she said. 'It's hard. It's better than the bed.'

'All right.'

She moved forward like a dancer and kissed me on my hot cheek. Then she moved almost religiously to the wooden chair and bent herself across it. Her bottom, thin like the rest of her, was arched up. 'I'm ready, Arthur,' she said from between the legs; her's and the chair's. I went forward and tapped her on the bum. 'There,' I said with finality. 'Now I must be off.'

'Arthur,' she threatened, still curled over, her hair flung on the floor. 'Do it properly.'

'That was,' I said.

'A tickle,' she said. 'I want a real one. If you don't I am coming to the Shunter's Arms and I shall tell your wife what a perverted beast you are.'

I really thought I was going to faint. 'You wouldn't,' I

moaned. 'You couldn't do anything like that. Tell Pamela?'

She looked around the leg of the chair. 'Listen,' she said nastily. 'You've known me only a few hours, but that's long enough. You know damned well I would tell her.'

Anger swamped fright within me. I raised the cane high over my head and brought it down with a fearful whack on her buttocks. It was terrible. She shot up into the air like a high diver in reverse, emitting the most devastating scream I have ever heard. Then she let go another one.

In a moment there were answering screams from beneath our feet. Bedlam came from below the floorboards. Screeches, barks, hoots, howls and other animal cries.

'Christ!' she exclaimed. 'You've woken the pet shop!'

We stood naked, transfixed, staring at each other with immediate hatred. 'Get out!' she said. 'Clear off bloody quick, you sadistic bastard. That really hurt me. Get out, do you hear!'

I was only too glad to go. I half dressed and stumbled down the stairs with the cacophony of animal noises unabated at my ear. She shouted something after me to the effect that her Bertram would be round to sort me out, presumably with his dustman-devouring machine, but I took no heed. In the street windows had been thrown up and people were shouting for the police. 'There's a burglar in the pet shop!' some nincompoop bawled, as though anyone would burgle a fucking pet shop.

When I got back to The Shunter's Arms Pamela was asleep but had ceased snoring. In the morning we made our first married love and I enjoyed every moment.

'I'm sorry about last night, darling,' she whispered.

'And so am I,' I said. 'Very, very sorry.'

I meant it too.

14

The next six months were the most careful and happiest of our lives together. The two rooms above the greengrocery shop in Newport were like paradise garnished with the lingering smell of brussels sprouts. Every morning, while she was still in our bed, Pamela would drop a small wooden basket, attached to a clothes line, from the street window and her uncle below in his shop would obligingly load it with mushrooms and tomatoes for our breakfast. On Saturdays he would put some potatoes in as well and we would sit up in bed, listening to the High Street sounds below, and peel potatoes for chips.

I say this time of our lives was *careful* because, for me, after the disasters attending our wedding and honeymoon and indeed my existence before that, it was a period when I tried to put my life, and with it hers, on a calm and steady course. Every day I went to Cardiff Technical College where I was doing my navigation course, and she would go to the confectionery wholesalers in the town where she had a job. We would return at about the same time in the afternoon, my bus getting into the bus station just before hers, and we would always meet under the omnibus company's clock, and walk home together.

On Mondays we went to the pictures and sometimes on a Thursday too, for the programmes in those days used to change mid-way through the week. Saturday nights we went dancing and had fish and chips at midnight. I had a lot of studying to do at home and sometimes when I was working out navigation problems with little counters on the table she would go off to see her family. When my birthday arrived she gave me a set of toy ships and plastic arrows (to represent the winds of the sea) which I used instead of the counters.

My mother came to see me one evening and found me alone in the place, arranging the ships and the winds on the table, and she thought it was a sign that we were un-happily married. But I had never been more peaceful, more content.

Happiness and the free availability of chocolates at her place of work had given Pamela a dumpier form since our wedding, but she was warm in bed, so I did not mind. No women had appeared on my moral threshold since the strange and frightening Belinda in Swindon, except Joanne, the model from the Technical College, and I cannot, in all fairness to myself, take her into account.

At the college I always found it difficult to distinguish between one corridor and another and one morning, opened a door, and walked in on an art class painting a naked lady model. To be confronted with a creamy pair of breasts almost at the tip of my nose first thing on a Monday morning was naturally an unexpected bonus and a shock. She was only inches from me as I stood, transfixed, at the door, her golden hair pulled back severely over her neck, her face poised in the special light provided for the assembled artists, her stomach caved in and diminishing to a dainty fan of fair hair at the top of her legs. She was in a sort of strong pose, like one of the Trojan Women, and one leg was bent up on to an orange box. I stood involuntarily and took her in and she turned minutely and whispered to me to go away and shut the door. I did and sat uncomfortably all the morning working out the complexities of the Davis Turn, which is the quickest way to turn a ship around in mid-ocean, so that it arrives back at a point it has previously left.

This is, of course, the operation adopted should anyone fall overboard from the vessel and have to be sought for, but that day I found it difficult to concentrate. In later years when twice I was called on to perform this manoeuvre, I did so very badly, and we never found the unfortunate men we were seeking. I thought at those times that in a way their drownings were at least partly attributable to a naked torso viewed so many years before.

The day following the indiscretion I saw the model sitting two tables distant in the college canteen. She was alone, nibbling tea, staring straight ahead. The art students were gathered at a table across the gangway, glancing salaciously at her and making wet remarks from the edges of their mouths, which I thought was odd because she was dressed in a sweater and skirt now and previously, when she was naked, they had been silent.

Telling myself that what I was doing was gallant and courteous, I sauntered from my place to hers and sat down in front of her. She glanced up with huge dull eyes that brought no tone of recognition.

'Look,' she sighed, indicating that she had said the same thing many times. 'I don't want to be bothered in my break.'

'Oh, I see,' I mumbled. 'Well, I'm very sorry. I thought the mob across on that table were annoying you.'

'I never notice them,' she said. 'Thank you all the same.'

'And there's another thing,' I went on, half-rising.

'I thought there would be,' she said. 'Well I'm very sorry, but I'm busy until the year after next.'

'No, it's not that,' I protested sitting down again. 'I just wanted to apologise for bursting in on you yesterday when you were in . . . in . . . in the art class. Posing.'

'Oh it was you,' she said more reasonably. 'Well somebody else having a look doesn't worry me at all. What difference is another pair of eyes? It's just that there's a hell of a draught comes through that door and I feel it in some nasty corners.'

'Yes, I expect you do,' I commiserated. 'Anyway I'm sorry. I got the doors and the corridors mixed up. I was looking for the Navigation Department.'

'Is that where you are?'

I felt pleased that she had extended the conversation of her own accord. The artists had stopped sniggering now and were looking across at me with hate and envy.

'Yes, Navigation,' I said. 'Fourth officer's ticket.'

'You're not going to be much of a navigator if you can't find your way around this place,' she said. 'Walking in the wrong doors. You'll be landing up in the wrong country.'

'Sorry,' I repeated. 'I'm just clumsy like that.' I glanced up and she was regarding me with amusement. Encouraged I said: 'Anyway, I must say you looked really terrific.'

'Keep your hands on the wheel, sailor,' she said. 'And your eyes on the stars.' She finished her tea and got up, gathering her big embroidered bag and a woollen shawl from the chair. 'Back to work,' she sighed. 'Now, don't get lost whatever you do.'

'I'll get a chart,' I said.

She went and I looked across and got the supreme male satisfaction of seeing the expression on the artists' faces. I rose, shrugged, and walked by them, slightly expanding my chest. I only did it for show, of course. With her I thought that would be the end of it. But it wasn't. Naturally.

Summer had come to the coast and, for those parts, it was a good summer. Our window was open to the sounds of the street and in the evenings little clouds of coal dust drifted in from the docks and settled on the petals of our potted plants. On Sundays we would go down to the cliffs or the lighthouse, or lie in bed late and then go to the putting green in the park in the afternoon.

One Sunday both our families went on a charabanc outing to Barry Island and sat sweating on the beach, drinking beer and eating sandwiches. Each faction had tried to outdo the others with the size, variety and number of sandwiches, and the result was a horrifying wall of bread built as though in defence against the advancing tide. We had brought our own lunch and we drew a little apart from them because they were so conspicuous with their bread bastion and their piles of beer bottles.

My mother sat nibbling tidily at the distant end of this rabble, staring out to sea as though she expected her ship to arrive at any tide. My father, stripped to the waist, for the benefit of Pamela's aunts and other female relatives, went around opening beer bottles with his bare hands, a feat much admired that day.

There was a medieval callousness about Pamela's family. Her grandmother fell down some steps while returning from the toilet on the promenade and although this was in full view of everyone, including the old lady's husband, all they did was sit, continue to chew their bread and swig their beer and shout advice and encouragement through their full mouths. Pamela and I, who were some distance removed at the extreme of the tribe, eventually retrieved her and brought her breathless and distressed into the camp. Then, at the end of the day one of the nieces, Nora, a somewhat looney girl of about fourteen, went missing and no attempt was made to find her on the crowded beach. A random argument took place as to whether, at her age, she would qualify as a lost child and be available at the Lost Children Enclosure. But nobody went to look. It was eventually decided that she had, in all probability, drowned in the sea and there was, therefore, no point in expending any energy in a search. Once again Pamela and I had to make the effort but we failed to find the girl. Everyone boarded the home-going charabanc cheerfully convinced that Nora was now floating face down towards Porthcawl on the afternoon tide.

With only a minute to go before departure the girl turned up with a dubious looking fairground attendant and was rejoined with the family who showed, if anything, a certain disappointment at this mundane end to what might have been an interesting occurrence.

It was the putting green, naturally, that I remember best, because of what happened years afterwards. We would go there on reasonable days and pay our twopence for the hire of the golf balls and the putters. It was in a very pleasant part of Newport Park with seats and flower beds arranged all around and a bandstand like a birdcage set at one edge. It seemed to be the only place we ever discussed ourselves. At home we never talked about our lives, not seriously, not about the bigger aspects such as what we were going to do. We knew, for example, that before long I would have to return to the sea, because my course at the college was all but finished, but neither of us mentioned it until one September day at four o'clock as we were knocking the balls towards the sunken cocoa tins thoughtfully provided by the council's parks and cemeteries department.

'What's going to happen to us?' she said pushing a long putt almost to the edge of the first hole.

'How do you mean?' Mine was short for I was never as good as her. She was always right up to the hole, or beyond it. Never short.

'Well, *us*,' she repeated. 'Something's got to happen hasn't it? You know that. We're just going along, living, at the moment.'

'Don't you like that?' I said surprised. 'I'm happy just living. I thought you were.'

'You're going back soon,' she said. 'To sea.' It was almost a question; not quite.

'Yes, I suppose so.'

'Well, *are* you?'

'Yes. That's the general idea, isn't it, Pamela? That's why I'm doing the navigation.'

'Right,' she said. 'But you've never really *said*, have you? You've never actually *mentioned* going back. All I see you doing is working out figures and writing down things and playing with those little boats and arrows.'

'But what is there to say,' I argued. 'I thought we both *knew* that. You helped me when I applied. You wanted me to be an officer.'

'We weren't married then.'

'I see,' I said. I touched her hand to show that I did, but she nudged me away and said: 'I'm putting.' She swung the club much harder than she needed.

'What can I do?' I asked. 'I'm working as hard as I can because I thought this is the way to make sure we have decent lives, that we have the things we want. A house for a start. So we can do better things.'

'Better? You mean so we don't have to go on any more charabanc outings to Barry Island?'

'If you like,' I said feeling my temper rising just below my chin.

'You're a snob,' she sniffed. 'I always knew it.'

'Shit,' I said. 'It's *you* who who wanted me to do it in the first place. To go to sea. What do you want me to do now? Tell me what you want. Would you like me to get a bike and be an errand boy? Or work on the railway?'

'Fore!' The bellow came from behind us and we looked up to see a gathering of people in slow collision at the previous hole of the putting green. 'Hurry up,' called the man. 'It's not the Open Championship.'

'Open arseholes,' I said under my breath.

'Don't say that,' rasped Pamela. 'And don't say "shit" either, like you did just a minute ago. You're not on the deck now, you know.'

She walked angrily away from the green and I followed her, stunned by the quarrel, the first we had fallen into since our wedding day. Head down she was walking along the park path in front of the people sunning themselves on the benches. I went after her and the putting green attendant came after us and demanded his putters and balls back.

'Give the man his balls back,' said Pamela and she turned away and I saw she was laughing. I put my arm around her and we walked away from the park and went home to tea.

But on the Monday I went to the college knowing what I would not admit before, that I was studying for a life of separation. It had always been obvious, it had stood out like large clouds, but I had not turned my head in that direction.

Perhaps intuitively, before our wedding, she had thought that marriage in short bursts was better than the long grind of the everyday thing that she saw and heard all about her. When I signed with the shipping company she had said: 'Every time you come home, pet, it will be like a new husband.' But those first months had been better than we had hoped, far better. Away from our families, up there in our rooms above the greengrocery, we had lived an unworried summer. I really loved her, even though she was putting on weight, and I am sure at that time she loved me very much.

All through the Monday morning lecture on the North Atlantic Drift I was mentally going through the alternatives. Insurance man, Kleen-ezee Brush Salesman (a neighbour did this and earned good commission and had a house full of free, or stolen brushes), council work, the railway, building work, even the horrifying prospect of the Food Office. I saw myself returning each day, Fridays with my wage packet, to our eyrie above the brussels sprouts, and see her evening smile. But the more I thought about it the more the smile began to fade. What was I to do?

I heard hardly a word about the North Atlantic Drift and when I went out at the break I saw the bright shawl of the model moving among a group of students in the main corridor. She was walking away from me, but I hurried and caught her up, pretending I did not see her until the last moment.

'Oh, you,' she said. 'I've been looking for you.'

'Me?'

'Yes. Have you been adrift again?'

'No, I've been on course, more or less.'

'Listen, I'm having a few people around my place to-night. I wondered, if you weren't doing anything . . .'

'What time?' I demanded so loudly and quickly that several students turned and looked. 'What time?' I whispered, making it worse.

She told me eight o'clock and I went home and told Pamela I had a special evening lecture. She said she would go and see her mother and I saw her go off with my guilt lying like stale bread in my stomach.

The first of the autumn channel fogs came up that evening and the girl lived in a street near the docks. There were coils and layers of mist sniffing about the alleys of the district when I got to her door. I had not dared to put on a clean shirt or change into my best suit and I stood outside trying to tug the creases out of my collar. As I reached for the knocker the door opened and Joanne was standing there behind a baby's cot which was blocking the entire passage.

'Oh good,' she said happily. 'You've come. Just in time too.'

'For what?' I asked looking suspiciously at the infant.

'We want to take little Haroun just up the street to Mrs Richards. She's going to look after him.'

I leaned forward and examined the baby. The baby examined me from the frontier of his sheets. He was brown with black eyes.

'Haroun,' I said flatly. It was neither a question nor a statement; just a label.

'Yes,' said Joanne. 'He's a Persian. Well, half. His father's Persian.'

'And his mother?'

'Welsh,' she said. 'It's me.'

The hopeless, leaden, feeling I had already come to know, and which, God knows, I have become more and more familiar with over the years, caught hold of my chest.

'Where's his father?' I inquired. 'Inside?'

'Yes,' she nodded. 'Five years.'

'I meant was he inside the house,' I pointed out, but it did not matter then.

'No, he's inside Cardiff Jail. Brian will help you carry the cot to Mrs Richards. But don't be too long will you, because it's getting a bit foggy.'

Brian, not altogether to my surprise, turned out to be Chinese. He called himself Blian. He was the only man I ever met who could not pronounce his own name.

We trundled the cot out into the street, Brian clucking with concern, Joanne holding the door open and waving a miniature goodbye to the baby. With reluctance I took hold of the feet end of the contraption and said: 'Where is it? Just across the road?'

'Down stleet,' said Brian and Joanne nodded and mimicked, 'Down stleet.'

Fog in my face, I turned and we set off towards the docks at an appropriate rickshaw pace, at first letting the cot run along on its own wheels. After a few hundred yards, however, one of the castors came off and we went into a skid and had to pick the cot clear of the pavement for the rest of the journey.

It seemed miles. Far from being just down the street, it

was down numberless streets, around corners and through dreadful alleys that I had never dreamed existed. The fog thickened and the hooting of a ship in the channel started the baby crying. We stopped at the low entrance to a dripping alley and Brian turned and said with concern: 'Baby cly. You make baby cly.'

Ignoring the charge, I said: 'When are we going to get there? The kid will choke in this stuff.'

'Soon,' he nodded. His face looked sinister in the fog. 'All soon.'

We began our jogging again, along the slimy pavements, passing hunched people who stared at us and our baby, or did not see us at all. Several women called after us through the fog that we had no right to be transporting a child on a night like that, but they, and we, were gone before it mattered. Brian threw out a right arm like a turning driver and we went at an angle across the main Dock Road where it reached the wharves.

Coming upon the familiar street and dodging with the cot and little Haroun between the buses and blindly-driven cars, I had a real and sudden fear that I might be recognized. My numerous relations and Pamela's too lived in this part of the town. What if they spotted me in this ridiculous situation when my wife thought I was at an evening lecture? Then I thought: 'Christ! *What if Pamela sees me?*'

I felt myself freeze from my ankles upwards. Only my fear kept jogging along the pavement. My head dropped down almost on my chest, with my eyes hinging up to see where I was going. Then, at a fish shop on the corner, I saw Pamela's idiot cousin, Nora, the one we lost at Barry Island. She was coming out of the lit steam and into the unlit fog, her newspaper packet of chips spread like a giant handkerchief in front of her nose. I tried to take evasive action, but I stumbled and although I recovered the movement attracted her attention. Pushing Brian, at the front, abruptly, I sent him staggering forward, and little Haroun let out a concerned wail.

'Arthur!' I heard the girl call through the fog. 'Arthur

McCann – is that you? Arthur . . . Arthur . . .'

'Down the cutting,' I snarled at the startled Chinese. Obediently he wheeled and we staggered down a steep and rutted cutting between two warehouse walls, the cot bouncing like a dinghy, the child howling, our feet splashing and slipping through mud and water. Through the eerie fog, at the top of the slope I could hear the cousin calling 'Arthur? Is it you Arthur?' She was the only one who consistently got my name right.

Almost aching with breathlessness, our shoes soaked, mud clinging to our shins, we reached a swiftly gurgling sewer outlet, which we were obliged to ford. The fog was like wool down there and we could hear large ships moaning almost at our shoulders. I would only have been mildly surprised if we had collided with a tanker. The baby had stopped crying and his blackberry eyes were now regarding me madly from the defensive edge of his blankets.

Brian was cursing in what I took to be appropriately Fukien as we mounted the slimy slope to the streets on the other side. When we regained the houses he confessed he was lost and we spent a further ten minutes wandering with our cot and baby in the fog, not daring to ask directions, until he at last recognized a street, and we delivered Haroun, now asleep to the doorstep of Mrs Richards. A small, ragged boy told us that she had gone to the off-licence, and refused us admission until she returned, which she did after a further five minutes, festooned with Guinness bottles and packets of crisps.

We bore the cot to a downstairs room containing another six cots, all pushed against each other like some sort of infant traffic jam. Mrs Richards decided there was no room for even one more, so we carried our burden upstairs and lodged it among another snarl-up in a front bedroom. There were babies behind bars in every room, some white, some black, some yellow; crying, sleeping, wetting, crapping, trying to stick their fingers in their neighbour's eyes. There were alien twins in a pram in the hall and another child blissfully sleeping in a sea hammock slung from the toilet cistern to a coathook on the landing. It was the first time I realized how overpopulated the world is.

'Blian go sod off home,' announced Brian when we were in the street again. I did not discourage him and he kindly directed me back to Joanne's house. I returned carefully, avoiding the vicinity of the fish shop where Nora might still be lurking behind the smoke screen of her chip-bag. It was much quicker going back, however, and damp, but relieved, I arrived once more outside the door from which I had started that terrible journey.

She answered my knock. She was wearing an oriental dressing robe, a wide channel open down her naked front, the large flanks of her breasts pushing it wider at the top.

She smiled and her eyes brimmed with pleasure. 'Was he a good boy?' she asked.

'He liked his little outing,' I said. 'Blian has gone home to have a nervous breakdown.'

'Come in,' she whispered. 'Come and get those foggy clothes off your back.'

Needless to say we both ended naked, posing on a dais for the Dock Settlement Art Circle. That marvellous moulded body was inches from the end of my cock, but every time I moved a millimetre some undiscovered Ukrainian Utrillo would howl a complaint. When it was finished, after two hours, I had a glass of Tizer and a rock cake and went home to my waiting wife. When I got there her grandfather was sitting at our table and his wooden suitcase was standing threateningly at the bedroom door.

'He has decided to separate from gran and he's got nowhere to go. He wants a divorce,' explained Pamela practically.

'Divorce!' I cried. 'Jesus Christ, they're both over eighty!'

'There's no age limit,' sniffed the old man. He had been weeping copiously over our tablecloth but that had not prevented him eating two-thirds of my supper. 'I should have done it ten years ago.'

'Ten years? You were seventy-three then, for God's sake.'

'I've tried to make a go of it,' he moaned. 'But it's no good. We just don't laugh at the same things any more.'

I stared at the dirty old figure, then looked up at Pamela who was soggy around the eyes. 'He's getting lines like that from television,' I said to her. 'They don't laugh at the same things any more! I knew there'd be trouble when your mother got that set. It gives people ideas.'

'She's always too tired,' he went on ignoring my remarks, concerned only with his monologue. 'Excuses, excuses. She . . . she . . . she turns away from me in bed.'

I sat down heavily and stared at him. 'She's eighty-one,' I said slowly. 'That's the best excuse I've ever heard.'

'Eighty-two,' he corrected. 'What am *I* doing with a woman of that age anyway?'

I glanced at Pamela who was nodding as though she understood perfectly. 'Can I have a cup of tea?' I asked. She went towards the stove, still looking sadly at her grandfather. I leaned closer to him: 'Have you met anybody else?' I asked nastily. 'Somebody who's more *you*? Together you can reach for the stars.'

'No,' he answered, but so shiftily that I didn't believe him. 'It's been fifty-eight years of hell,' he complained. 'I want to start my life again.'

'It's a bit bleeding late, isn't it?' I retorted and Pamela reproved me from the kettle. 'Arthur, don't be so brutal. Poor old man. He's all cut up, can't you see.'

I got up from the table and went across to her. 'If he had the strength to walk down the High Street we could take him to the marriage guidance council. I'm told it's very good. Get her to go too. Better still get a couple of bloody ambulances to take them. That would be something new for the do-gooders.'

'Poor old chap,' she whimpered over the steaming kettle. 'Look at him crying.'

'Look at him eating the rest of my supper,' I said more to the point. 'I suppose you think he's going to stay here.'

'Where else can he stay? He can't wander around on a

night like this. He'd catch his death.'

'He'll catch his death at our bedroom keyhole,' I said.

She caught her breath. 'You nasty bugger,' she said. 'How can you say such a thing about an old man?'

'Easily.'

Her face was sweating and red in the steam. She still had not taken the kettle off the boil. But then she relaxed and her voice became soft. 'Let him stay tonight,' she said. 'He can sleep on the couch. Tomorrow we'll take him back and try and get it straightened out between them.'

'Let's take them down to the cemetery,' I answered. I found I was whispering. 'Let them sit on a couple of graves and talk it over. Maybe they'll see sense then.'

But the next morning I had a letter from the shipping company offering me a voyage on the S.S. *Rotterdam Emperor* to the Gulf ports, Valparaiso, and Rio. I tore up the application form I had cut from the previous evening's paper, offering me a new dazzling life in insurance, and cabled my acceptance. Pamela and I made it up before I went, but the old man stayed and I stuffed our keyhole with cotton wool that night.

15

That was in the autumn of 1947. I went back and sailed to Port Everglades, New Orleans, and down to the Latin places, even to Port Desire, where I saw the grave of my great-grandfather buried, as I've said before, in a ship's barrel, but with some honour by the indigenous Indians. On the memorial post he is described by a native name, three miles long, which translated turns out to mean White-Voyager - who - die - when - bitten - on - the - elbow - by - devil - dog. It was explained to me by a tribal archivist that the 'elbow' was a euphemism for arse, which was a forbidden word on memorial stones, and in fact did not often occur. That he was also screwing a local lovely at the time of the rabid dog's fatal bite is also deleted out of delicacy, but the facts are well established in the history of Port Desire. The name of the girl, which I also now forget, is mentioned with others on the stone in the sort of fashion of our own memorials: 'Sadly missed by Debbie, Kath, Beryl, Doreen' or whatever they were called, 'And his children in Port Desire and Moonlight Bay.' Moonlight Bay was just up the road, towards Rio de Janiero.

I felt an odd sense of affront at my ancestor who had travelled so far from home, after saying he was only going to Bristol for the day, and had spread his happiness and semen among alien people. After all, he had known a life before this even if he failed to acknowledge or remember it. There was his wife, lying mouldy and alone in Barry Municipal Cemetery, and he was out here in exciting foreign parts. It did not seem fair. My annoyance was such that for a few pesos I commissioned an obliging mason to chip an extra line in the old stone which said bluntly: 'And remembered vaguely by his wife Annie, his children and all his relatives in Wales.' That put the record right and I was glad.

That going away from Pamela, after our happy six months, was, I suppose the hinge of my life. It turned me from baffled boyhood to fugitive manhood. In 1950 I got my third officer's ticket, in 1955 my second officer's, in 1962 I was the mate of a tanker, I passed my master's certificate four years later and my extra master's in 1969, which meant that I could be left to take a great ship across the deep waters by my own judgement. Because of the unfortunate wreck of Mr Cohen's Rolls-Royce I am now reduced to first officer again, but there is time. I think.

My life, over this period, became more unfathomable than any ocean I traversed. I have tried everything, I suppose, on this odyssey of twenty years and more, even if I appear to have learned little. My solitariness has been of my own making for the sea has given me many acquaintances and no friends to speak of. I speak of it as solitariness because it has been spiced with pain and misgivings;

solitude is serene and that I have never been.

For that whole year after my marriage, a year bravely borne, I kept the faith, but one thick day in the middle of a Hamburg August I threw it away and went with a woman from St Pauli. We lay under the very roof tiles of a house, sizzling like chops in an oven, the German sun baking our every jerk and slippery movement. When I walked away all the people were going home from their work for the day, filling the tramcars and pavement cafés which were even then sprouting among the ruins of the war. They were like pigeons filling the city; they seemed free and I was still sweating under my clothes.

I knew it would ever be thus, that I would walk, detached from the good, ordinary world, from some woman to some ship and from some ship to some woman and never find peace or really know my wife.

From that time I simply let these things happen to me. There seemed nothing else I could do. Sometimes they were unspeakably sordid, at others hideously laughable, and there were others when I found something of the comfort and love a man needs when he is always voyaging. I became used to waking in the middle of the night with strange arms about me.

But if I am the world's prime fool, and I fear that after Angie there can be little doubt, then I've got there by my own efforts. Some men spend their existence in pursuit of conquests and never do battle with themselves. If only I could have stepped back and studied myself intently for a while, instead of going off like a randy rabbit at every whim of my sexual organ. But I didn't. I have gone alone into strange cities and countries to find company, sympathy and sex and sought out my own peculiar disgraces. Some men feared to go ashore alone, rushing off in gay gangs to find the sunken bars and hideouts where sailors always seem to go. There have been times when I've brought misfortune upon myself, almost lying back and enjoying it, and others when ill-natured chance was just waiting for a victim to walk by, and along I came.

I am, after all, the very man who, promised an orgy of witchcraft and sex – for which I had, I might say, paid good money in advance – sat blindfold on a mountain track in Turkey waiting to be taken to the secret place. But they didn't come back for me, as they promised, and when it began to rain I took the blindfold away to see a ten-year-old goatherd regarding me with total interest.

That was my own fault and doing. But in San Peso, in Central America, it was with the most decent motives that I took an eleven-year-old girl from her mother in the street. Those mothers sold their daughters to any man who had the money. I've heard men return to ships laughing at how they made those children squeal. But, when I had paid the mother, I took the girl down to the San Peso beach and paddled with her in the warm sea and built her a sandcastle. True she became very agitated at all this strange behaviour, and was crying when her foul mother turned up with the police. The British consul said to me after he had recovered me from gaol: 'You're a fool McCann. A bloody fool.'

Even now I can remember some of my women only by remembering the ships. Memories of Lisa of Naples are prompted by a mental picture of the S.S. *Aegean King*, my first oil burner. Alice of Sydney, whom I called the Great Australian Bight, smiles at me through the smoke of the *Southern Cape*; I can still see Natalie, the American girl in Panama, running weeping alongside the canal, trying to keep up with the ship as we left Balboa; rushing blindly to a point where the concrete slid quickly into the canal. I wonder what happened to Natalie? Suzanne of Saint Nazaire conjures the S.S. *Atlantic Castle* (my first triple-screw) and, after years, I look with an outrageous optimism at the iron bridge by Singapore Harbour, thinking that I might see the lovely Eurasian face of Doris Da Souza enmeshed in its iron, weeping and waving at the departing *Malacca Envoy*.

Sometimes when I am making chart calculations on the bridge the very corner of my eye touches some cape or channel, some inlet with a small port at its head, and the lines and whorls on the official Admiralty chart become pieces of real land, touching the sea, the geometric blocks become buildings and streets that I can see clearly, perhaps from many years before. They become some place where something happened, sometime. Where someone was walking down a street and I happened to be walking towards them. Just a temporary bit of life that never comes again and maybe is forgotten. Maybe not.

On that first voyage, after my marriage, I wrote to Pamela from every port, a page a day composed in my bunk, I thought of her and I conscientiously tried to dream of her, except I could not.

When I returned after four months I found that Pamela's grandfather had sundered himself from his wife more irrevocably than even he had intended. He had died. Pamela found him in an untidy pile outside our bedroom door when she got up one morning. He died as he had lived, with his eye to the keyhole. My own father was not long behind him. He expired heartily, laughing at one of his own jokes in the Donkeyman's Arms. I flew home from Antwerp for the funeral and never have I seen such open satisfaction around an open grave. The grins were almost elbowing their way through the prayers.

As a climax my Uncle Cedric, with a spontaneous fling, threw his false teeth into the grave and they sat grimacing on top of the coffin. No one made any movement or comment, even the vicar, who, burying people in that area as he did, had probably seen everything. Eventually when the men were about to shovel the earth on top of my dad, the vicar leaned quietly towards Uncle Cedric and clearly pointed out that if he wanted the teeth back he had better retrieve them right away or they were gone for ever. But my uncle shook his head. After the funeral, when we had gone back to the house, I found him in a corner and asked him why he had thrown the teeth. He began to cry and said: 'My boy, your father had everything else of mine that was movable, so I thought he might as well have the teeth as well. They say that in the Hereafter there is weeping and gnashing of teeth, and I want that bugger to do plenty of gnashing.'

My mother, of course, saw but said nothing. After that she took to her knitting needles and chair by the fire, like someone watching over the eternal flame, and never moved from the house again. They found her dead there one morning a few months later, half way through a jumper that would have only fitted my father. She had a drawer full of scarves and socks and sweaters all his size, all folded away. It was a shame and a waste, because he would never have needed them; not where he had gone.

Pamela and I began to play our game which went on over the years, until the events of last autumn on the putting green, brought play to what I suppose is a definite end. I would return from a voyage and she would embrace me and ask me when I was going back. When once I challenged her about always asking me that same question she was hurt and said that she only wanted to know how long we would have together before I had to go away again. There was no hurry intended.

She continued to live in the two rooms, although her uncle sold the greengrocery business and it became a baker's shop, which meant that our home was a good deal warmer and smelled both wholesome and wholemeal. She still lowered the basket from bed but a loaf and half a dozen pastries now came up instead of the tomatoes and mushrooms of the former days. The little place always looked exactly the same on the day of my return as on the day I left. She changed nothing, and she added nothing. We would spend a couple of weeks, or sometimes if I was back at the Technical College, a couple of months, in a void, a segment of what marriage is to many people everywhere. We did not row very much, but neither did we make each other laugh. We had a television now and it had taken her love from the cinema. I left her once watching 'Peyton Place', although she did rise and kissed me before I went through the door. I went to Australia, New Zealand, India, and Liverpool; I had seen two men die and another go mad;

I had watched women weeping with the despair of hunger and children screaming because their mothers were crying and they were starving; I saw a policeman shoot a boy in the leg because he had stolen a driving mirror; I saw a flooded village and a town where the people shuddered as they prayed for rain. When I returned she was still hunched before 'Peyton Place' the ghostly tele-light on her quiet face, and what could have been the same Mars Bar half-eaten in her right fist.

She would always say: 'Have a good trip?'

'So-so.'

'Meet anybody nice?'

'Not that I can think of. Did you?'

'No. I don't meet anybody. I'm all right here.'

And I really thought she was.

The sailor knows very well the perverse comfort of loneliness. He hugs it to himself, wandering strange, alien cities where no one even turns their eyes to see him. Each step is a hope for some vaguely adventurous miracle, that he will meet some temporary love, some companionship, some pretended homeliness, some hastily made familiarity; an emergency thing with a simple bed and an embrace at its end. Loneliness is a sensation spiced with doggerel and self-pity, two things the sailor treasures. At sea he has the nursing ocean and the comfort of belonging to it, but in a foreign place he will wander, as I do, miserably because he feels shunned by everyday land people; jovial, busy men, children engrossed in play, shopping housewives, people laughing in cafes, priests and girls of eighteen with thirty-eight inch busts.

I gave this matter much thought over the years of my voyaging, and devoted considerable space to it in my accumulating novel 'All The Coloured Lights Of The World by Arthur McCann'. The girl in every port is a careless and untrue generalization composed by some fanciful man who had never ventured beyond his own backyard. For myself I felt short-changed by the temporary affiliation, come and gone with the morning or the impatient banging of the next customer on the door, even though I took it because it was available. I wanted a good, decent, settled domesticity. In as many places as possible. I wanted someone to whom I could go *home*. Wherever I was.

The Split Legs Go-Go Bar on New York's East Side is, I confess, scarcely the sort of locality where a man searching, as I was, for comfort, love, honesty, friendship, and sex, – in a package – could seriously hope to fulfil his mission. But there, in Angie I found, and I say it again now, openly, ashamed as I am, the finest combination of those qualities I needed in my approaching middle age. Angie was so nearly right for me. So nearly.

It was, as I say, hardly the venue for the meeting of two true people. I told her at the time that neither of us ought to have been there, with the mad lights, the three girl dancers twirling their breasts in a cage and the sore music. By rights we should have met in a park or by a river, introduced by a chance mutual friend, but since this could not be we had to make the best of the Split Legs Go-Go Bar. It was a place full of lost and aimless men and hard, predatory women. Somehow I felt that we were different, and, as it transpired, we were. As far as I was concerned our being there at all was a temporary membership of some sub-strata of society, and we would soon be able to escape and to walk happily in that park or by that river, where we so rightly and obviously belonged.

Our conversation over the first drink was, I suppose, as banal as all such conversations are in those dim holes.

'It must be very uncomfortable for those girls dancing in that cage,' I observed. 'They look like they're hanging up to cook.'

'Shit, it is,' said Angie. 'Wednesday night the bottom fell out of the thing and they all dropped out on to the floor. That's dangerous.'

'Why did you say that?' I asked seriously. She looked a good girl, soft featured, eyes genuinely friendly in the half light, her hands white and nervous, playing with a cigarette packet. Her shoulders were naked, sprouting from a lovely red dress and her hair was very dark and curling modestly around her face.

'Say what? About the girls falling out of the cage? Because it happened. It occurred.'

'No,' I said. 'Shit. Why did you say "shit"?'

She smiled, but down at the table. 'I guess that's not very ladylike,' she said. 'You don't like that sort of expression?'

'I've heard worse,' I admitted. 'I'm a ship's officer, after all.'

'Gee, are you? That's real nice.'

'But I didn't like to hear it coming from you. Somehow you don't fit in with that sort of thing in my picture of you.'

'Right,' she nodded as though I had found her out. Her head went nearer the table and I had a funny feeling she was crying. I felt sure I was right because she excused herself and went to the wailing girls in the go-go cage and borrowed a Kleenex from one of them. She returned brushing her eyes with it. 'Sorry,' she said touching my hand as she sat down. 'The smoke worries my eyes a little.'

'You were saying . . .' I said.

'Oh yeah. Sure I was. You're just right, Alvin . . .'

'Arthur.'

'Boy, how could I call you Alvin! I must be going crazy.'

'Easily confused,' I conceded.

'Sure. Thanks. Well, I was saying, Arthur. Arthur. Now that *is* right. Arthur?'

'Spot on,' I said.

'Well, I think you're absolutely, one hundred per cent, right about me saying "shit". It's a tough expression, I suppose. But, working here, I just try to be professional, that's all. Most men I meet in here would have said it first anyway.'

It was then, when she said that, there came a thought that this was not destined to be the usual emergency relationship formed and frequently finished over an expensive martini in a place full of noise and hideous lights. I had a sudden feeling that she was real. All the subsequent things could never remove that sensation of discovery that I knew then.

'How long have you worked here?' I asked. 'I know it's a corny question, but I really would like to know.'

'Sure,' she laughed quietly. 'It's a corny question, but it's a nice corny question, and I guess you *are* interested.'

'I'm interested in you,' I said.

'You damned British,' she mimicked quite cleverly.

I laughed. 'Well, that's all right, then isn't, it?'

'Sure it is. I've been here ten days. It's the usual old story, I'm sorry to say. Little girl from Turniptown, big city, needs money. Just that. When I've got enough I'll get out and do the things I want to do.'

'What do you want to do?'

'Well I want an apartment. Nothing crazy, just a good little apartment, double locked, and with a security guard down in the lobby. And I want to go to art school because I'm going to be a commercial artist when I'm a big girl.'

'How big are you now,' I murmured. 'I mean how *old* are you?'

'Twenty-two,' she shrugged. 'I guess that's a little hoary to start thinking about commercial art, but I don't think I've gone too far yet.'

'Oh no,' I encouraged. 'I wouldn't say that's too old. Don't say that word again, will you?'

'What? Shit? No, you know we've agreed that. We don't like that expression.'

'No,' I corrected. 'Hoary. I know how you meant it, but it still sounds terrible coming from you.'

For a nasty moment I thought she was going to be angry, but then she subsided into good-natured laughter, and rolled her head from side to side. 'Oh, Arthur,' she laughed. 'You're a good man! A real, good man. I guess you're just what Angie's been looking for.'

The affair took a strange turn after that. I did not stay at the bar, or I could see it degenerating into just another of those grubby little things that, God knows, I have known well enough. I told her I was going and she did not try to detain me, nor did she ask me to buy her another drink. She just took my fingers and said she hoped we would be able to talk again and I said I intended that we should. I asked her to have lunch with me the following day, for I thought this would put the association on a civilized footing, away from the artificiality of the Split Legs Go-Go Bar, and she smiled and said she would like that, so we fixed it.

When, now, I think of the parts of this affair that I like to remember, that I can *allow* myself to remember, the sweetest moment of all was the next day, in the English Bar of the Barclay Hotel when she came in from the Lexington Avenue sun, and I was waiting for her. She was wearing a superb camel coloured suit and a wide-brimmed hat. Her face was more beautiful without the hysterical lights and her smile was full and honest. My inside seemed to fill up suddenly with warm water as she came through the door. Every man in the place stopped and revolved towards her and I knew that every man wanted to see who was the lucky one she had come to see. I stood and waited for her (I was in uniform) and she came deftly across the floor and took both my hands. The faces of all the men about me collapsed with envy and I knew it was one of the best moments of my life. Even taking into account all that followed, if there were only that moment that was worth anything, then I could console myself with the memory of it.

The head waiter at the English Bar was German, although his father had been a prisoner in Bedfordshire during the war. All the others were Puerto Rican or Negro. Around the walls were some nice prints of Brussels and Environs. We drank Bourbon, the food was chilli con carne, and the piped music drifted originally from the South Seas. I was the only English connection in the place and I was Welsh.

'People come here when they want to get some feeling of England,' she said. 'It's cute, don't you think?'

'Cute, but not English,' I said.

'Maybe you ought to tell them you're English and they'll give us a free bottle of champagne, or something very English like that.'

'Cider more like it,' I said, abruptly remembering the dance hall of that wedding night. 'They make it out of little apples and sometimes they call it West Country champagne.'

'Gee, I like the sound of that. West Country,' she mused over the words. 'England is somewhere I've always wanted to visit, you know, Alvin. I think I would be at peace there. I can just imagine all those castles and toadstools and things.'

'Oh, we have them all over the place,' I said. 'Castles and toadstools.'

'And those bars with the grass roofs.'

'You're thinking of Honolulu.'

'No, I am not. They have grass roofs and funny old windows.'

'Oh, I see. Pubs. Thatched roofs. No go-go girls, I'm afraid.'

'Maybe I could work in one of those if I went to England.'

A minor but guilty pain started within me at the thought of her turning up in Newport.

'It's all strictly amateur,' I said hurriedly. 'You wouldn't earn enough to go to art school in an English pub.'

'You're going soon? Leaving New York?'

'Day after tomorrow. Thursday.'

'So soon?'

'As soon as we finish loading. We'll be out of Hoboken on the mid-morning tide.'

'Hoboken? But that's not very nice. Why couldn't your ship be over on Manhattan?'

'It's not that kind of ship,' I said.

'You'll be back some time?'

'In three weeks. I'll be coming back regularly now, just doing the trip between here and home.' I said it carefully. She was going the way I wanted her to go without any help from me.

'Oh, that will be nice. Maybe we can see each other.'

'I had that in mind,' I said.

16

It was a beautiful American afternoon, with Manhattan shining like a forest in the sun. We went down to the pier on the West side, and went on the tripper boat up the Hudson and down the East River, sitting hand in hand, among all the people from Milwaulkee, Dallas and China. Even knowing what I know now, I still think it was one of the most romantic afternoons of my life, and I prefer to believe that Angie felt so too.

We made the long oval voyage of both murky rivers, paddling among barges and cargo ships, a liner going out and one coming in to take its place. The man at the wheel sang some songs through the loudspeaker and then told us to look and see where the Mayor of New York lived among the surprising city trees, and to see the windows of Frank Sinatra's apartment. Our heads turned left and right and left again with the rest.

At Riverdale I bowed quietly towards the place where Mrs Nissenbaum and myself when young had lived and loved. She did not haunt me now, not after these years, but I still remember her and Errol Flynn and the afternoon when my lovely big lover screamed from the bed: 'Oh my God, he's just eaten the French letter!' He was a greedy little dog and he had gobbled it up after I had dropped it from our vicinity. He was dead by the time we got him to the veterinary surgeon's, who told us that it was a rare occurrence, as if we didn't know, and charged twenty dollars, and that was all those years ago. God knows what it would cost today.

Naturally I did not tell Angie about Errol Flynn, but she noticed that I had become reflective as we rounded the wooded suburbia at the top of Manhattan Island.

'I knew a woman at Riverdale, once, many years ago,' I said. 'That's all. Just after the war.'

'The war?' she said with the puzzlement of those young

enough not to remember it, or even after it. 'You must have been a kid.'

'Sixteen,' I said. 'My first trip to sea. I got torpedoed. I think I must have been the last one. I was picked up and I came to New York and this lady looked after me.'

'How old was she?'

'Thirties, I suppose,' I said. 'She was amazing.'

'And you sixteen? I *bet* she looked after you. And torpedoed. You've seen everything, I guess.'

'Just about everything,' I agreed modestly although I wish, now, I hadn't said it.

I showed her my ship, lying over against the afternoon smoke of the wrong side of the river, but when we went under the bridge and chugged alongside Welfare Island I did not tell her that it was there that Mrs Nissenbaum, in her flying voluminous pink, descended heavily to her abrupt death. That I wanted to keep between Mrs Nissenbaum and myself.

When we got back to the city I told her I had to go out to dinner that night with a shipping agent and his wife. This was true, but she held both my hands and said with concern: 'Oh, really.'

'I'll see you tomorrow, if you can,' I suggested.

'Sure,' she smiled. 'It's a shame about tonight, though. I was hoping you could come in and talk.'

I stopped myself saying I would try. It would be good for her to wait until tomorrow, I thought. It would show that I didn't care for her in the background of the Split Legs Go-Go Bar. It would be good for us to be apart for a few hours; for the next day I would put my plan to her.

'I'll see you tomorrow,' I repeated. 'Be good, won't you?'

'If you mean you want me to promise that I won't take any man home, okay I promise,' she smiled. God, when I think of it now, I writhe. As I said later to Mr Trombone, she was some girl, and he said, 'Sure, some girl.'

All through dinner with Mr and Mrs Svensen that evening I kept thinking of her sitting in the mayhem of the Split Legs Go-Go Bar, while I sat in the sub-dued restaurant where we dined. Afterwards, with my own perverse leading, we went in that direction to find a taxi for the Svensens, and we actually waited outside the Split Legs Go-Go Bar until an unoccupied cab pulled up. I knew that Angie was within a few feet, but I would not let myself even look in that direction, nor hear the raw sounds coming from its cavern. When my guests had gone I stood uncertain, tempted, for a moment, and then walked resolutely away.

I had made up my mind to ask her as soon as we met the following day. She was only a minute late and she came to our meeting place in Central Park, by the fountains where I had walked with the late Mrs Nissenbaum. She was wear-ing a lime green trouser suit and a wide straw hat. Angie that is. Once again she looked wonderful.

We sat down on one of the seats facing the water and I said immediately: 'Angie, will you live with me when I'm in New York? I mean, have a proper home together.'

'Are you married?' she asked coolly.

'I was,' I said staring at the lake. 'My wife died in a car crash two years ago.'

'Oh, Arthur, I'm sorry.'

'One of those things,' I said. 'Part of life.'

'Why do you just want to live with me then? Why can't we be married?'

I thought I had better kiss her while I thought of an answer. I did so gently, feeling the soft lips and the New York sun on the back of my neck.

'I'm afraid,' I said simply, drawing back. 'My life takes me everywhere, and it's the only life I know. My marriage was a disaster, Angie, because we were strangers. I often wonder if she crashed that car purposely.'

'You mustn't say that. You mustn't blame yourself, honey.'

'I do. I've been in misery since it happened.'

'It's not the Split Legs Go-Go Bar you're afraid of?' she asked. 'You're not afraid to risk me because I work there?'

'You won't work there any more, will you, please,' I said. 'I went crazy thinking about you there last night.'

She kissed my neck. 'I'll quit,' she said. 'You know I don't belong there. I'll quit right now.' She clapped her hands. 'There! Split Legs Go-Go Bar, I quit!'

'Shush,' I said. 'Someone will hear you.'

'I don't care,' she laughed. 'When can we start?'

'What? Living together?'

'What else, crazy?'

We threw our arms about each other and held each other, and when we looked up there were two old ladies, with dogs and carrying red balloons, as people in Central Park curiously do, and they applauded us while we shrank with embarrassment.

'You *will* be coming back, won't you?' said Angie anxiously. 'All the time, I mean. Every three weeks, like you said.'

'I'll sign a ten year contract with Cohen Overseas Lines,' I promised.

'What about in England?' she said. 'You won't be unfaithful to me with women in England, will you?'

'Nobody's got a hope,' I said exultantly. I held her at arms length in the bright park sun, and thought what a marvellous catch I had made. Oh, God.

'Where will we live?' she said. 'If we're *living* together, we've got to have somewhere to *live*. I'll keep house for you and go to art school while I'm waiting for you to come home, and maybe I'll get a part time job somewhere.'

'No clubs or bars,' I said.

'Never,' she promised. 'I told you, mister, I'm the original girl from Turniptown.'

Immediately, my arm around her comfortable waist, we began to walk from the Park towards the city. 'We can get a service apartment, can't we?' I said. 'Just for now. For the first few weeks. Then you can look for somewhere better. Maybe a bit out of New York in a nice neighbourhood.'

'Can I join the tennis club?' she laughed.

'If the other wives will let you.'

'I won't be your wife,' she sulked. 'You've only got me on trial.'

'And you've got me on trial,' I said. 'Let's not hurry it, darling. It will be all right in the end. I know it will.'

'You know? You really know?'

'I do,' I said seriously. I felt as though I were swimming through the city's summer air. I wondered briefly if Pamela was watching Peyton Place, but I did not dwell on it. And that is what we did, God help me, that very afternoon. We went like babbling teenagers into the city, hand in hand across the road in front of the Plaza, patting the buggy horses on their bored noses and joyfully dodging the traffic. I must have looked strange running like that with her, laughing in that young way. We slowed down and jogged along in front of the Fifth Avenue Shops, among all the people, and it occurred to me that this delight is what I should have felt long ago with my wife.

We went to some agencies and by four o'clock we were looking out of our own window at an avalanche of back walls on the West Side. The place was small and the furniture minimal. Someone had fashioned their initials in the grit on the window pane and the carpet had so many holes it looked like a good cheese.

'It's sure crummy,' she laughed. 'But it doesn't matter. We've got it, and that's all that counts.'

Because, until then, we had always been together in public places our contact had been inhibited, but now, in that dusty room in the basement of that glamorous city, I pulled Angie to me and felt her for the first time. Jesus, to think I did that.

We kissed and my hands travelled slowly over her. From the tight bottom up the curve of her back, from her firm waist to the joyful breasts.

'There's a bed in there,' I said against her neck.

'You randy pig,' she laughed. Then she relaxed her clutch and said soberly: 'I don't want it like that. Not right now, Arthur. I want to be *domestic* with you. I'm

227

your wife and I don't just want to be rushed into the sack in the afternoon. Wives don't do that.'

'Some wives do.'

'Not with their husbands,' she laughed. She pulled herself close to me again. 'Listen, honey. I haven't got a thing of my own here. I need to go and get a couple of suitcases from my room.'

I should have gone back to the ship for an hour, but I had a good first officer, so I telephoned instead and told him I would be back the next morning. The company would not have liked it, if they'd known (for one thing Mr Cohen's Rolls had to be stowed), but I did not want to let her out of my sight now.

We took a cab to a street beyond Washington Square and seeing it again reminded me of the day when I walked alone through the crowds on the day the war ended, and the man I had talked to on the park bench. The bench was still there. I could see it from the cab. She asked me to wait while she went into an old apartment block. She was very quick, returning in five minutes with another girl, a lovely blonde, helping her with her cases.

'Sandra,' she said when we were all standing on the pavement. 'This is Arthur. Arthur, Sandra.'

I thought that she actually sounded so proud. Considering the difference of twenty years between us, and considering also that hardly a person in my life had ever actually been proud of me, I felt flattered and more loving toward her than ever. The brilliant blonde smiled and said: 'I guess you're just what Angie's been looking for.' She turned and kissed Angie on the cheek and said: 'Bye, honey. If he treats you bad, you can always come back here.'

'Sandie's fantastic,' said Angie when we were back in the cab again. 'But she's just crazy. Lots of men. And she loves them all.'

'Does she work at the Split Legs Go-Go Bar?' I asked. The window to the driver's seat was ajar and I saw him hunch his shoulders in a laugh. Angie briskly leaned forward and shut the glass.

'She does sometimes. But she does some modelling and men are always giving her money.'

'Did men always give you money?' I asked. I always make it difficult for myself.

'Sometimes,' she nodded. 'But for nothing.'

'True? For nothing?'

She turned to me. 'I told you I've only been at that place ten days, nights, and I'm straight from the sticks. I would only do it for love, Arthur. I can get dollars without that.'

Naturally I believed her. We took her luggage to the apartment and then we went out to a street market and bought some rugs and two pictures for the walls and pots and pans, and cleaning things.

'Do you want to have dinner out tonight, or shall we eat at home?' I asked when we had returned.

'There's a lot you don't know about me,' she said sadly. 'And one of the things is I never learned to cook in Turnip-town. When you get back next time I promise I will.'

'That will only be three weeks.'

'I'll get through Cordon Bleu in that time,' she boasted. 'I make good coffee, though.'

'We'll go out,' I said catching hold of her. 'As it's our wedding night and when we get back I'll sit in my arm-chair and you can make the coffee.'

So we went. We went to Sardi's where I had last gone with Mrs Nissenbaum. We even sat at the same table by the door. I felt like a ghost sitting there and the recollections flying back again. I smiled at the head waiter as though he ought to recognize me. All that time ago. Sitting there, a trembling boy, wondering what was happening to me, and opposite that marvellous blown up woman who had been both mother and lover to me for those few weeks. Now it was I who was getting old, and sitting in Mrs Nissenbaum's place was this fresh, lovely and familiar girl, in her turn to be a substitute for the real thing for Arthur McCann.

All through dinner I could scarcely take my eyes from

her. She smiled at me indulgently through our conversations. I told her about places I had been and carefully selected things I had done in all my years of traipsing the seas. She told me about Turniptown, about the school, her home and her parents. The next summer, we vowed, when I got my long leave we would go together to see them.

Afterwards we walked back through the city and I got both my feet caught in a patch of unmarked gluey stuff at a place where some building work was going on. I pretended I could not move from the spot, picking up my feet in turn with the thick strings of glue yawning from the pavement to my soles. She was wearing a splendid ice blue dress, but she sat on the gutter and laughed into her hands at my antics.

Then we went to shop windows along our way and selected furniture and chattels that we would purchase when we had our real home. We even found a crib for our first child and it was then that the possibilities of the whole thing really came to me. It was the Captain's Paradise. If only I could keep Angie and Pamela on the separate sides of the Atlantic I could have the sexual domesticity I needed so badly. I told myself that I knew it could work. Poor sod.

By midnight we were back in our close apartment and the door bolted behind us. The curtains did not fit when I pulled them across, but that district was mostly in darkness and the people sleeping.

Angie made the coffee and she sat placidly in my lap on the one comfortable armchair in that doleful room. I had my arms complacently about her, as though we had been familiar with each other for a long time. It was a new and comforting feeling, we told each other. She glanced at her watch. 'I'm going to get ready for bed,' she said. 'Stay here, husband, and smoke your pipe.'

'I don't smoke a pipe,' I said.

'We must get you one,' she said, getting up from my lap. 'The image demands a pipe.' It was marvellous, I thought, feeling the small flesh of her buttocks leave my knees. She leaned towards me and kissed me on the mouth. 'I'm going to put my nightdress on, like any decent woman. Understand? It's a pity you haven't got any pyjamas. We could be really quiet and domestic then.'

'I'll go out and see if there's a midnight pyjama store open,' I said.

She regarded me from the side of the chair: 'It's a great game, isn't it?' she said.

'I think it is. Keeping house,' I said.

'Keeping house, that's it,' she smiled. 'A game for people who have never played before.'

'We'll get better at it as we gain experience,' I said.

She yawned beautifully: 'Darling, I must go and get my clothes off. I've had such a busy day in the house.'

'I won't be long,' I said. 'I've had a hell of a day at the ship.'

She laughed briefly and went into the bedroom. I was slotted into that chair, thinking about what was coming. That lovely body in a soft nightdress. Waking up in the dark and smelling her hair, feeling her flesh against me. My dream had evoked a creeping erection. I wriggled to accommodate it. To hear her rustling movements in the next room and to see her slim shadow projected from the door to the floor a few feet from me, increased my anticipation. Then the doorbell rang. Eight times.

Something was going to happen to spoil it. I knew it. I was about to get a bucketful in my face again. Angie came to the bedroom door, wearing a lovely pink nightdress that went down to her feet. She had a dab of cream on her nose. I stared at her, letting the doorbell ring another fusilade, taking in the beauty of her and having the painful suspicion that I would have to be content to remember her like that. Whoever was outside that door was going to kill it for us. It was like the Gestapo demanding entry.

'Angie!' screamed a voice from the landing. 'Oh, Angie!'

'Sandra,' she caught her breath and her breast and

231

moved forward from the bedroom door. I went to help her, slipping my arm about her waist for one last feel while we were about it. We opened the door and the blonde I had seen that afternoon was standing there, weeping, blood running from the corner of her mouth, hair hanging in hanks. She stumbled in.

'Angie,' she sobbed and fell into my girl's embrace.

'Oh, Sandie, come on in, honey. Come in. What happened?'

'Yes, come in Sandie,' I said lamely. I thought I felt the floor breaking up like a cracking ice floe.

She was already in, shaking in Angie's arms, pressed against that soft nylon where I ought to have been.

'What happened, baby, what happened?' Angie kept asking.

'What happened, baby?' I sighed.

We put her down in the chair and Angie told me to get some coffee. As I went into the kitchen I hit my groin in the narrow entrance and I thought I felt my thing grunt with injury added to insult and disappointment.

When I returned with the coffee Angie was kneeling before her friend, wiping the edge of her mouth with a handkerchief.

'She was attacked, Arthur,' she explained. 'Have you got the coffee?'

I gave her the coffee and she gulped at it as though she had been bombed.

'It was Leroy,' she said to me. I blinked.

'Leroy is a friend of hers,' explained Angie, half turning and looking up at me. Anger and jealousy, that her concern had gone from me to the woman, swamped me.

'The swine,' I said feelingly.

At this, Sandra threw her arms wide and howled 'I love him!' She began to weep copiously. She slopped the coffee from the cup all over my stockinged feet (I should explain that in my domestic role I had taken off my shoes, my jacket and my tie. I had a sad but convincing suspicion that this would be the total of my divestment that night).

No one even noticed my hot, wet socks, although I leapt at the pain. 'The bastard,' sobbed Sandra. 'But I love him. I love that mad guy, Angie!' Her hysterics increased and Angie, like a flamingo, enclosed her in her pink nyloned arms again. Christ, there was I in a room with two ravishing creatures and all I got was coffee on my socks.

'He'll kill you one day,' warned Angie. 'The pig will kill you, Sandie.'

'I love him,' bawled Sandie again, 'And he loves me.'

'There's different ways of showing it,' I said consolingly. They took no notice of me.

A small, apologetic Mexican-looking man with a tearful moustache was standing at the open door when I turned that way again. He had apparently been standing there for some time and was taking in the embrace of the weeping Sandie and the consoling Angie with huge interest.

'Señor,' he asked, when he saw I had spotted him. 'Can anybody join?'

'It's Leroy,' I sighed defeatedly. 'He hit her.'

'But I love him!' confirmed Sandra from the room.

'But she loves him,' I told the Mexican.

'That's okay then, señor,' he said preparing to go away. 'I was just getting worried, that's all.' He waved an in-effectual Latin hand. 'Adios,' he said.

'Adios,' I nodded, shutting the door.

Leroy, I said to myself. Leroy. Over the years I thought I could remember that name. Leroy. Then I saw the coloured whore of my youth laughing into the telephone and saying 'Leroy, that skunk!' No it couldn't be the same Leroy! He couldn't have come back to fuck things up again for me, not after all these years.

'I'm scared,' shivered Sandra. 'I'm scared to go back. He'll kill me. I just wish I didn't love him.'

'Sounds like it's a risky thing,' I said.

'Arthur,' said Angie severely. 'I don't think you realize just how serious this is. This guy's a no-good. He'll harm poor Sandie if he can. Look at her now. All blood and bruises.'

'I can't go back to that room,' said Sandra. 'I'll die in there with him.'

'You've got to stay,' said Angie decisively. Then, as though she realized for the first time, she looked unhappily, apologetically at me and said: 'I'm sorry, darling. But she's just *got* to stay.'

'I'm going,' said Sandra leaping up from the chair. 'I'm a selfish slut. Crashing in on you two tonight!' Then she collapsed into the chair again, simultaneously with my hopes, and sobbed: 'There's nowhere else I could go. Nobody I could turn to. I'm scared, Angie, honey. I'm real scared.'

There was nowhere anyone could sleep in that apartment except in the bed, on the floor or on the table. We all three slept in the bed. Sandra and I on the flanks and Angie in the middle. It was far worse than sleeping alone on your first night.

I lay awake, sore eyed, through most of the dark hours, holding my woman and genuinely trying not to commit accidental indecent assault on the other one. It was a very close fit in that bed and we sweated a lot through the night. But they both slept deeply. I attempted to manoeuvre Angie's body more to my advantage, but every move seemed to end with my arm or my leg being trapped in some deadening way. Eventually I moved towards her lovely sleeping face, my loins howling for her, and she turned a full turn like a slow splendid fish and cuddled close into the warmly breathing form of her friend on the other edge of the bed.

In the morning Sandra was optimistically transformed. She would be able to handle Leroy, she assured us, because he was a great guy really. It was just that he drank. It was not wise to approach him too early in the morning, before the air had got to his lungs, because he could be difficult, but if she left it a while he would be amenable later. So she stayed with us until it was time for me to go back to the ship for my voyage home. She gave me a daughterly kiss on the cheek and thanked me overwhelmingly for allowing her refuge. Angie came quietly down the stairs with me and at the door, in a great gallery of morning sun cutting between two tall buildings, she kissed me like a true wife.

'Gee, I'm so sorry, Arthur, honey,' she sighed. 'But I'll make it up to you when you get back. You'll know you've *really* got me then. And nobody will bother us.'

'Unless Leroy is on the rampage again,' I said.

'I don't blame you for being sore,' she whispered. 'But you were marvellous. Only an Englishman could be like that. I love you darling.'

These last sentiments were keenly observed by a red haired youth and an elderly down-and-out who paused in their pavement journeys to listen and to see the lovely flamingo lady say goodbye to her sailor. They nodded approvingly, as interlopers quite often do in New York, and continued their passage. I went down the street to get a cab to Hoboken.

She stepped from the doorway, attracting even more passing attention, and waving, called: 'I'll be waiting, honey!' Immediately, furtively envious men stared at me from every side and I waved and called back: 'I won't be long, baby!' If only they had known the greyness of my heart. Three weeks, five thousand miles and my wife Pamela, stretched between that moment and my return to that marvellous girl. I prayed she would stay and be there when I opened the door again.

I found a cab and we went across the bridge to Hoboken. She didn't blame me, she had said, for being sore. I was sore. But not in the right place.

17

All the way down the river and out to the sea, as far as the Nantucket Light, my mind was with her and on her. I hardly remembered to slow to drop the pilot and I would not have done so if that anxious man had not tugged my sleeve some nautical miles out. When I went below I wrote a long sad chapter of 'All The Coloured Lights Of The World by Arthur McCann', and slept grumpily through the beginnings of one of the most terrible storms I have ever known at sea.

The ship, the S.S. *Cohen Prince*, was twenty-three years old and ten thousand tons, flagship of Cohen Overseas Lines. Travelling as a passenger on that trip was Mr Isadore Cohen, President of the Company, who had a Rolls-Royce motor car in the hold, and my job in his pocket. He had come aboard only minutes after I had arrived in my taxi from Manhattan. He was a fault-finding man at the best of times and he indicated that I must have arranged the storm especially for him.

On the fourth night out, when the wind had raised itself to force ten and the ship was rolling and dipping like a randy elephant, the Rolls in the hold broke loose.

At eleven o'clock I was on the bridge when I was told that the car had burst some of its retaining ropes and was tugging at the others. We were light on hold cargo that trip and I knew that it had room enough to career about if it became free. It was a silver Rolls with every finery and embellishment that Cohen money could demand, and I knew the man loved it. He took it to Europe with him and left his wife in America. Nothing must happen to that car.

'Get two men down into the hold and secure the bloody thing,' I said to the bo'sun.

'I've tried sir, but they want danger money.'

There was no time to argue. 'Get that car secure, bo'sun,' I said. 'If we've got to pay, we've got to pay.'

The bo'sun wanted danger money as well for ordering the men down there in the first place. When all the negotiations were complete, I stumbled from the bridge and went to see the situation for myself.

Few things are more frightening at sea than cargo adrift in the hold of a rolling and pitching ship in the darkness of an Atlantic night. In the awful light down there two seamen and the bo'sun were clinging to the hold ladders while the car plunged and jerked, like a stallion trying to break out of a stall.

'Secure it!' I bellowed. 'I didn't send you down to admire the thing.'

I heard one of the men say 'bollocks' under his breath but this was no time to stand on ceremony. The front of the huge car was rearing up almost pawing the air with every yawning movement of the ship, the wind was hooting through the open hatch over our heads, the lights were swinging like acrobats. I had been at sea more than twenty years and I felt sick. With every fall and rise of the bow we had to hang on and be swung around like hanging cargo ourselves.

'Double danger money for the man who secures it,' I shouted.

Both men nodded and at the right time jumped into the floor of the hold and scrambled towards the enraged vehicle like hunters. At that moment it tore itself clear of the holding ropes at its rear and in a frightening charge went down the steep temporary hill of the hold's floor, collided with some piled bags of bone meal fertilizer, and then, as the ship reared into the sea again, rolled backwards to its original site. The two men scattered as it charged at them, one slipped and fell flat on the bottom boards. The bo'sun and I shouted, as though he wasn't aware of the danger, and he swivelled and rolled out of the way as the car charged back on its path again. The other seaman had taken refuge behind some piled bags and was crouching petrified. The berserk vehicle began its hideous journey again.

At that moment Mr Cohen, president of Cohen Overseas Lines, summoned no doubt by his toadying steward, appeared at my shoulder arrayed in the only fur dressing gown I have ever seen. I had an illogical vision of my grandfather and the giant sloth he vowed he had seen in foreign places.

'My life! My Rolls!' shrieked Mr Cohen. 'Why is this happening to my Rolls-Royce?' His face was green in the nasty light.

'It's come free of its ropes, Mr Cohen,' I muttered. 'We're trying to secure it.'

'Put the handbrake on!' he howled. 'For God's sake put the handbrake on. That's fifty thousand dollars worth of automobile.'

At that moment the Rolls seemed to bunch itself like an athlete at the wind-up for a supreme effort and then it went banging down the length of the hold and hit the fertilizer sacks with the most spectacular explosion. Sacks burst under the ramming and clouds of the fertilizer were flung into the meyhem. Metallic clatterings told us that bits were falling from the car, and behind me Mr Cohen was moaning and muttering short Hebrew prayers.

'You go,' he said suddenly, cutting into his devotions. 'You go. You're the assholing captain.' He dug me between the shoulder blades as he swung side-faced towards me with a heave of the bulkhead.

'Me?' I asked. 'But I can't, sir. I'm in charge of the ship.'

'You won't be mister, if you don't stop that car pissing about,' he warned. 'That vehicle has been through every major city in Europe and America without a scratch. I'm not having it written off in the middle of the ocean!'

I don't know why I went down there, but I did. I would have been well within my rights to refuse, even on account of my age and not even considering my rank. But I went anyway. I suppose there was some motive of impressing the owner and my crew, and somewhere in the decision was the thought that I had to be back in New York three weeks from then.

She rolled and then, in that penitent way that ships have even in the worse storms, I felt her steady and steam straight and true as though she were on a minor lake. I knew it would last fifteen seconds at the most. I saw the car go by, backwards, through the clouds of choking fertilizer dust. The man on the floor was trembling like a shipwrecked mariner on an island of crates, just beyond the vehicle's reach.

I dropped down on to the floor of the hold and immediately made a run for the car through the fertilizer dust filling my eyes and my throat. It had to be then or never. I was not even sure in my mind what I was going to do, but I knew they were all watching me. Running at it, I swooped and picked up one of the trailing ropes which had previously held it secure. Then, when I was almost there, the wretched ship pitched forward again, at a hell of an angle. It was as though the car had been waiting for me. All the God-knows-how-many tons of that grinning silver bulk was suddenly coming my way.

For a moment I froze then I jumped like a frog, clean over the charging nose. I even heard the bo'sun laugh as I went hurtling through the thickly fertilized air, hit the pointed roof of the bonnet and slid brilliantly down the other side. I was sprawling on the floor when the car hit the sacks again. It would be charging back at any second and I was in its path. Like some funnyman I tried to get to my feet, but the sudden lifting of the ship threw me forward on to my face again. The car was coming back. I could hear it and turning my apprehensive eyes I saw it careering towards me. In that moment of fright I was actually swimming on the floor of the hold, my legs and arms performing an authentic breast stroke, which miraculously carried me a fraction to one side. When the wheels were only feet away and running at me, I twisted and felt them go by my head.

'Oh Jesus,' I was praying. 'Oh Angie! Oh, Pamela! . . . Oh, Mrs Nissenbaum!'

Somehow I managed to get to my knees, then my feet. The car was right back into its first position now, a missile loaded into its launcher. At a queer monkey gait, I began to climb the steep uphill slope, trying to make for the bags of fertilizer which would offer me sanctuary. Then, I was running downhill, as the bow dived again. Running, scrambling, staggering, with that bloody car snorting down at my heels. I made it to the bags by two seconds at the most. I fell forward just as the bonnet and the bumper slammed into them again. All around the bags were exploding and the choking dust was in my throat, my nose and my eyes. I couldn't see the car any longer, only hear its metallic destruction of itself and most of the things around it.

'Oh, Angie,' I managed to cough again. 'Oh, Pamela . . . Oh, Mrs Nissenbaum.'

'You're the first person they've ever had in this hospital suffering from bone meal fertilizer gassing,' said Pamela at my bedside. 'There's a doctor who says he's going to write up your case for one of those medical papers. With pictures of your lungs and windpipe.' She sighed. 'It's just like you Arthur. When you get your picture in the paper, it has to be your inside.'

'Nobody will recognize me, you mean,' I said. Speaking was still painful for my throat, despite all their pumpings and pummellings it still seemed lined with broken glass.

'Well, hardly,' she sniffed. 'Not from your lungs they won't.'

'But it will have a caption, I expect,' I argued painfully. 'It will say whose lungs they are.'

'That's not the same,' she said. 'Not the same at all.'

'Well don't nag me about it,' I grumbled painfully. 'I didn't *arrange* all this you know, Pamela. I didn't actually *fix* it. God, I feel like a bag stuffed with sawdust.'

'They quite *like* having you in here,' she conceded. 'Being as they've never seen anything quite like you before it gives them a chance to do a bit of their experimenting, I suppose. That man who gave you the kiss-of-life . . .'

'The bo'sun,' I said.

'Yes, him. It was ever so amusing to hear him describe it. He kept getting mouthfuls of that fertilizer stuff as he was breathing into you. He said you kept spouting the muck out like a combine harvester.'

'Well I'm glad everyone was amused,' I mumbled. 'Mr Cohen wasn't though.'

'Scrap metal, that Rolls,' she confirmed. 'It's down at the dock now. They say it's the first Rolls-Royce ever to be wrecked at sea. He was quite nice, really, that Mr Cohen, for a Jewish gentleman that is. He felt he had to explain why he couldn't do anything but sack you, so he took me out for a drink at The Queen's Hotel and we got on so well that we ended up having dinner together.'

'Oh, did you?' I croaked nastily.

'Yes. It was a pity you had to mess up a job with a nice man like that, Arthur.'

'How's our flat?' I coughed.

'The flat? What a funny thing to say. It's all right. But very steamy and damp since the laundrette was put underneath.'

'A laundrette? The baker's gone?'

'Of course it's gone. You could hardly have a bakers and a laundrette in the same couple of rooms could you? The cakes would go soggy. As it is everything gets steamed up and damp upstairs.'

Every time I gathered myself to say a long sentence the bone meal rose in my gullet and blocked it and I had to lie still until the nurse came along to pummel me and make it come right up. It was a very nasty experience, like sicking up old porridge. It happened now and Pamela couldn't look, so she went off to the other end of the ward and, while the nurse was pummelling me, I could see her having a cheery laugh with a professional footballer with a broken leg who was in the bed near the window.

Eventually when another lot of fertilizer had been disposed of, she came back and stood at the side of the bed. 'I'm going then, Arthur,' she said. 'I'm glad you mentioned the flat because I wanted to have a chat with you about things anyway.'

'About the steam?' I said. 'We'll complain, darling.'

'No, not just that. Things in general. But I'll wait until you get out of here and you've stopped bringing up those wood-shavings. Then we'll have a nice talk.'

'Can't you tell me now?' I asked. 'Visiting time's not finished yet.'

'No, I won't now,' she said, kissing me briefly on the cheek, and turning to go. 'The last thing I want to do is upset you when you're ill.'

It was the last day of the season for the putting green in the park. In fact it was the last hour of the last day of the putting season; October, with the day going to ashes around us, and our lives too, although I did not realize it at the start.

I had said to her: 'When are you going to tell me whatever it is you are going to tell me?' She was quite fat now, in her thirties, but still pretty in her plumpish way, and although I still had thoughts of Angie in New York, I honestly think at that time I could have stayed with Pamela forever and been comfortable.

After all I had never actually *had* Angie, lovely as she was. I had only been in her close proximity. What you never have you never really miss. At that point I might have even given up the sea and got a shore job and tried to build a decent, everyday life with Pamela. We might even have a late child.

'Let's go down to the putting green,' she said.

'Now?'

'Yes, now. We can have a game and I can talk to you.'

'But it's three o'clock nearly, and they close it for the season about this time of the year. It's probably closed now.'

'Let's go and see,' she insisted.

So we went. A funny thing happened on the way. Well, not funny, but odd in its own fashion. A man with a terrible stutter came up to us in the street and asked the way to the bus station. It turned out that the poor bugger was not just a stutterer, but was deaf as well.

We had to yell at him and he kept stammering back telling us there was no need to shout. But it broke the ominous silence between us; we bent towards him as though he was a conveniently lost child and we both took turns at explaining and shouting, and trying to make out what he was saying, and somehow, it suddenly restored earth under our feet; it gave to us something we could do together, some common interest.

'You don't realize how well off you are until you meet somebody like that, do you?' I said hopefully. I was reluctant to let our new tenuous contact fall apart without making every effort to cement it.

'He's only lost the bus station,' she sniffed.

'He had a bit of a job to ask where it is,' I pointed out. 'And more of a job to hear the answer.'

'I suppose he was quite brave really,' she conceded. We were at the bowed iron gates to the park now. I could see the old, white man who looked after the putting green in the distance, beyond the closed tea kiosk and the band stand. 'You ought to have been braver, Arthur,' she said to my astonishment. 'All your life, you ought to have tried to be just a little bit more brave. Can you understand me?'

'Brave?' I said. 'What are you talking about?'

The old, white, man came towards us and I asked for the hire of two putters and two golf balls. He stared at us, first me then her, with aged astonishment. 'But it's packing up,' he said wheezily. 'Putting's finished for the winter. I'm just going out to collect the little flags and put the stoppers in the holes.' He glared at us challengingly. 'It's all finished, I tell you.'

I would have gone away, but Pamela said: 'It says on the notice that it's four-thirty when putting is finished, so even if this is the last day it's not four-thirty yet.'

'But it's nearly dark by then,' he argued. 'The council says that I can pack up when there's nobody else who wants to putt this afternoon, because it's the end of the season. Can't you see that?'

'We want to have a game,' said Pamela.

'It's chilly and it's getting dark,' he said. 'I was hoping to go home.'

'Hard luck,' she said uncharitably. 'We want a putt.'

'Trust you,' he snarled, as though we did it out of spite every autumn when he was ready to quit. 'Just trust you.'

Ill-temperedly he handed two putters to us and two chewed up golf balls and almost snatched the money from me. We walked away, leaving him hunched and scowling, and went to the small arrow marked 'Hole One' at the edge of the green.

'We didn't *have* to play, did we?' I said. 'The poor old bugger wants to go home for the winter. He's cold.'

'That's just your trouble,' she said. 'Backing away. Never getting in and getting things. That's what I was saying before.'

'What?'

'About you. You're just not brave enough.'

'Christ! Not brave enough? I'm the one who nearly got stuffed with fertilizer trying to save a bloody car in a force nine gale.'

'I'm not talking about that,' she said. She put her ball down and struck it truly towards the hole. It never looked like going anywhere but down into the cup and it did with a single, confident plop. I hit my ball sullenly, not hard enough. It rolled and stopped a foot short.

'What I'm saying, Arthur,' she went on, 'is that you, *you*, could have really *been* somebody. When I first met you that night I thought you might really turn out to be something important later on in life. Honestly I did.'

'I can't say I remember you showed it,' I grunted. My anger was low, for over it was a cold sludge of unhappiness; now I sensed what she was going to say to me. I prayed she wouldn't say it, because I really did love her.

She putted the scarred ball towards the next hole, carelessly, but laid it up to within three inches of the lip. 'Your trouble,' she sniffed more at the ball than at me. 'Your trouble, Arthur, is that you've spent your life trying to be *ordinary. Ordinary*, that's what. In everything. If you'd set out with a bit of guts to be *GREAT* you would have been *GREAT*. Or very nearly. I know it, Arthur. Instead

244

you've held back, sniffling along like some timid bloody hedgehog.'

I stared at her with genuine astonishment. She looked up at me. 'Your putt,' she invited. Then she looked behind us, and I did too, and the white, anxious attendant was following us, taking up the flags and filling in the hole which we had played. He put a neat little round of turf fixed to a tin base into the hole and stood belligerently with the miniature flag in his hand, waiting for us to continue the game.

I putted my ball in a dream. 'How can you say that to me?' I said. 'God Almighty, Pamela, I'm only in my forties and I've got my extra master's certificate. I'm a bloody sea captain, I'll have you know!'

'I'm cold,' called the old man querulously behind us.

We both looked at him. He looked cold. Pamela said to me: 'You could have been anything. *Anything*. An admiral! But you'd rather be a bus conductor.'

'I would not!' I protested. 'And there's no admirals in the merchant service, you ought to know that. But I am the master of a vessel.'

She walked to the hole and tapped her ball down carefully. 'I wouldn't count on that either,' she said. 'Mr Cohen says there'll be an inquiry about his Rolls breaking loose. He says cargo adrift is a very serious matter and the responsibility of the master of the ship. You could find yourself down to first officer again.'

The possibility had already occurred to me. 'Thanks,' I said miserably. 'That should give you something to laugh about.' I mechanically knocked the ball towards the hole and missed. I knocked it the other way and missed again.

'If you're going to play, play properly,' snorted the slowly pursuing attendant. 'I'm not hanging around watching you playing ping pong.'

'Sorry,' I called back apologetically.

'Sorry indeed!' she snorted. 'Sorry! Don't say sorry to him. That's you all over. Why don't you go and give him a kiss?'

'Lay off,' I said, glaring at her. 'The poor old sod's cold.'

'Go and rub his hands, then,' she said. 'Give him a hug. What you should do is to tell him to shut his trap and let us get on with the game. He's being paid. He's cheating the ratepayers if he goes off early.'

We played a few more holes in silence, the attendant, bending and following us like some peevish pilgrim crouching in prayer and collecting sacred flags at every few steps to some shrine.

'You've always been so . . . well, so wet,' she went on again. I turned my sullen face towards her and saw to my amazement that there were tears filling her eyes. I had never seen her cry.

'You're crying, darling,' I said moving towards her.

She backed away. 'Keep off,' she said. 'I'm crying for you because you're such a fool. You screw everything up in life because you're afraid of offending somebody or other. While you've been in hospital I've been reading that bloody great book you've been writing all these years . . .'

I froze in mid-putt and turned to her. 'All The Coloured Lights Of The World by Arthur McCann', I said. Nobody had ever seen it before. 'You've read it?'

'They brought it home with the rest of your things,' she said guiltily but still defiant. 'And I read it.'

'I wondered why you were so upset,' I muttered. The putter shook in my fingers and the ball wriggled drunkenly down the green. I heard the attendant snort derisively. I said: 'All those women and things. They're not real, you know, Pam. I only made it up. You mustn't get annoyed because none of it is real. It's only a book.'

'God give me patience,' she muttered. 'You're such a blind, buggering fool. Don't you see? It would have been a hundred per cent better if they had been real! Christ, I would have thought you had some blood in your guts anyway. Not just that sawdust.' She turned on me. I thought she was going to grasp me by the lapels. 'Can't you see? Can't you understand? I could have been happy with a man like that, no matter how many women he screwed in no matter how many places! At least he would be a man. Not a fucking ninny!'

'Swearing!' shouted the old man behind us. 'Swearing, abuse and disagreements on the putting green. It's against the by-laws.'

'Wrap up!' she snarled at him in a fury now. 'And stop sniffing after us or I'll strangle you and that will really be against the sodding by-laws.'

'Strangle me?' He stared at her horrified. 'But I'm sixty-six.'

'There's no age limit,' she bellowed. 'Clear off before I do it.'

Scraggy mackintosh hanging about him, he backed away towards his hut. 'I'll get the superintendent to you,' he trembled. 'I'll go and get him now. You can't threaten me like that.'

We watched him go. There seemed to be no more to say about him. 'I thought you were happy,' I said to her. 'All these years, I thought you were happy just being here and waiting for me to come home. You shouldn't have said you'd marry me if you weren't sure.'

She was about to strike her ball, but she swung the putter through the air over its head instead. 'You might as well know now,' she said. 'That I never did say I'd marry you. When I sent you that telegram it was to say nothing doing. The answer, Arthur, was "no". But you had to lose the bloody thing before you read it. I was going to marry Charlie Hughes, the butcher in Commercial Road, if you want to know, but he ditched me the night before you came home. Then you turned up like some shining Prince Charming, all innocent and happy, so I thought I might as well have you instead.'

'Oh no,' I breathed. I stared at her because I did not believe she was suddenly saying these things. 'Oh, no, that's not true. You didn't want to marry me?'

'Look, Arthur, I didn't. Get that straight. You were a romantic sop then and you still are now.'

'You mean I ought to have been tough with you?'

'Tough! Violent, that's what you should have been. And you should have gone around the world belting and kicking all those women like the man in your book, then you wouldn't have come home every time like some pent-up bloody missionary. God, you used to give me the creeps.'

'Perhaps I did,' I said desperately. 'Perhaps I did do that to all those women.'

'Too late to start making out you're a good fuck now,' she said blatantly. 'You don't know what it means. You're the only man I ever knew who folded his *socks* before getting into bed with me.'

'A person can be tidy *and* passionate,' I argued quietly. Then I realized what she had admitted. 'You've . . . you've had affairs then. With other men.'

'Yes, dozens,' she said firmly. She was still playing putting and she rolled the ball several feet, with a right hand bias to go ahead by something like six holes to nil on our game.

'But Pam . . .'

She looked up at me, at my lost face, and I could see she was really crying now. 'You twerp,' she sobbed. 'I've had the trousers off half the men in this town. What did you think I was doing? Waiting for you to come home and put that clean pillow under my arse?'

Her face collapsed in weeping. And then it happened. She took a huge, blind, angry swing at my golf ball with her putter and sent it soaring off, a foot above the ground. The old, white, attendant was just returning irritably through the dusk with the park superintendent and had reached the little gate at the end of the putting area. He opened it and put his leg through just in time to meet the skimming golf ball as it flew from Pamela's violent blow. It struck him on the knee and with a terrible screech of agony and fear he collapsed on to the gloomy path and lay writhing there. Stiff with horror I looked at him and then I felt the putter thrust into my hand. I now had two. I looked and saw Pamela running towards the far gate by which we had entered.

I turned again. The old, white man was flat on his back, his legs waving feebly in the damp Newport air, another man, presumably the summoned superintendent hurrying through the gate towards him. I turned and ran after Pamela.

If they caught me, I thought as I ran, I would explain that I was running after my wife to save my marriage, and not attempting escape from justice. She was always a good runner and she had gone out of the park gates and vanished into the gloom by the time I reached the road. I ran towards home, took a short cut across some waste ground to head her off, and emerged into the main street again. I was breathless already for the fertilizer dust was still in my lungs to some extent and they had warned me not to run. Now it rose up my tubes and clouds of it flew around inside me and even came out of my mouth. I stopped, bent and gasping. A timid hand touched me eventually and I lifted my choking face to see a recently familiar and puzzled countenance.

'Pl . . . . . e . . . . . eeese,' he stammered. 'Cccccc ould . . . you . . . ttttellll me . . . . . the bbbbbbbbbus sttttation . . . . . bus station.'

I straightened up and cleared the awful dust from my gullet. I wiped my wet eyes. He watched me with mute sympathy. Then I bent down near his deaf ear and called out the directions once more. I hope he got there that time, poor devil. I didn't see why he should suffer.

18

It was another three months before I was able to get to New York to seek my splendid Angie. At that time I was suspended on full pay pending the inquiry into the wreck-of Mr Cohen's Rolls-Royce in Mid-Atlantic. It had become known that I was not on the ship when the vehicle was loaded and had not personally supervised the stowing, as instructed by Mr Cohen. The reason, of course, was that I was in Manhattan trying to occupy one bed with two women.

I could not hope to find her at our apartment; I realized that. I had written to her half a dozen times but, like my letters so long before to Mrs Nissenbaum in that same city, no reply had been returned. The letters were all restored to me when I went to the flat by a whispering man wearing a black wig, fashionable rimless glasses and a Mexican tobacco moustache, who was in occupation.

'Here's your mail, mister,' he whispered admiringly handing them around the door. 'Did you write all those to that one lady?'

I said I had. 'That's a whole lot of writing to one lady,' he said so quietly I could hardly hear him. 'I don't think that I could write that many letters to any one person. How can you *say* so much to one person.'

'Why are you whispering?' I asked, glancing about me, wondering if perhaps the violent and haunting Leroy were still in the vicinity. He did not seem to think the question an impertinence. 'The world's too noisy,' he hissed. 'There's a pollution of noise. I'm trying to contribute something. If everybody lowered their voices it would be a better place. We talk too much anyway.'

'I see,' I nodded quietly. I took the letters and saw something else. There was one for me. With my mind entirely on what that note might contain I whispered my thanks and farewell, and he said I was not to mention it, a sentiment which, by his glare, I knew he meant. So I said nothing further. I went down and out into the street. Standing where, on that remote morning, I had kissed her face for the last time, I opened her letter. It said: 'Darling. You will never see me again, but, whatever anyone tells you about me, I want you to know that you made me happy for a few hours and that it really meant all I said it meant. Love Angie. P.S. It would never work.'

I felt a ball of joy and hope begin to bounce within me.

If she felt like that then – the letter was dated three months before – she could feel like that again. We would have the happiness we both needed and sought. All I would have to do was to find her again. It *would* work!

It was early evening and New York was full of people going home or going into bars before they went home. The Split Legs Go-Go Bar was unlit, but the doors were open and I went into the dimness of the place. It looked like all those establishments look when they're not operating; dusty, propped up with pieces of wood, threadbare, all the things you can never see in the soft lights at night. The Go-Go girls' birdcage was hanging awry, the door hanging open as though the occupants had escaped only recently. A man was, curiously, sweeping it out with a dustpan and little brush. The place smelled hollow and stale like a tomb. In one corner another attendant was industriously sawing a leg from a chair.

I remained and watched him for a moment unwilling to disturb him in mid-amputation. Eventually he got through it and glanced up at me: 'The things we do for the mugs who get in here,' he sighed. 'Look at that. There's this little guy who complains that chairs are too high, so we make him a shorter chair. Did you ever hear anything like that?'

'That's service,' I said. 'Do you know a girl called Angie?'

He looked at me suspiciously; 'I don't know any girls,' he said. 'I'm a married man.'

'I mean in here,' I said.

'Especially I don't know no girls in here. I just come in to saw the legs off chairs.'

I saw someone moving in the shadows beyond the bird cage. 'Who's that?' I asked. He stared obligingly. 'Mr Trombone, the boss,' he said. 'He knows all the girls, I don't.'

I caught the man at the door of his office. He was fat and soft and he said his name with a long final letter – Trombonee. I told him who I was and he seemed to know of me because his eyebrows, like a pair of fat, fair caterpillars, moved up on his head, and he invited me in.

'Angie,' he mused. 'Yes, Angie. I been thinking you might come by sometime. Would you like a drink?'

I refused, but he said: 'Maybe you ought to have one because I think it will all be better with a drink.'

'She's not dead is she?' I asked in fright.

He laughed. 'Dead? Angie? Oh boy, she's not dead all right. That's one thing she ain't – dead.'

I said I would have the drink and he poured one for himself as well. He seemed reluctant to go on with the conversation. But eventually he sighed: 'Sure, sure, Angie.'

'What's happened to her?'

'Angie's gone,' he said opening his hands like wings. 'Just gone. Vanished. Disappeared. But I can't say I'm surprised. You did something to our Angie, mister. Even you don't know what you did. The day you left for England Angie was sitting right there in that chair, where you're sitting now, and the tears were flowing.'

'Well, we'd grown to be very fond of each other,' I said feeling pleased. 'I'd hoped we might even get, sort of, married.'

'She was some girl.'

'Some girl indeed.'

'That's it,' he said quickly as though he had been waiting. 'Just *some* girl. And it would only be *some* sort of marriage.'

'Why?'

'Because Angie was a man, mister.'

'Fuck off,' I cried wildly.

'Fuck off, indeed,' he replied softly. 'Right off as far as Angie was concerned. Angie was the greatest thing we've ever had in the Split Legs Go-Go. The greatest female impersonator that ever wagged an ass through Manhattan. And I'm not kidding.'

I knew he wasn't. 'Oh, God,' I said dropping my head in my hands. 'Oh, shit, God.'

'You have my sympathy, friend,' he shrugged. 'I didn't go for it from the start. It was a bet. Here in the club. I was there when it was struck. I lost five hundred dollars.'

'Oh, God,' I said again. I was speaking through my fingers as though they were bars.

'The bet was that Angie – Angelo, whichever you like . . .'

'Angie,' I muttered miserably. 'Can I remember her as Angie? Please.'

'As you like, friend,' he nodded. 'At least that disposes of the difficulty of calling him or her, he or she.'

'Why me?' I asked. The question was more to God than to him. It wasn't just this, it was everything. Mrs Nissenbaum, Pamela, every bloody thing. But this was the worse.

'Why you?' he repeated. 'Well, it had to be a certain type of guy.'

'A cunt,' I said sourly.

'Okay, pick your own label. That's how it started out anyway. Angie wanted something she didn't have, namely a cunt. And you walked by baby.'

'But it's not possible,' I muttered. 'Christ, we were in bed. I *kissed* her! I had my hands on her . . .'

'Best boobs, either sex, in New York,' he nodded calmly. 'Unfortunately Angie had the smallest cock in New York too. Small, but complete in every detail.'

'Oh shut up, for Christ's sake.' I was really crying now. I got up to make for the door, but he put me kindly back into the chair and poured another whisky in my glass. 'Listen, buddy,' he said. 'You might just as well listen. You won't feel so bad about it if you listen. You won't want to go looking for him . . . her . . . now anyway.'

'All right,' I said wiping my eyes. They felt sore like they did when I cried as a child. 'Tell me all the funny details.'

'Okay, it was funny,' he acknowledged. 'We had customers here just about croaking at your expense. That was when Angie started crying. She really *liked* you. It's perverted, but there you are. She was pretty sick about it at the end.'

'That makes me feel better,' I said bitterly. 'Knowing she felt bad.'

'Well, it was a bet,' he said throwing his arms wide.

'Just a laugh. Angie was boasting that she could pass herself off as a woman well enough to spend twenty-four hours or more living with a guy as his wife. And she was good, boy, make no mistake about that. She looked more like a dame than my wife does.'

'I remember her,' I said hopelessly. For Jesus sake, the best person, the only person for that matter, I had ever felt completely at ease and happy with! Sitting contentedly in my armchair, waiting for her to undress. Listening to her. Kissing her!

There was a lot of dough thrown about,' he went on. 'Hundreds of dollars. Angie said as soon as the right guy arrived she would go to work. It had to be somebody who . . . well, who had a nice outlook on life. Some people, including me, didn't think she could do it, some thought she could. And she was good, boy. Was there ever anything so feminine? Sometimes I had to pinch myself to stop me pinching her ass.'

'You should have tried,' I said miserably, calmer now, numb from it. 'It was a nice arse as they go. As long as you didn't know.'

'That's right. Be philosophical,' he encouraged. 'It ain't the end of everything. I lost five hundred bucks, remember that. All you're without is a good screw and your pride. That was the trouble; that's why I didn't think Angie could swing it.'

'Swing it?'

'Pull it off. Oh, shit. *Do* it. I thought that when it came to the clinch the guy would smell a rat. But you didn't. You were too trusting. I guess that's what you wanted to be, and you have my sympathy. There's too little trust in the world, Mr McCann.'

'There's going to be even less now,' I said.

'Ah, now, don't let it ball you up too much. She was real sorry, I can tell you. I had to mop up the tears, so I know. Angie felt that in you, she had found something decent and loving. I mean that. I've got no reason to give you that crap if it's not true. Those sort of words don't come easy to the manager of the Split Legs Go-Go. Decent and loving. There I said it again.'

'Thanks,' I said. It did not make me feel any better. I cringed inside. Fancy kissing a man! And going on a river trip! Holding hands! Buying things for the apartment! Planning a suburban home! The tennis club! No wonder she couldn't cook. I ought to have got her to do some carpentry.

'The danger was,' he said, going back, 'that you would find out once you were in the sack.'

'I think I might have,' I said. 'Even me. Even I can count up to two.'

'That was the reason that Stanley, the other guy. . . .'

'Sandra?'

He looked embarrassed again. 'Yeah, sure, Sandra,' he said. 'That was the reason that they fixed for Stanley – Sandra – to burst in on you and have to stay the night.'

'I slept with the pair of them. I mean the *two* of them,' I admitted dolefully.

'I know, I know,' he said decently dropping his eyes. 'I heard.'

'They cuddled each other.'

'They're old friends,' he shrugged.

'Ugh!' I shook my head. 'I want to be sick.'

'Why be sick?' he asked. 'So you shared a bed with two other human beings. In India they sleep ten in a bed. And I want to tell you mister, that Angie was real sorry. She wouldn't even take the money she won. It all went to some charity fund. She was sitting right there, where you are now, and she sobbed her heart out. She said you were the only decent, straight, loving person she had ever met. For her to say that was really something. She just had to mean it. She said for a few hours she had felt happy and secure and clean, and all sorts of crazy things like that. And she was sincere. That guy . . . that girl, really was sincere. You gave her something different, something she'd never experienced before.'

'It was mutual,' I sighed. I got up. I felt heavy, sick and

sad. I smiled wryly at him and we shook hands. 'Thank God there weren't any children,' I said.

As I walked that mile down Lexington I felt them all laughing at me from all the tall windows. Aircraftwoman 842912 Rose Kirby, Mrs Nissenbaum, Monique, Annette, Belinda, Joanne, and Pamela all pissing themselves to die, catcalling, with their arms about each other's shoulders. All my women. All mine. And there too Mr Gander and Angie, howling and holding hands. And above them all my father, my bastard father, laughing the longest and loudest of all.

Well I knew then. I knew what I was and I knew what women did to me. What had they wanted me for? A junior dickie for Rose, a walking memorial for Mrs Nissenbaum, a native bridegroom for Monique, a masseur for Annette, a sadist for Belinda, a pram pusher for Joanne and a romantic wet for Pamela. But now they had made me hate. Arthur McCann had turned at last.

There was a young woman on the corner of Lexington and Forty-second, an auburn haired girl like Greer Garson, for God's sake, telling a taxi driver that she had left all her money at home. I heard her say it but I looked resolutely the other way and walked on. She called 'Oh, excuse me, sir . . . excuse me.' But I didn't turn because she could have been calling some other mug. There must have been other mugs on that street and she was very beautiful. Just like Greer Garson who I had prayed would wait for me.

I walked on three more firm paces. She was still calling. I stopped and then slowly returned to the cab. She smiled brilliantly when she saw me coming. I paid her fare and she touched my hand while I was doing it.

Her name is Margaret Durbon and if you would care to meet her then it's easy. She is the secretary of an organization called 'No Sex Before Jesus Comes Again Society'. I can give you her address but you're wasting your time. And that's another pitiful story.